TRIPLE
THREAT

CH

Also by Camryn King

Stiletto Justice

Published by Kensington Publishing Corp.

TRIPLE
THREAT

CAMRYN
KING

KENSINGTON PUBLISHING CORP.
www.kensingtonbooks.com

DAFINA BOOKS are published by

Kensington Publishing Corp.
119 West 40th Street
New York, NY 10018

All Kensington titles, imprints, and distributed lines are available at special quantity discounts for bulk purchases for sales promotion, premiums, fund-raising, and educational or institutional use.

Special book excerpts or customized printings can also be created to fit specific needs. For details, write or phone the office of the Kensington Sales Manager: Kensington Publishing Corp., 119 West 40th Street, New York, NY 10018. Attn. Sales Department. Phone: 1-800-221-2647.

Dafina and the Dafina logo Reg. U.S. Pat. & TM Off.

ISBN-13: 978-1-4967-0220-3
ISBN-10: 1-4967-0220-4
First Kensington Trade Paperback Printing: November 2018

eISBN-13: 978-1-4967-0221-0
eISBN-10: 1-4967-0221-2
First Kensington Electronic Edition: November 2018

10 9 8 7 6 5 4 3 2 1

Printed in the United States of America

1

A year ago today, Mallory Knight's world had changed. She found her best friend dead, sprawled on top of a comforter. The one Leigh had excitedly shown Mallory just days before, another extravagant gift from her friend's secret, obviously rich lover, the cost of which, Mallory had pointed out, could have housed a thousand homeless for a week. Or fed them for two. Leigh had shrugged, laughed, lain back against the ultra-soft fabric. Her deep cocoa skin beautifully contrasted against golden raw silk.

That day, when the earth shifted on its axis, Leigh had lain there again. Putrid. Naked. Grotesquely displayed. Left uncovered to not disturb potential evidence, investigators told her. Contaminate the scene. *With what, decency?* She had ignored them, had wrenched a towel from the en suite bath and placed it over her friend and colleague's private parts. Her glare at the four men in the room was an unspoken dare for them to remove it. That would happen only over her dead body.

She'd steeled herself. She looked again, at the bed and around the room. Whoever had killed Leigh had wanted her shamed. The way the body was positioned left no doubt about that. For

Mallory, the cause of death wasn't in doubt, either. Murder. Not suicide, as the coroner claimed. But his findings matched what the detectives believed, what the scant evidence showed so . . . case closed. Even though the half-empty bottle of high-dose opioids found on Leigh's nightstand weren't hers. Even though forensics found a second set of prints on one of two wineglasses next to the pills. Even though Mallory told investigators her friend preferred white wine to red and abhorred drugs of any kind. She suffered through headaches and saw an acupuncturist for menstrual cramps. Even though for Leigh Jackson image was everything. She'd never announce to the world she'd killed herself by leaving the pill bottle out on the table, get buck naked to do the deed, then drift into forever sleep with her legs gaping open. Details like those wouldn't have gotten past a female detective. They didn't get by Mallory, either. Beautiful women like Leigh tended to be self-conscious. What did Mallory see in that god-awful crime scene? Not even a porn star would have chosen that pose for their last close-up.

The adrenaline ran high that fateful morning, Mallory remembered. Early January. As bitterly cold as hell was hot. Back-to-back storms in the forecast. This time last year, New York had been in the grips of a record-breaking winter. Almost a foot of snow had been dumped on the city the night before. Mallory had bundled up in the usual multiple layers of cashmere and wool. She had pulled on knee-high, insulated riding boots and laughed out loud at the sound of Leigh's voice in her head, a replay of the conversation after showing Leigh what she'd bought.

"Those are by far the ugliest boots I've ever seen."

"Warm, though," Mallory had retorted. "I'm going for substance, not style."

"They'd be fine for Iceland. Or Antarctica. Or Alaska. Not Anchorage, though. Too many people. One of those outback places with more bears than humans. Reachable only by boat or plane."

Mallory had offered a side-eye. "So what you're saying is this was a great choice for a record cold winter."

"Absolutely . . . if you lived in an igloo. You live in an apartment in Brooklyn, next door to Manhattan. The fucking fashion capitol of the world, hello?"

Mallory had laughed so hard she snorted, which caused Leigh's lips to tremble until she couldn't hold back and joined her friend in an all-out guffaw. Complete opposites, those ladies. One practicality and comfort, stretch jeans and tees. The other back-breaking stilettos and designer everything. They'd met at an IRE conference, an annual event for investigative reporters and editors, and bonded over the shared position of feeling like family outcasts who used work to fill the void. Leigh was the self-proclaimed heathen in a family of Jehovah's Witnesses while second marriages and much younger siblings had made Mallory feel like a third wheel in both parents' households. To Mallory, Leigh felt like the little sister she'd imagined having before her parents divorced.

That morning a year ago she'd stopped at the coffee shop for her usual extra-large with an espresso shot, two creams, and three sugars. She crossed the street and headed down into the subway to take the R from her roomy two-bed, two-bath walkup in Brooklyn to a cramped shared office in midtown Manhattan, a five-minute walk from Penn Station in a foot of snow that felt more like fifteen. She'd just grabbed a cab when her phone rang. An informant with a tip. Another single, successful, beautiful female found dead. One of many tips she'd received since beginning the series for which she'd just won a prestigious award. "Why They Disappear. Why They Die." Why did they? Mysteriously. Suspiciously. Most cases remained unsolved. Heart racing, Mallory had redirected the cabbie away from her office down to Water Street and a tony building across from the South Street Seaport. The building where Leigh lived. Where they'd joked and laughed just days before. She'd shut down her thoughts then. Refused to believe it could be her best friend. There were nine other residences in that building. She'd go to any of the condominiums, all of them, except number 10. But that very apartment is where she'd been directed. The apartment teeming with police, marked with crime tape.

"Knight."

Jolted back into the present, Mallory sucked in a breath, turned her eyes away from the memory, and looked at her boss. "Hey, Charlie."

"What are you doing here? It's Friday. I thought I told you to take the rest of the day off and start your weekend early."

"I am."

"Yeah, I see how off you are." He walked over to her corner of the office, moved a stack of books and papers off a chair, and plopped down. He shuffled an ever-present electronic cigarette from one side of his mouth to the other with his tongue. "That wasn't a suggestion. It was an order. Get out of here."

He sounded brusque, but Charlie's frown was worse than his fist. It had taken her almost three years to figure that out. When she started working at *New York News* just over four years ago he was intimidating, forceful, and Mallory didn't shrink easily. Six foot five with a shock of thick salt-and-pepper hair and a paunch that suggested too many hoagies, not enough salad, and no exercise, he'd pushed Mallory to her limit more than once. She'd pushed back. Worked harder. Won his respect.

"I know it's a hard day for you." His voice was softer, gentler now.

"Yep." One she didn't want to talk about. She powered down her laptop, reached for the bag.

"She'd have been proud of you for that."

"What?" He nodded toward her inbox. "Oh, that."

"'Oh, that,'" he mimicked. "That, Knight, is what investigative journalists work all of their lives for and hope to achieve.

Helluva lot of work you put in to get the Prober's Pen. Great work. Exceptional work. Congrats again."

It was true. In this specialized circle of journalism, the Prober's Pen, most often simply called the Pen, was right up there with the Pulitzer for distinctive honor.

"Thanks, Charlie. A lot of work, but not enough. We still don't know who killed her." A lump, sudden and unexpected, clogged her throat. Eyes burned. Mallory yanked the power cord from the wall, stood and shoved it into the computer bag along with her laptop. She reached for her purse. No way would she cry around Charlie. Investigative reporters had no time for tears.

She was two seconds from a clean escape before his big paw clamped her shoulder and halted her gait. She looked back, not at him, in his direction, but not in his eyes. One look at those compassion-filled baby blues and she'd be toast.

"What, Callahan?" Terse. Impatient. A tone you could get away with in New York. Even with your boss. Especially one like Charlie.

"Your column helped solve several cases. You deserved that award. Appreciate it. Appreciate life . . . for Leigh."

"Yeah, yeah, yeah. Out of my way, softie." Mallory pushed past him the way she wished she could push past the pain.

"Got a new assignment when you come back, Knight!"

She waved without turning around.

Later that evening Mallory went for counseling. Her therapists? Friends and colleagues Ava and Sam. The prescription? Alcohol. Lots of it. And laughter. No tears. At first, she'd declined, but they insisted. Had they remembered the anniversary, too? One drink was all she'd promised them. Then home she'd go to mourn her friend and lament her failed attempts to get at the truth. After that she'd go to visit her bestie. Take flowers. Maybe even shed a tear or two. If she dared.

Mallory left her apartment, tightened her scarf against the

late-January chill, and walked three short blocks to Newsroom, an aptly named bar and restaurant in Brooklyn, opened by the daughter of a famous national news anchor, frequented by journalists and other creative types. Stiff drinks. Good food. Reasonable prices. Not everyone made six figures like Mallory Knight. In America's priciest city, even a hundred thousand dollars was no guarantee of champagne kisses and caviar dreams.

Bowing her head against the wind, she hurried toward the restaurant door. One yank and a blast of heat greeted her, followed by the drone of conversation and the smell of grilled onions. Her mouth watered. An intestinal growl followed, the clear reminder she hadn't had lunch. She unwrapped the scarf from around her head and neck, tightened the band struggling to hold back a mop of unruly curls, and looked for her friends.

"In the back." The hostess smiled and pointed toward the dining room.

"Thanks."

"Heard you won the Pen. Way to go."

"Gosh, word gets around."

"It's one of the highest honors a reporter can receive, Mallory so, yeah, a few people know."

She turned into the dining room and was met by applause. Those knowing people the hostess described were all standing and cheering. After picking her jaw off the floor, Mallory's narrowed eyes searched the room for her partners in crime. A shock of red hair ducked behind . . . Gary? Special correspondent for NBC? Indeed. And other familiar faces, too. The *Post*, *Times*, *Daily News*, the *Brooklyn Eagle*, *Amsterdam News*, and other local and national news outlets were represented. Highly embarrassed and deeply moved, Mallory made her way across the room, through good-natured barbs, hugs, and high fives, over to Gary, who gave her a hug, inches from the dynamic duo who'd undoubtedly planned the surprise.

"You two." Mallory jabbed an accusatory finger into a still

shrinking Sam's shoulder while eyeing Ava, who smiled broadly. "When did you guys have time to do all this?"

"Calm down, girl." Ava shooed the question away. "Group text. Took five seconds."

Ava. Her girl. Keep-it-real Holyfield. "Thanks for making me feel special."

"You're welcome." Ava munched on a fry. "Always happy to help."

Just when Mallory thought she couldn't be shocked further, a voice caused her to whip her head clean around.

"Can I have everyone's attention, please?"

There stood Charlie, red-faced and grinning, holding up a shot glass as two tray-carrying waiters gave a glass to everyone in the room. Her boss, was in on it, too? All that insistence that she get out of the office? Damn, he was trying hard to make her cry.

"She doesn't like the spotlight, so next week I'll pay for this. But I was thrilled to learn that a celebration was being planned for one of the best reporters I've ever had the pleasure of working with, Mallory Knight." He paused for claps and cheers. "Most of you know this, though some may not. The hard work done on the Why series has resulted in three women being found and reunited with their families and two arrests, one of which a cold case that had remained unsolved for fifteen years. Good job, kiddo."

Mallory accepted his hug. "Thanks, Charlie."

"Speech! Speech!" echoed around the room.

"As most of you know, I'm a much better writer than I am a speaker. At least without a lot more of these, so . . ." Mallory held up a shot glass holding pricey liquor. "Hear, hear."

She downed the drink, swallowed the liquid along with the burn that accompanied its journey down the hatch. Holding up a hand quieted the crowd.

"Okay, I . . . um . . . thank you guys for coming. The Pen

means a lot. But your support means a lot more. Um . . . that first toast was for me. Let's do one more for another IR, Leigh Jackson. Everybody here who knew her knew she was . . . pretty amazing."

Mallory blinked back tears. "She was the inspiration behind the series and why I have this award. She held up a second shot glass. "To Leigh!"

For the next half hour Mallory accepted congrats and well wishes from her colleagues, accompanied by a medium-rare steak dinner and more vodka. The crowd thinned. Mallory grew quieter.

Sam squeezed her shoulder. "You okay?"

Seconds passed as she pondered the question. A slow nod followed. "As of a few seconds ago, I feel a lot better."

"Why?" Ava asked.

"I just made a decision." Mallory looked from Ava to Sam. "I know I said I'd let it go. But I can't. Whoever killed Leigh is not going to get away with it. I'm going to find out who did it, and make sure they pay for her murder."

Sam's expression morphed into one of true concern. "Oh, no, Mal. Not that again."

"You think a cold-blooded murderer should walk around free?"

"You know what she means." Ava's response was unbowed by Mallory's clear displeasure. "Or have you forgotten those first couple months after she died, when you were so bent on proving Leigh's suicide was murder that you almost worked yourself into a grave?"

"But I didn't die, did I? Instead, I got the Pen." Mallory's voice calmed as she slumped against her chair. "I'd much rather get Leigh's killer."

"I know you loved Leigh," Ava said, her voice now as soft as the look in her eyes. "And while Sam and I didn't know her as well as you did, we both liked her a lot and respected the hell out of her work as a journalist. You did everything you could right after it happened. Let the police continue to handle it from here on out."

"That's just it. They think it's already handled. The death was ruled a suicide. Case closed."

There wasn't a comeback for that harsh truth. Mallory held up a finger for another shot. Ava's brow arched in amazement.

"How many of those can you hold, Mal? You're taller than me, but I've got you by at least thirty pounds."

Mallory looked up to see Charlie wave and head to the door. Ignoring Ava, she called out to him. "Charlie!"

He waited by the hostess stand, the area now cold and crowded from the rush of dinner guests and a constantly opening door.

"What is it, kiddo?"

"Can't believe you knew about this and didn't tell me."

"Had you known, you wouldn't have shown up."

"That's probably true. I appreciate what you said up there. Thanks."

"Think nothing of it." He looked at his watch. "I gotta run. See you next week."

"One more thing. The new assignment you mentioned earlier. What's it about?"

Charlie hesitated.

Mallory's eyes narrowed. "Charlie . . ."

"Change of pace. You're going to love it."

"What's the topic?"

"Basketball."

"You want me to cover sports?" Incredulity raised Mallory's voice an octave.

"Told you that you'd love it," Charlie threw over his shoulder as he caught the door a customer just opened and hurried out.

"Charlie!"

Mallory frowned as she watched her boss's hurried steps, his head bowed against the wind and swirling snow. His answer to her question only raised several more. *Why would Charlie want an investigative reporter on a sports story? Why wasn't the sports editor handling it? Freelance writers clamored for free tickets to sports events. Why couldn't he give the assignment to one of them?* She wanted to continue doing stories that mattered, like those on missing women and unsolved murders that had won her the Pen. And Charlie wanted her to write about grown men playing games? Her mood darkening and shivering at the blast of cold wind accompanying the next customer through the front door, Mallory walked back to the table, hugged her friends goodbye, and began the short walk home. She lived less than ten minutes from the restaurant, and, although the temperature had dropped and snow was falling, she barely noticed. Mallory's thoughts were on her dead best friend, the botched closed case, and how to regenerate interest in catching a killer. Because whether officially or not, for work or not, Mallory would never stop trying to find out who killed Leigh Jackson. Never. Ever. No fucking way.

2

Mallory awoke to a gloomy Saturday morning and a foggy brain from too much vodka. The forecast called for rain that could later turn to snow. Appropriate, she thought, since she'd decided to visit Leigh this morning. It hardly seemed right for the sun to shine while she visited what remained of a light that had been extinguished way too soon. She rolled out of bed with a groan, pulled on boots, threw a coat over her pajamas, and dashed to the corner coffee shop. A long, hot shower and double shots of espresso helped wake her up and clear the fuzziness from her mind.

Thirty minutes later Mallory was outside again. She carried an umbrella but didn't open it as she walked to her car. Rather, she welcomed the cold drizzle on her face, the wind whipping her misbehaving curls about her. Disheveled. Unruly. How Mallory felt right now. She started up her trusty Toyota and since it hadn't been driven in almost a month, she let it idle until the engine warmed up. While sitting there she checked her voicemail and was surprised she'd missed calls. Obviously, the restaurant had been loud and she'd slept harder than she realized. Just as she pulled away from the curb, her phone rang. She plugged in her Bluetooth and turned up the volume on the stereo.

"I'm alive."

Sam chuckled. "Just checking. Last night you had me a bit concerned. I know this is a tough time. How are you really?"

"I'm okay. Heard from Leigh's mom last night, Mrs. Jackson."

"How's she doing?"

"I don't know. I missed it. Probably best since I was three sheets to the wind."

"More like three blankets."

"Remind me next time that vodka is not my friend."

"Wonder what she wanted."

"Checking in on me, probably, same as you."

"That was nice of her to think of you."

"She also mentioned having something to give me and wanting me to stop by."

"That's why you're up so early?"

"Early is relative, Sam. It's after ten. I'm going to visit Leigh and wanted to try and beat the crazy Saturday traffic. Her mother doesn't live far from there so I hope to see her, too."

Seconds of silence. Mallory imagined her mystical friend Sam—the former IR-turned-lifestyle-column-writer after marrying her alternative music husband and having the baby named after a star—twirling a honey blond lock while trying to tactfully suggest that Mallory need not go to the cemetery to honor their friend. That Leigh was now a beautiful spirit, sparkling even, who was everywhere and nowhere at the same time. Mallory saved her the trouble.

"I know what you're thinking. That the whole funeral/coffin/graveyard thing is for the unenlightened. The unevolved."

"Mallory, I would nev—"

"I know you wouldn't. Not in those words. But I know how you feel about life and death, and I actually appreciate the perspective. It helped me cope with her loss. But I don't view going to the cemetery the same way you do. I went there once before, about a month after the funeral."

"And?"

"It brought me peace."

"Then go, Mal. Honor Leigh in whatever way that works. Just remember to take care of you in that process."

"Thanks, Sam. I'll try."

Mallory hung up and concentrated on driving. Even with her deliberate caution due to the wet pavement, thick traffic, and her paranoia from rarely getting behind the wheel, she still made it to the Queens cemetery in less than forty-five minutes. It took her another thirty to find the section where Leigh was buried and about the same time to find the simple slab of granite that marked her grave:

Leigh Serenity Jackson
Sunrise: June 15, 1985
Sunset: January 21, 2017
God granted us serenity. She rests in his arms.

Mallory blinked, swallowed hard and ground her teeth in an attempt to stanch her roiling emotions. But nothing could allay the tears. Reading that last line brought them down in a torrent, unstoppable, unwilling to be dammed. She fell to her knees before the stone. Cried. Stopped. Cried some more. The first time in more than a year since she'd allowed herself the luxury. Somehow being here with her best friend made it okay.

Reaching out, she touched the cold stone with a gloved finger and traced the letters etched in the gray granite. She ran her fingers along the roses that outlined the words and just then, noticed a bouquet of live flowers nearby, probably blown from their intended spot by the wind. Mallory reached for the pink and purple arrangement, dug a shallow cavern in the earth, and placed them there, supported by the stone. Moments later, or hours, who could tell, the stream of tears slowed to a trickle. Mallory pulled a crumpled napkin from her jacket pocket, blew her nose, wiped her eyes, and took a deep breath to get a hold of herself.

"Well," she said firmly, her shoulders squared as she sat in front of the tombstone. "Now that we've got that out of the way . . ." She tried to smile but it wilted like the fading flowers near the stone. She took another deep breath with lips pressed tight. She wouldn't cry again. Enough of that. Instead Mallory pulled the band from around damp, wayward curls, brushed them back and doubled up the band in her effort to tame them and pulled her jacket hood over her head.

"I probably look a mess," she said, her eyes focused on Serenity. "I can hear you now, clucking your tongue like your mom does and saying, 'Ghul, ya shamin'." It was a phrase that loosely translated to, *Girl, you are a shame*, or, *Girl, you should be ashamed (of yourself)*. "Well, I'm not. At least not about the way I look. I felt bad for not visiting you earlier. You know, on the day it happened. Sam thinks it's silly for me to come here anyway. She didn't say it like that, but that was her meaning. Miss Woo-woo thinks I can talk to you from anywhere, and you'd hear me.

"I don't know if that's true, if you can hear me or even if you still exist out there." Mallory shrugged, feeling strangely comfortable and relaxed. She pulled her legs up and rested her chin on her knees. "Part of me thinks that when you die, it's over. The other part hopes that you're still . . . somewhere. That somehow you know what's going on."

She paused to watch a flock of birds fly overhead in perfect symmetry. Heading south to warmer weather she supposed, even as she pulled the strings of her hooded jacket tighter around her and wished for earmuffs. She shifted and leaned on the cold, hard tombstone that verified her friend had once had a place in the world. It was a sorry substitute for the vivacious Leigh Jackson. That's what Mallory would have told anyone who asked. But of course, no one had. She had told Leigh's mother Barbara of a conversation with Leigh that took place not a month before the murder. How when she died Leigh wanted to be cremated, the same as Mallory, her ashes flung into the wind near the Caribbean island of her ancestors' birth. Nobody'd heard her then either. Leigh was given a traditional Jehovah's Witness funeral and looked positively stunning in a lacy white dress—one she wouldn't have been caught dead in while living, Mallory thought semismiling at the pun—and was buried in a simple white casket with pale pink interior and silver trim. Mallory had never seen Leigh wear pale anything. Unlike the service her parents had planned, Leigh's life had not been subdued. She laughed loudly, partied endlessly. She loved vibrant colors that matched her personality, paired with the highest designer heels she could find, and anything bling. There were no words to describe how much Mallory missed her friend.

"If you are somewhere having a voyeuristic experience of my life, then you know that my *Why They Disappear/Why They Die* series won the Pen. Hardly feels like a notable accomplishment considering the fucked-up circumstances that led to its creation. I got to tell your story though, and dozens of others who are dead and/or missing. A few got found, young runaways believed to be dead, a couple murderers arrested. So, that's good. The main reason for doing it though was to generate enough interest for the cops to take notice, maybe even get a lead strong enough to have your case reopened. That didn't happen and I feel it's my fault. Hell, if my investigative journalism skills can't help me find your killer, then just how good am I, you know?

"Everybody thinks it's time for me to give up, let it all go and move on with my life—Ava, Sam, Charlie. Especially him. Next week he wants to talk about a new assignment, new story. He's proud of the series but thinks doing it has driven me a little crazy. We both know that's a lie. My insanity began way before you left."

Mallory tried to laugh, but choked on the lump in her throat.

"Maybe they're right. Maybe it's time for me to let go. What about you, Leigh? Is that what you want?"

A gust of wind blew over, causing leaves to swirl and Mallory's hood to fall back. She didn't notice that the rain had turned to snow until flakes hit her face. She looked at Leigh's name etched on the stone, then up at the bare, swaying branches, then back at the slab.

"I didn't think so." She shook her head and stood. "Guess I should be going even though I hate to leave you, my friend. Silly, I know. You've managed to be out here a year without me.

"Can you really hear me, Leigh?" She looked around, waited for another gust of wind, a crow to caw, something. Instead, it seemed quieter than ever, and suddenly a bit spooky, too. Mallory shivered. "If you can hear me, do me a favor, okay? Help me find the person who put you here and send them behind bars, where they belong. You and whoever that is are the only ones who know. If you can hear me, then it's possible that you can communicate, too. Find a way. Help me out. Help me help you," she finished dramatically, quoting one of their shared favorite movie lines as she swiped a final tear. "I love you, Leigh."

Mallory kissed her fingers, touched them to Leigh's name and hurried back to her car. Once inside she started the car, cranked the fan to high, and received a blast of cold air for her trouble. She turned the vents away from her and reached for the phone she'd left in the car, along with the bag that held it. *Missed call.* She tapped the screen to reveal a number that was unfamiliar. After turning on the wipers to clear snow-covered windows, she made a U-turn, headed out of the cemetery and engaged her Bluetooth. As soon as the call was answered, she knew who it was—Leigh's mom.

"Mrs. Jackson, it's Mallory Knight. I received your message the other night and totally intended to call you back. I'm so sorry."

"No need to apologize, Mallory. I know you're busy, writing award-winning columns and all."

"Oh, you saw that, huh?"

"I did and was happy for you. I know how hard you work."

"Thank you, Mrs. Jackson."

"I'm sure Leigh would have been delighted as well. And you can call me Barbara."

"I hope so, Barbara. She is the reason behind the series, and continues to be my inspiration in finding criminals and getting justice for their loved ones. I just left her, in fact."

"You visited the cemetery?"

"Yes. I just left not five minutes ago."

"I was there earlier in the week, on the anniversary, still somewhat in disbelief that my daughter sleeps in the arms of Jehovah."

"You left the flowers."

"I did."

There was silence then as both women remembered the challenge that was Leigh and her mother's relationship, from completely different perspectives. "How are you, missus . . . Barbara?"

"Gaining strength every day, child. Which is actually why I called."

Mallory nodded as though Barbara could see her. She'd talked to Leigh's mom less than a half a dozen times. The question that had plagued her since getting her call was about to be answered.

"I thought they were all gone but a week or so ago I found a bag of Leigh's things and remembered you wanting to have something that belonged to her. At the time you asked it was just . . . well . . ."

"It was probably an insensitive thing to do. There's no need to explain."

"We all were hurting and still in shock. I can't say time has healed the wound but it does make the pain more bearable. Anyway, when I found the bag I thought of you. I know what good friends the two of you were and I believe Leigh would appreciate my giving it to you."

"Barbara, thank you so much. I would love that."

"Is it possible that you can come by for it? I don't drive much since having a seizure, and don't like to take the subway either."

"I'm sorry to hear about your health. That's not a problem at all. In fact, I'm still in Queens and can stop by right now."

"Okay, then. Hold on a moment." Mallory heard a garbled conversation and thought that Barbara had placed her hand over the receiver. "We'll only be here another half hour or so, but if you can make it within that timeframe . . ."

"I can."

"Okay, Mallory. We'll see you shortly."

An accident and a GPS gone wild put Mallory at the Jacksons' Jamaica, Queens doorstep at three fifteen, exactly twenty-seven minutes from when she'd hung up with Leigh's mother. Parking in front of a single-family, one-story home with a fenced-in front yard and chipped cement steps leading to the front porch, she killed the engine and hurried through the gate and up the stairs to ring the bell. She waited, and when no one answered she added a gloved, muffled knock on the locked, metal screen door. Still no response and no sound from inside. Mallory turned and headed for her car, pulling out her phone to leave a message. Closing the gate, she heard the front door open.

"Mallory?"

She turned and though it was rounder, darker, and framed by a black and white knitted cap, saw a face so reminiscent of Leigh's that it took her aback. She'd only met Barbara in person once before and had commented then on how the two looked more like sisters than mother and child.

"Hi, Barbara," Mallory said in greeting while retracing her steps back to the porch. "Sorry I didn't get here sooner. A detour caused by an accident got me all screwed up."

"No worries." It was said with a small and fleeting smile.

Like Leigh's, Barbara's skin was flawless, a warm and inviting cocoa brown. As she came closer, however, Mallory noted the dark circles beneath Barbara's eyes and a shock of gray hair not covered by the cap, gray that Mallory didn't remember being there when they'd met before.

"It looks like you're leaving, so if you'd like, I can come back another time."

"No need for that." Barbara slid a strap off her shoulder, bringing Mallory's attention to a large, bulging black duffel bag with faded white stripes. She placed her hands beneath the bag and offered it to Mallory.

"I don't know what all is in there. Undoubtedly inappropriate though for her younger sisters. I never could understand Leigh's showy extravagance or where that came from. We've always been simple folk. But not her. There was something about that girl, always chasing, wanting more. Especially right before it happened. She just . . . she changed. I tried to . . ."

The door behind Barbara opened. A middle-aged man— tall, lean—wearing all black and sporting a full beard stepped outside, giving a curt nod to Mallory before turning to lock the door. Mallory assumed it was Leigh's stepfather and prepared to speak, but he closed the screen and stepped past her before she could form a word.

"I'll go now," Barbara said hastily, shoving the duffel bag into Mallory's chest as her eyes followed the man's quick movements. "We're late for service."

"Sorry I kept you waiting." Mallory followed Barbara down the walk. "Thank you for thinking of me."

A slight glance was the only acknowledgment Barbara gave

her before she got into the car Mr. Jackson had already started, which he began backing up almost before Barbara's door fully closed. Mallory watched him pull out, watched the car drive away while still clutching the duffel bag she'd been given. She got in her car and just sat there, digesting Barbara's words.

There was something about that girl, always chasing, wanting more. Especially right before it happened. She just . . . she changed.

All the way home it nagged at her, the comment on a continuous loop in her head. Leigh was ambitious, but so were a million other professional women in New York. She'd set her sights high and wanted the good life. And while she wasn't above using her womanly wiles to gain an advantage, Leigh believed in a hard day's work. She was smart and worked her butt off. But in the month or so before she died, Leigh had been different. Subdued. Preoccupied. Mallory had noticed. So had Barbara. When asked, Leigh had brushed off Mallory's concern. Had her mother also tried and failed to get at the truth? What had Leigh been hiding? And who killed her, so no one would find out?

3

By the time Mallory arrived back home, the peace of spending time with Leigh had been replaced by a burning drive to investigate. Mallory shed boots, coat, scarf, and gloves and plopped down right on a rug in the living room with Leigh's black bag. With a deep breath, she unzipped the bag and began removing its contents. The items inside were signature Leigh. Bold, colorful tops. A politically incorrect cropped jacket made of real sable. Corset belts and heeled thigh-high boots that were more like stilts to Mallory's mind. Crystal-laden jewelry, silk scarves, CDs, a boatload of bangles, a couple small purses, a metallic clutch. Chargers for several electronic devices. Mallory frowned as she thought of those items and wondered if they were with the police, locked up as evidence in a case gone cold. Mallory set the CDs and a thin silver bangle aside, then reached for a mirrored jewelry box in the bottom of the duffel bag. She opened it and pulled out a thin booklet within a gold-plated case. *An appointment book? A journal?* Flipping through the pages, it appeared to be a bit of both, an appointment calendar with writing covering many of the lined pages. Mallory frowned at the familiar cursive written in black ink. It was definitely Leigh's handwriting. Her friend was big on email and texting but outside of their work, Mallory couldn't remember Leigh reading or writing much of anything.

Along with the book there were a couple other items inside, including a gold object shaped like a jigsaw puzzle piece. It was solid, heavy. *A paperweight perhaps?* Mallory turned the piece over. It was the size of her hand, beautifully sculpted and smooth on both sides. She thought of her friend and loved it at once—a fitting memento. Not only as a gift from one journalist to another, but a nod to the puzzle that Leigh left behind. Mallory walked over to the fireplace mantel and set the piece next to a favorite picture of her and Leigh, taken just weeks before her death. Leigh's pretty brown eyes stared back at her, twinkling with joy and a hint of mischief. Still viewing the picture, Mallory again picked up the gleaming puzzle piece.

"This is cool, Leigh, and different," she whispered into the room, as if hesitant to disturb the quiet. "Is it real gold? If so, then . . . thanks."

Mallory glanced from the gold piece over to the gold appointment book and finally once again at the picture of her and Leigh. With purpose, she strode into the kitchen for a cup of tea. Once done, she returned to the living room, picked up the appointment book or journal or whatever it was and got comfy on her leather couch beneath a fleece throw. For a moment, she simply held the book.

Do I have a right to read what's in here?

More questions followed. *Was she about to unveil secrets Leigh thought to take to the grave? Was it a coincidence that a year after Leigh's death Barbara had found a duffel bag of her things? Or that she'd called on the day Mallory sat at Leigh's gravesite, asking for help?* Mallory didn't think so. At the gravesite Mallory had asked Leigh to help her. She hadn't really thought it possible. But her former best friend and colleague just might help her after all.

Mallory took a deep, fortifying breath and began to read. With each word, she heard Leigh's lilting voice. Saw her smile.

January 1. Across the squares marking the month's first week, Leigh wrote of their friend, Sam.

Samantha says writing down wishes make them come true faster. True? We'll see. Here goes.

Mallory didn't remember the conversation but had no doubt it happened. Sam had been a mantra-chanting, visualizing, meditator since Mallory and Leigh met her and Ava while participating in the Tunnel to Towers 5K Run and Walk. Mallory mostly ignored her ramblings and Ava flat out called her cuckoo. Sam was undeterred. Considering she now freelanced from home as the wife of a computer analyst and the mother of an adorable two-year old, she also seemed to have been right.

Mallory studied the page. There were doodles of stars, hearts surrounding a declaration. *Today is the first day of the rest of my life!* She could imagine Leigh's squared shoulders as she wrote the words, could almost hear the passion with which she underscored the word today. Written confidently, with sure, clean strokes, with no clue that the rest of her life wouldn't last that long.

New job. Mallory knew she'd been looking.

True love. A never-ending search.

Can only go UP from here. Mallory took a sip of tea and pondered the sentence written after "true love." That New Year's Eve had seen both she and Leigh complaining about their love lives. Pretty much rock bottom, as Mallory remembered. Up was the only way to go.

Get fit. Really, girl? From a totally objective perspective, Leigh's body was flawless. Her face was like that of an angel. She didn't need it, but Mallory never observed Leigh in public without makeup. Leigh Jackson was one of the most beautiful women Mallory had ever seen, in person or in print. That she was even more beautiful on the inside was how she and Mallory became best friends.

The last week of January.

Penned in yoga classes. The title of an album by Leigh's favorite neo soul artist. A comment in the fourth Saturday box.

Invited to a Navs game. Another chance to see Christian . . . Heck yeah!

In February, there were more personal notes about New York's basketball team, the Navigators, and hooking up. With who? Not the attorney-turned-politician whom Leigh had dated for about six months before he'd abruptly ended the relationship. Mallory remembered meeting him once and not being impressed. When they broke up and she'd asked what happened Leigh had simply answered, "I didn't like his politics."

Mallory continued through the planner. The next few weeks seemed to focus on appointments for work, dinners and events and messages about "getting up," "moving up," "staying up," and other similar phrases containing the two-letter word. Some phrases fit within the sentence but others were odd, one-liners and rhymes that looked to Mallory like some type of code. Hidden messages for Leigh's eyes alone, that only she could understand. Like the lines written on March's page.

Madness. Yes, crazy the love. Caught up. Impossibly.

Inexplicably. Both of us feeling the scorch of the heat. Yet jumping headfirst into flames.

April and May were all about the Navigators in the playoffs and being in love. Mallory paused to reheat her tea. She leaned against the counter, watched the water begin to bubble and thought back to that time more than a year ago when Leigh stopped talking about her love life. Mallory pushed for information. Leigh admitted she was seeing someone, a man she'd refer to as The Mister or Special Friend. Mallory thought the man was probably married and warned Leigh to be careful. Not long after that, Leigh moved into the luxury condo. Mallory had called Leigh a kept woman, told her she deserved better than to be somebody's sidechick. Their friendship had wavered, restored only when the two friends agreed not to talk about it. Mallory picked up her mug and slowly returned to the living room, more than ever wanting to know the identity of Leigh's mystery man.

June was all about the Navigators and Christian Graham, their star player. Leigh was a huge basketball fan and Christian was her favorite player. She called him a triple threat—smart, successful, gorgeous. Mallory remembered her excitement when he joined the team. It was contagious. She lived the regionals, breathed the playoffs, and scored tickets to two of the three home games. That's when Mallory had felt sure Leigh was dating Christian, that he was her special friend. Leigh had never confirmed it outright. For Mallory, it felt obvious. How else could she have gotten a floor seat and special passes? When she remained tight-lipped, Mallory had given up asking. Other than not wanting Leigh hurt or used, she couldn't have cared less. But Christian was single, Mallory contemplated, often photographed with the country's latest "it" girl—actress, singer, dancer, mogul—always gorgeous, mostly rich. Sneaking around to be with him made no sense. Unless he had something to hide, Mallory suddenly thought. Something he'd kill for to prevent going public.

There were other appointments, numbers, and names. Mallory pulled her iPad over and opened a page to jot down notes. Two hours later and halfway through the appointment book/ journal, her mom called with the latest shenanigans of a half-sister Mallory barely knew. That conversation zapped what was left of her energy so after hanging up, drained and hungry, she took a shower, ordered a pizza, and went downstairs to get lost in mindless TV.

She entered the living room to a screenshot of the evening news. Another woman dead. A person of interest named. Mallory's hand flew to her mouth.

Isaac Bankole—one of several names that just moments before she'd read in Leigh's journal.

4

Mallory arrived at the office that Monday morning having forgotten all about Charlie's mention of a new assignment. She'd slept in Sunday morning, then spent the afternoon learning all she could about Isaac Bankole, the person of interest mentioned on the newscast she'd heard, and one of the names she'd gleaned from Leigh's appointment book. Afterwards, she'd called Ava, gotten voicemail and no callback. First up on her things-to-do list was to text her girl and suggest they do lunch. What she'd found out so far told Mallory one thing. Bankole was too much for one IR to handle.

"Knight!"

"Callahan."

"Get in here."

Mallory finished the text on the short jaunt from her desk to Charlie's office. She moved a stack of perpetually present folders from one of two overflowing chairs facing his equally cluttered desk and sat down.

"What's up, boss?"

"I told you on Friday. A new assignment I want covered in your column."

"Oh. I'd forgotten about that."

"Thought you might."

"Why do you think it needs to change, the column? Having just won the Pen, readership numbers will only climb. People unfamiliar with the *Why* series will want to check it out. I don't know that now is the right time to switch topics."

"I think it's the perfect time."

"Why?"

"For the same reasons you gave. You just won the Pen. People will be on the lookout for the 'Knightly News' column, will follow what you write. Some will want to read what got you the award. For those folks, there are the archives, every article carefully filed. Others will turn to your page to see what's happening now. And the only thing happening now, at least as far as New Yorkers are concerned, is basketball and the Navigators ruling the playoffs."

"And?"

"I want you to find a way to work the sport into your column."

"You're kidding, right?"

"Stop acting surprised. I told you Friday night."

"I was hoping it was the vodka effecting my hearing."

"Sorry to disappoint you. Besides, I've been telling you for months. It's time to switch gears, give your mind a break from the mayhem. A chance to lighten up and give the readers a reason to smile for a change."

"Okay." Said in that long, drawn out way that suggested it was anything but.

"I want you to do a serious piece on Christian Graham."

"The sports section isn't big enough for his ego? Mine is a serious column. He doesn't fit in it."

"How do you know?"

Mallory's mind went as blank as her expression, words from Leigh's appointment book suddenly filtering through her brain.

"Exactly. You don't. Not until you've done your homework

and found an angle that, you know, humanizes the guy. Something that shows he has heart."

Mallory worked to keep her expression and tone bland while the investigator inside her with Graham on a list did backflips. Charlie moved a couple piles around, pulled out a folder, and slid it across the desk.

"What's this?"

"An angle, perhaps. About the foundation and the kids it serves."

"Sounds like a far cry from the murdered and missing."

"Not too far. Kids get killed and disappear."

"Christian's Kids?" Mallory asked, referencing the bold type on the front of the folder.

"The ones in the program have dodged that fate. That could be the positive part of the story. But their lives haven't been easy."

Mallory flipped through the folder's contents. "Today's troubled youth, huh? You might be right, Charlie. I'll give it a shot."

She rose to leave.

"Whoa! Wait a minute. What's going on?"

"What do you mean?"

"That was way too easy."

Mallory needed a few seconds. Whatever she said next had to sound convincing. She walked over and closed his office door, then leaned against it.

"I visited Leigh this weekend."

"You what?"

"Her gravesite."

"Oh."

"I went there. Hard to imagine all that beauty buried six feet deep. Seeing a stone instead of her face. Talking to the ground. It did something to me." *Made me more determined than ever to find out who killed her.* "Brought back a flood of memories, of her and all of the others. All of the missing and murdered women I covered over this past year."

Mallory pushed off the door, slid her hands inside her jeans pockets. "Besides, you aren't the only one who thinks I need a break, who feels this series has become much too personal. So I'll take you up on the challenge." She walked to the door and turned. "When is this going to run?"

"Next week."

Mallory gave a curt nod, left his office, and smiled all the way to her desk.

After checking her phone and seeing Ava's thumbs up response, Mallory fired up her laptop and placed Christian Graham's name in the search engine. More than fifty million results showed up, along with images of his godlike physique. She tapped uneven nails on the well-worn desktop, scrolled through the links, and tried to figure out how to best use this opportunity to benefit Leigh. *Go for a one-on-one interview, bring up Leigh's name, and watch his reaction?* No, too limiting. If he reacts, then what? If he doesn't, end of conversation about her. She continued surfing, logged on to the charity website. Christian's Kids—a diverse group of bright-eyed, smiling, happy children if one went by the photo on the site's. . . . She read the foundation's mission, scanned the curriculum. Thoughts of a series for the column began to form, one that opened with a story about Christian, then segued into the foundation and the children it benefited. That would hopefully give Mallory the time she needed, time and access, to either incriminate or eliminate him as a suspect in Leigh's death.

Mallory wished Leigh were here to write the article. She'd followed the guy since he was drafted by the Navigators in their first-round pick. Leigh could have written the article without references where Mallory would have to do some heavy lifting to find a unique angle on a guy that stayed in the papers, lived in the news. Christian, she read, had been a mainstay in sports news since bursting onto the scene as a seventeen-year old high school junior. Writers waxed effusive on his natural talent. Headlines continually screamed his praise. "Graham Leads Cadets to Wildcard Upset." "Eastern Regional Graham Grabs MVP Honors." "Graham to the Big Brawn on a Full-Ride Scholarship! Multiple Recruitments." His stats were impressive. He'd led college championships while maintaining a 4.0 GPA, and been first pick in the draft. He was the Most Valuable Player who'd led the New York Navigators to NBA victory for three years straight, with a new contract for more than one hundred million dollars. Mallory paused at the number, remembered the homeless man with the bent shovel who cleaned their walks for change. She thought of America's wealth and its misplaced priorities, teachers who earned an average of fifty thousand while a millennial earned more than ten times that much for bouncing a ball. It hardly seemed fair but that wasn't her story. Mallory bypassed the articles touting his millions and refocused on ones that highlighted the man.

She scanned a bio. White father. Black mother. Their son—six five, one ninety, ten percent body fat—a glorious and perfect blend of the two. A true goddess magnet, evidenced by all the images of him with beautifully flawless women draped on his arm. Several stories in and all the high praise started to bug her. Then she realized it was more than that. There wasn't much written that was truly personal. That gave the reader a glimpse behind the larger-than-life persona and a chance to see the human standing behind it.

She clicked a tab and returned to the foundation website. At the bottom of the home page was a section highlighting the foundation's annual fundraiser. Mallory sat back, her mind's eye scanning Leigh's appointment book. Hadn't this event been written there? Her brows scrunched with the concentration to recall her best friend's conversations about Christian, the Navigators, basketball, conversations that Mallory usually blanked out. She clicked on tickets, looked askance at the prices. The least expensive ticket was five thousand dollars, heady Mallory thought, even for a fundraiser. But not for the wealthy. The event was sold out.

How could someone like Christian relate to the under-privileged children his foundation served? Didn't think he knew what a deprived life looked like from what she'd read. Grandfather a retired banker. Mother a real estate whiz. Grew up in Nassau County. Private schools. Privileged life. Were the reasons behind the non-profit like those of so many others who ran them? A wise though worthy tax write-off? *Probably.*

Who are you really, Christian Graham? She wasn't as inter-ested in who he was when the world was watching, as in the person who showed up behind closed doors, when the public could not see him.

5

Fifteen minutes, a delivered drink order and a coveted booth at the crowded restaurant, and still Ava wasn't there. Mallory ignored the waiting groups shooting daggers. Any other day, she'd be fine at the bar. Not today, though. She was not going to budge. The booth was the most private spot in the room, she was a regular and tipped well to gain favor. Five minutes and a third of the way through her cranberry and sparkling water spritz, she yanked her cellphone off of the table and began to text.

"Calm down, Mal gal, I'm right here."

Mallory looked up as Ava reached her and leaned down for a hug.

"About time you got here. You know I only get an hour, right?"

"Did Charlie see you and start a timer? Why are you tripping?"

"Why are you trying to be MIA? I called you yesterday."

"I know."

"You didn't call back."

"That's true." Mallory frowned. "Hey, can't a girl take time out to get her groove on with a handsome hunk who's hard and willing?"

"I thought Sam and I convinced you to stop trolling those online dating sites."

"I found this one while trolling the grocery store. Six feet of charming chocolate, thick lips, dark eyes. Muscles rippling every time he moved, mine clinching each time he smiled."

"Oh, Lord."

"He was at the meat counter picking up steaks. I offered to cook them. Dinner was great, dessert even better. My phone was off from the time he arrived until he left this morning just before dawn."

"Well, it's obvious he made you happy. Your disregard and tardiness are forgiven. Is this one and done or do you want seconds?"

Ava shrugged, and motioned to a waiter. "We'll see."

The two studied the menus, then placed their order.

Mallory watched the bubbly blonde walk away. "I might have a date this weekend."

"What? With who?"

"Christian Graham." Said casually, offhandedly, like a throw-away line.

"Shut the front door. Is that why you called yesterday?"

"Indirectly." Mallory eyed a group of businessmen being led to a nearby table. Ava followed her eye and then tapped Mallory's arm. "Focus. The tea. Spill it."

Mallory laughed. "It's not what you think. Charlie wants me to do a human interest-type story on him. Like you and Sam, he feels I need a shift in focus."

"This is for work?" Ava slumped back in her chair. "Darn it, Mal. I thought you meant a real date. But who knows? Play your cards right, or in this case your questions, and it just may turn into one."

"I'm hoping it will turn into something . . ."

The waiter returned with Ava's drink. She reached for it. "Something like what?"

Mallory shifted in the booth and lessened the distance between them. "Like a lead, perhaps," she continued softly, "into who killed Leigh."

Ava almost choked on the sip of soda. She picked up the napkin to cover her cough.

"Are you okay?"

After taking another more careful sip, Ava replied. "In hearing that segue, maybe I should be asking you that question."

"That probably did sound a bit disconnected."

"You think?"

"But it isn't. Not after what I found out this weekend." Mallory told Ava about the duffel bag she'd gotten from Barbara, and its contents that had belonged to Leigh.

"I've only read through the first six months so far," she finished. "But I made notes of what I thought was important— names, places, events that might mean something."

Mallory pulled out her tablet and opened a file. "A few times, I ran into what looks like a series of random numbers. Like this," she said, pointing to the screen. "I can't figure out what they mean, if anything at all."

Ava stared at Mallory's laptop screen. "Phone numbers, maybe? With extra ones added in some kind of sequence that only she knows?"

"You might be right in which case it would take forever trying combinations to try and get the right one."

Ava tapped the mouse to scroll down the page. "What are these?"

"Some of the addresses that were in there."

"Did you check them out to find out who lives there?"

"Only this one." Mallory tapped the screen. "It belongs to an accountant who is also a murder suspect."

"No way!" Ava hissed.

"I couldn't believe it either. It hadn't been an hour, maybe thirty minutes after seeing his name in her appointment book that I heard it over the news. A person of interest is how the reporter framed it. But I did a background check on the guy, Ava. And it was shadier than a full-grown oak."

Ava pulled out her phone and began rapidly typing.

Mallory watched her. "What are you doing?"

"Checking the other addresses."

Mallory reached for her phone. "Good idea."

The first one she checked matched a yoga studio in lower Manhattan. The second one was the workspace of an up-and-coming designer. The third and fourth addresses were high-rises in Manhattan. The fifth address drained the blood from Ava's face and took Mallory's breath away. Silent screams assailed her insides as she and Ava looked between themselves and the screen.

"Are you thinking what I'm thinking?" Mallory asked when she could trust herself to speak.

"Of course." Ava clicked on the website link next to the address. "There's only one reason you make an appointment to see this kind of ob-gyn practice."

"Leigh was pregnant?" It was said not so much as a question but an impossibility. An incredulity. *Both of us feeling the scorch of the heat.* An inexplicable chance.

"At least she thought she was." Ava sat back against the couch. "What if she was, and the father of the child didn't want to have it?"

Mallory's eyes narrowed as she processed this news. "Then you kill her, and make it look like a suicide."

The two ladies continued talking, plotting, their heads close together, their voices low. The food arrived, but Mallory had lost her appetite. She thanked Ava for playing detective and keeping what they'd discussed between the two of them, accepted the now boxed lunch from the waiter and headed back to work for another pow-wow with Charlie. To think that not one but two lives had been taken when Leigh was killed made Mallory twice as determined to nab the killer. Mallory believed the answer might lie within the names found in Leigh's appointment book. Christian's name was one of several mentioned in that book. Mallory wanted to know why, was determined to learn if he was Leigh's secret. For a reporter to get more than a press kit and a pat interview with a bad boy who was also basketball royalty might not be easy. Even for an award-winning one.

The fundraiser.

That was it! A place for casual conversation. To observe, scrutinize. Unlike Leigh, Mallory hated dressing up. She'd feel as out of place as Cinderella had one minute past midnight but so be it. The prince was giving a ball and one way or another, Mallory would be there.

6

"Absolutely not."

Similar to Cinderella's plight, going to the ball wasn't going to be easy. Mallory learned this as soon as the question passed her lips.

"Charlie, you didn't even let me finish the sentence."

"Didn't have to. To any question regarding basketball and Saturday night, the answer is no. Graham's fundraiser is one of the hottest tickets in the city. The paper only got one and it's got my name on it. If not me, Josh is next in line."

Josh was the sports editor. It made perfect sense that after the editor, he'd be in line for the paper's sole Holy Grail. That didn't stop Mallory from fighting to usurp his position, and Charlie's too.

"Look, you're going to rub shoulders with the athletes and hobnob with celebrities. It's prestigious. Huge. I get that. But for me, it's not about any of that. It's about the paper, and my column, and how we can build on the momentum gained by my winning the Pen. I've got an idea on how to do that, how to grab our readers back from the *Reporter* and reclaim the number one spot."

There was no love lost between the *New York Reporter* and

New York News. They'd battled for years, scrapping like boxers and fighting for stories to gain the edge and be the first papers New Yorkers opened to get their news. Mallory knew Charlie loved at least one thing more than basketball—being number one and beating his nemesis, Rob Anderson, the editor at the *Reporter*.

Charlie leaned back in the chair, his soft beer-belly straining the buttons on his wrinkled white shirt. "I'll probably regret asking, but tell me this idea."

Mallory grabbed the few folders that accumulated on the chair she'd sat in just hours ago and held them as she sat.

"You wanted a soft story, right? To make people feel good." Charlie gave a slight nod. "Instead of a single article solely focused on Graham, think of a four-part series that starts out about him but then highlights his foundation. After reading what you gave me I checked out the website and read about some of the children his center serves. Reading about them reminded me of the missing and runaway teens I covered last year, many with situations similar to those kids. Low-income families living in less than desirable neighborhoods. Often being raised by single, working mothers. One link told the story of a kid who fits that profile but is doing amazing stuff. She's into horticulture. Growing a rooftop garden in her Queens neighborhood. The article seemed to suggest that the difference in her story and the girls I ended up writing about was a center that helped turn her life around. Christian's center."

Charlie worked an unlit electronic cigarette from one side of his mouth to the other. "Keep talking."

"I thought I could do comparable stories in a way that 'Knightly News' retains its brand of serious journalism on issues that matter, that directly effects our communities. One kid makes it. Another doesn't. Why? Answer the question. That way I continue the theme of what got me the Prober's Pen while using the center's success stories as a bridge away from a topic that you suggested I needed to take a break from."

"At first you weren't keen on making the change. Now you're almost gung ho. What happened?"

"I've had time to think about it and am now using a woman's prerogative of changing her mind." Mallory said this lightheartedly but Charlie's expression didn't change. "For over a year I've been single-minded. As you've pointed out, I can use a break and the readers could use something lighter too, a little love for a change."

Charlie eyed her speculatively for several seconds, then sat up and rolled closer to his desk. "I'm glad you appreciate the angle I suggested, maybe even embraced it. And this from a woman who professes to not like sports."

"Liking sports and covering those who play them are two different things. Besides, before the New Year even got here you shot down the story I really want to do."

"The one on your friend Leigh Jackson?"

"I believe the suggested series title was Catching Up on Cold Cases."

"I know what you wrote. I also know how you think and what you believe to be true about her. I get that she was your friend and I'm really sorry about what happened to her. But there's no more story there. That case isn't cold. It's closed. Over. End of story. The public's moved on."

Mallory heard the words in the silence that followed. *And you should, too.*

"Attending the foundation's fundraiser is the perfect event from which to frame this story. It should, hopefully, afford me a whole picture of both the man, and his mission."

Charlie shook his head slowly. "I don't know, Knight. Graham's annual gala is everything, and it's not just about hob-nobbing. It's about positioning the paper for future interviews, networking and, you know, stuff like that."

Mallory remained silent, her expression neutral, waiting. She'd delivered a sound argument, thrown all her rocks, used all her bullets. By remaining quiet, Charlie wouldn't know that the chamber was empty.

"And . . . included with the ticket may have been a suggestion that stories focusing less on his bad boy persona and more on his humanistic, philanthropic side would be appreciated."

"So we're his PR team now?" Mallory asked with raised brow. "The ticket was incentive for you to publish articles that reshape Graham's public persona into that of a nice guy reeking of kindness and humility?" She snorted.

"Okay, I'll also admit that I'm a Navigators addict who worships Graham. He's the god of the goal, Mal! You do know that, right?"

"Really, Charlie? That's like asking if I knew President Obama passed the Affordable Care Act."

She paused, softened her voice.

"I know it's a hot ticket. I know you love all things Graham and that I'm probably not the only one who'd like the chance to attend his soiree or even better, for a one-on-one with New York's media darling. Not as many journalists were rushing behind me to cover the latest Jane Doe runaway-turned-sex-slave. But it begs the question, what if there'd been a Christian's Kids center where she lived? What if she could have run away to a place like that for support? The column could get more celebrities and people with big bucks thinking about using their dollars to make a real difference in this country. To help save lives."

"Any other female, Knight, and I'd have no doubt that the motive was self-serving."

"You know me. Between getting shot and wearing heels, I'd rather take a bullet."

"But to get the story . . ."

"I'd walked in them the length of the Macy's parade." *To potentially catch a killer, twice as far.*

Charlie turned and opened a drawer behind his desk, then swiveled around and tossed an envelope toward her.

Mallory picked it up. "Is this the ticket?"

She opened the envelope and pulled out a gold-embossed invitation on linen stationery. "I get to go?"

"It's not just any gala, but the annual fundraiser for his charity," Charlie explained, casually, a slight frown the only indicator of the pain turning over that ticket must have given him. "Wear something fancy."

"Right up my alley." Mallory's sarcasm dripped off every word.

"You asked for it."

Charlie pushed back from the desk, his twenty-year old mentor's chair squeaking under his bulk as he rolled across the mat. It was an obvious dismissal. Mallory remained seated.

"Anything else?"

"No, that's it."

"Then you'd better get out of here before I change my mind."

Mallory jumped up and headed back to her desk thinking, *be careful what you ask for. Sometimes you might get it.*

7

Mallory hated shopping. At times like these, she really missed Leigh. Her diva girlfriend wouldn't be in angst about what to wear to a black-tie event that Charlie dubbed "high-brow." Leigh's dilemma would be which one out of the plethora of dresses in her huge walk-in closet would best dazzle and make her stand out in the crowd. After receiving the invitation from Charlie, Mallory had worried about the situation for all of five minutes before deciding to rely on her little black dress stand-by. Then she'd thrown herself back into writing and investigating, what she did best. The center at the heart of the Christian's Kids foundation and the contents of Leigh's calendar note book had consumed her for the past two days. Christian Graham? Other than a potential suspect in Leigh's demise? Not so much. Which is why at eight p.m. on a Wednesday night she was still at work, pondering part one of the four-part series she'd pitched to Charlie and searching for a way to write about a man who to her came off as a bit of a jerk, in a way that revealed more positive qualities while remaining true to the "Knightly News" brand.

It wasn't easy. She'd been at it for over an hour and still had only half of a typewritten page. She huffed in exasperation and dropped her head in her hand.

The shrill sound of the office phone startled her. "Mallory Knight."

"So . . . what's the plan?"

"Sam? Why are you calling the office, especially at this time of night?"

"You didn't answer your cell."

Mallory had silenced it before going in to speak with Charlie and belatedly realized she hadn't turned it back on. "Plan for what?" she asked, while reaching for her cell phone and firing it up.

"Tracking down Leigh's killer."

A gentle huff was the only sign of Mallory's anger.

"Ava told me about the appointment book you found in Leigh's things, and how you felt one of the men named in it might have something to do with her murder."

"Did she also tell you that I'd asked her to keep it to herself?"

"Don't be mad at her, Mal. You know there're no secrets between the three musketeers. And while she believes you may be onto something, she's also concerned that once again this search will consume you, that you'll stay so focused on Leigh's death that you'll forget to live your life."

A pause and then, "I'm worried, too."

"Don't be. It's okay. And I'm not mad at Ava."

"Good. So how do you plan to check out these guys and find out their connection to Leigh?"

"Background checks on the internet and then meeting them, striking up a friendly conversation, mentioning her name to hear what they say about her."

"You think it will be that easy to get guys to talk?"

"I don't know. We'll see. My first test is this weekend. Christian Graham."

Sam laughed. "That one should be obvious! You're how I found out Leigh was a die-hard Navigator. That she spent hundreds on game tickets and bled black and gold."

"I think there was more. I think they may have dated."

"I can see that. Leigh is . . . was . . . stunning. Definitely his type. But you don't think he—"

"I don't know. That's what I'll be finding out."

"How? Joining the press after the game to try and nab a private conversation? And even if you do, I doubt he'll cop to a murder, no matter how nicely you pose the question."

"You're so bright. That's why we're friends." They laughed. "I'm going to his annual fundraiser Saturday night to do an interview for my column."

"You're featuring Christian in 'Knightly News'?"

Mallory laughed. "Thank you for sounding appropriately shocked."

"It's just such a stretch from the usual gist of your column. He's not female, missing, or dead."

"It was Charlie's call, not mine. But I've found a way to make it work." She told Sam about the series. "The longer the contact, the more info I'll get. Visiting the center, speaking with the employees, maybe a little secret sleuthing . . . who knows what I'll find out.

"All right, Sherlock, whatever and however. Just be careful. Promise me that."

"The most dangerous aspect of this Saturday night will be me in heels."

"That brings up the most important question. What are you wearing?"

"You have to ask."

"Don't tell me the little black dress."

"Okay, I won't."

"No. Way."

"Why not? It's totally fine."

"You're not going for fine. You're going for knockout. And the event is this weekend? We've got to go shopping."

"I don't think—"

"You won't have to. I'll do the choosing. You'll try them on."

"Just bring me over something and I'll wear it."

Tomorrow. Six o'clock. Brooklyn Mall. End of story. Meet me in the atrium. Don't make me come get you."

8

If Christian Graham weren't six foot five with a dazzling smile, a dimpled chin, and eyes that pulled one into his gaze, he'd still enter a room and command it. Even without the tailored suit he wore, the Rolex watch, or the diamond cuffs that peeked from beneath his jacket sleeve when he bent his arm, there was something magnetic and enigmatic about him. Graceful, panther-like movements, long legs, smooth and strong stride, And so it was on this late Saturday morning as Christian entered the Atlantic Grill on Broadway, just blocks away from the ball player's newly purchased multi-million-dollar penthouse on Fifty-Eighth, fan reactions rippled along his path to a corner booth. He paid little attention to them, a brief nod or slight smile the only acknowledgement, if at all. His eyes were hidden behind designer shades. All other eyes in the room were on him. Nobody approached him to ask for an autograph, though, or to take a selfie. Five years in and New Yorkers knew the rules. On the court or during public appearances, he belonged to the fans and the city. When he navigated said city as a private citizen—leave him alone.

As Christian reached the booth, a man stood in greeting. Broad shoulders, like the ball player's, skin a few shades lighter, same chestnut hair except streaked with gray, hazel eyes that mirrored those behind the sunglasses and twinkled as if holding mischief and secrets. He held out his hand.

"Good morning, son."

"Hello, Dad."

The two men shook hands while sharing a shoulder salute then settled into the booth with Christian's back to the room. He removed his glasses. Dad's request. They made small talk while placing their order. Christian opted for green jasmine tea but his dad, Corbin, ordered coffee made the way the son knew his father liked his women—Black and strong with two teaspoons of sweetness.

Corbin watched Christian text away on a phone that constantly vibrated, buzzed, and beeped. "Looks like you need another assistant."

Christian shook his head, thumbs tapping and sliding across the screen. "Folks and their last-minute ticket requests. They know this event sells out every year."

"I was surprised to get your text wanting to meet. Figured you'd be either too zapped after last night's game or too busy with tonight's preparations."

"I've got people to handle all that."

"Yes, but you are your mother's son."

"Controlling?"

"I was going to say responsible."

Christian showed a dozen reasons why a popular toothpaste company paid him millions to represent their brand. "I like responsible, but when it comes to my shit, I'm controlling, too."

"Ah, then that's where you two differ."

"Right, because Mom controls her life," they finished together, "and everybody else's, too."

"So, you didn't go out celebrating after last night's comeback?"

"Yeah, in a cryo chamber."

"Ha!"

"It's not time yet to cut the net."

Corbin nodded. "That'll happen if you win the championship."

Christian's eyes flew from the phone to Corbin's face in a blink. His expression was one carved in stone. "When we win. Not if, when."

"Of course."

"Other than your body taking a beating, you good?"

Christian shut off his phone and placed it on the table. "I'm all right. Dudes wreaking havoc on my whole left side trying to reinjure my shoulder."

"I told Pete that I thought you went back too early."

"Why? It wasn't broken."

"It's your body, and I trust the doctors. Rebecca showed me the picture you took with the kid from your center while there. It was probably Zoey's idea, but your mom took the credit, saying visiting him is how you were raised. Her words. It was a good story. Shined a spotlight on the foundation and let people know you do have a softer side. And a shot much preferred to the other ways in which you sometimes make news."

Christian's bad-boy antics often netted publicity that tarnished the otherwise stellar Graham name. He didn't give a damn; he had told his mother that on more than one occasion. People were going to think what they wanted, believe what they wanted. He'd made this city's basketball team a force to be reckoned with, one that overshadowed every other sports franchise in New York. That was his job, and what he owed the fans. As for the kid, Brandon, he'd been housed at another hospital altogether. Going to see him had nothing to do with his PR manager Zoey, Christian's upbringing, or a photo op to soften his image. Christian needed answers. He was trying to save lives. Maybe his own, who knew? But he let his father's assumption ride. Probably best.

"Speaking of the foundation, DeVaughn told me the bank bought four tables this year. Thanks for that."

"Are you kidding? If I didn't spend the bank's money so the execs could schmooze with you, I'd probably get terminated."

"You need to retire anyway. Help your brother run the center."

"Rebecca's still smarting that she didn't get that role. She's a much better fit than your uncle."

"Maybe, but the foundation was Pete's idea."

"I know."

"He did everything, managed every aspect of getting Christian's Kids up and running. I think having the foundation to focus on is what brought him out of the depression he faced."

"He does seem a much happier man these days. Of course, that might also be from a having a wife half his age."

"Stop hating on Pete, Dad. Melissa's good for him. Finally made him a father."

"She made somebody one."

Christian chuckled. "Still won't get that DNA test, huh?"

"No. I think he's afraid of what might be found out."

"If it doesn't matter to him, then it shouldn't matter to you. He believes he's lucky to have her."

"She hit the midlife crisis jackpot and, as such, is truly the lucky one."

"Okay, now you sound like Zoey."

Christian said this even though his statement was true. Groupies were known for poking holes in condoms and hoping for pro player cash kids. Melissa was an A-tier groupie who had seen more naked basketball players than a reporter in their locker room. Christian also had doubts about the child. But Pete was happy, so Christian was tickled pink.

"Honestly, though, I would feel better with you taking a more active role. At least on the financial tip. You know I love my uncle, but I think for him spending money is almost better than fucking."

"Oh, I can assure you that when it comes to my brother and his love for the dollar, he'd say it was infinitely better than any prize between a woman's legs. But I don't want to deal with his territorial bullshit. He directs that center as though he carried it nine months."

"I'll handle uncle. Better yet, I'll set it up for you to go over the books when we're out of town. He just started acting like he has sense again. Don't want to throw him off normal."

"Don't worry about it. I know how to work around him."

"Y'all's sibling rivalry. Man, I swear."

The conversation lulled as their food arrived.

"So that's why you're buying me lunch," Corbin asked. "As a bribe for my services?"

"I invited you here because you're my father. And I love you."

"Ah, thanks, son. I love you, too."

"And to tell you to check out those books first chance you get."

"Motherfucker," Corbin grumbled as both men laughed and began eating.

Neither knew it then, but a time was soon coming when there would be no more smiles.

Not now, though. For Christian, today was a feel-good one all the way around.

The crowd was dense in the Mandarin Oriental hotel's massive ballroom. As he had earlier in the day at the restaurant, Christian waded through a sea of admirers with charm and finesse. Tonight, he was resplendent in a tailored black tux complemented with white and silver. His stride was slow and confident, with a casualness carefully honed years ago to hide the fear and uncertainty he often felt within. Some might say he'd worked his ass off and had earned the right to be arrogant. But he wasn't, not really. Every admiring glance he got now helped to cover the pain of childhood rejection, of being too white to be black and too black to be white. Now he commanded respect from every race, creed, and color. As far as Christian was concerned, it was about damn time.

He continued through the crowd, barely got more than a step or two before being stopped for a hug or handshake, a selfie or kiss. He accommodated all requests with the skill of a politician. He looked each person in the eye and in a room of more than five hundred people, called many by name. Those who approached were mindful of the injury sustained during the rumble with Golden State and stayed clear of his shoulder. The pain was pretty much gone, but there was still a weight being borne on its breadth: Brandon's father, Danny, being shot, the kid trying to commit suicide on top of it. The whole situation was beyond fucked up. That answers continued to elude him bothered Christian more than he let on. In this instance, the foundation's name was more than a catchy moniker. Christian truly cared for the kids who came to his center. Brandon reminded him of his younger self and occupied a special place in his heart. Which is why, after hearing the news during his own health crisis, he'd been driven to Queens to be at Brandon's bedside to let the kid know that his life mattered, and that it was totally not cool to ingest a near-fatal amount of super sweet Kool-Aid mixed with industrial-strength disinfectant.

That was earlier in the week. Since then his ever-present publicist and PR manager, Zoey Girard, had lost sleep over the visit, trying to erase any link between the rumored suicide by a preteen who regularly came to the center and a murder attempt on the boy's father. He hadn't found out until the next morning that Pete had been questioned by detectives. They'd wanted to talk to Christian but his uncle had flatly refused. Being shuttled out a side door hadn't been to protect him from gathering fans but to keep him an arm's length from the law. Frustrating, but Christian understood what they were trying to do. Some might label him an asshole, but Christian's Kids as an organization had a spotless reputation. All of them wanted to keep it that way. So, the official story for Brandon's hospitalization wasn't near suicide but an allergic reaction. They didn't lie. The kid was no doubt allergic to murder and had reacted to someone wanting to kill his dad.

"Christian!"

"Can I get a pic?"

"Can we get a selfie?"

He turned to find a half dozen sexily dressed young women on his heels, cell phones at the ready.

"Hello, ladies. Whoa!" He turned to protect his shoulder as one particularly aggressive female elbowed her way through the others and wrapped an arm around him as if it were her due. "Tell you what, give me the camera. All of you come around. No, we're doing one group shot," he replied to clamors from those, including Miss Aggressive, who wanted an individual pic with the legend.

"Come on, shorty." He motioned to a vivacious looking Latina on the group's perimeter, the prettiest and quietest one among them. "Stand here to make sure that you get in the shot."

He'd barely tapped the screen before Zoey appeared at his side, taking the phone and asking which girl it belonged to.

"Can you sign my—"

"No, he can't." Zoey took Christian by the arm, the one not attached to the injured shoulder. "Sorry, ladies. Christian is needed elsewhere."

"Thank you for rescuing me, but that was a bit rude."

"No, a bit rude would have been my blocking the path as I saw them make a beeline over. Anyone of those girls is a lawsuit waiting to happen."

"How do you figure?"

"Jailbait, dude. Not one of them is over eighteen."

"You're bullshitting me."

"Nope. I rescued you from a sixteen that could have gotten you twenty. But that's not why I came over. Not the only reason, anyway."

She'd walked them to an area along the room's perimeter where there was a modicum of semi-privacy.

"What's wrong? Is this about Brandon?"

"Brandon's fine, and yes, his mother got the money you requested be sent. She's appreciative. Look, I don't have much time. I've scheduled a press conference to happen in thirty minutes."

"What?"

"While everyone's eating. Look, Christian. I know you wanted tonight to be all about raising money. This press conference is indirectly about that, too. News sharks keep circling the kid's story. They printed what we gave them about an allergic reaction, but we think some of the keener ones smell blood. Rather than have them coming at you all evening, or trying to dig up shit on their own, we're going to have the conference, lead off with how well Brandon is doing, and thank them for affording the family the privacy they need."

"What about Danny?"

"Brandon's father?" Christian nodded. "What about him?"

"Just wondering if anyone has made the connection."

"No, thank God. One of the times that kids taking their mother's last name is a good thing."

"That's fucked up, Zoey."

"Sorry," she said with a slight chuckle behind her insincere apology.

Rich bitch, Christian thought but didn't utter, knowing if he had, Zoey would only have laughed. Having known each other since they were in grade school, their families were close, and she got a lot of leeway when it came to her skewed views on race, her lack of compassion, and sometimes lack of tact. There was nothing good about neighborhoods filled with single mothers and many boys who didn't even know their fathers, let alone carry their last names. A woman who suckled from a trust fund titty couldn't possibly understand what women like Karen, Brandon's mom, went through. What it was like to be poor and Black in America. These thoughts were processed as he half listened to Zoey prattle on about spin, before something stole his attention altogether.

Tall. That was his first thought about her, as it was the first attribute that caught his eye. She appeared just over Zoey's left shoulder walking to the bar, towering a head of long silky hair and a bare shoulder over the women around her. With the gentle lighting and distance between them, he couldn't make out her nationality. Hispanic, Indian, maybe Middle Eastern? Just that she was tall and, from he could tell from her side profile, beautiful.

". . . Ten, fifteen minutes max. After that you'll be seated at the head table next to . . . Christian? Are you listening?"

He cut his gaze back to Zoey. "Yeah, I heard you."

Zoey's eyes narrowed. She turned in the direction of his gaze. "Oh, that."

"You know her?"

"Not personally, and you should steer clear, too. She's a reporter, an investigative journalist, and from what I've heard a good one. She just won some type of prestigious award, which means when she looks for answers, she finds them. Avoid her like the plague."

9

Not even thirty minutes and Mallory's feet protested the wearing of four-inch heels. She'd balked at the shiny, strappy stilettos, but Sam had insisted they went perfectly with the dress. They did, in that last Saturday when Sam brought them over to her, Mallory hadn't wanted to purchase them, either. As she'd stood in front of her bedroom mirror, however, with her friend and colleague standing by like a proud mama bear, Mallory had admitted that every shopping suggestion Sam made had been a good one. Even Leigh would have approved. The one-shoulder dress, with its empress waist and flared skirt, played down her bubble butt and healthy thighs, and the color, which reminded her of a premium merlot or cabernet, brought out the golden hues of her sun-kissed skin and complemented her amber eyes. Mallory hardly ever wore makeup. She rarely straightened her rebel curls. Yet tonight, she stood at the edge of the bar wearing mascara, blush, and a shiny lip gloss, with hair that had been conditioned and flat-ironed into silky submission and now fell gracefully over her shoulders and midway down her back. Reaching for the club soda with lime the bartender served her, Mallory mentally thanked Sam once again. She felt out of place in the hoity-toity setting, but knew she looked the part.

Sipping her drink, Mallory scanned the well-heeled crowd and caught sight of Christian. He stood with a beautiful blonde, their heads turned in her direction. Looking at her? Mallory thought it possible until a man walked from behind her over to where they stood. Then the man and the blonde headed in her direction, passed her and continued toward the exit and in the direction of where she'd been told a press conference would be held. His assistant, Mallory wondered? A girlfriend? Didn't matter to her one way or another. Were she in the market for love, which she wasn't, a professional athlete was the last type of fish she'd try to reel in. Who'd want to sign up for that type of pressure? Even among several contemporaries in the room, Christian stood out. He was never without an audience. Women buzzed around him like flies. No, Mallory didn't envy that woman one bit.

Turning away from the star of tonight's show, Mallory scanned the crowded ballroom. The largesse, opulence, the inevitable waste went against everything she'd ever stood up for or believed in. Mallory had grown up solidly middle class yet even then sometimes felt privileged beyond what she deserved. So few with so much when so many had nothing. A mini-exodus caused her to check the semi-gauche, jeweled watch purchased from a street vendor. Game time. The press conference was set to start in less than ten minutes. Time to position herself in the path of his majesty and get the one-on-one.

Securing the clutch purse strap over her shoulder, Mallory stepped away from the bar and entered the throng of rich or well-connected people milling about, choosing the shortest path to the exit doors, even though it meant navigating through the crowd. A jazz trio played light and airy music from their spot in a far corner; tinkling ivory floating over the steady drum bottom was the perfect accompaniment to the low din of voices. Mallory imagined Leigh here and felt a pang in her gut. She would have loved this atmosphere, would have given Christian competition for commanding the room.

"Mallory?"

She reached the exit nearest the hall leading to the press area, and although she heard her name, kept walking. Maybe it was her imagination, and one of the rats Manhattan was known for hadn't snuck into a party well above his pay grade.

There was movement in her peripheral vision. Again, she ignored it.

"Hey, Mallory. That is you!"

A glance and then, "Oh, hi, Rob" She could hardly stand to be civil to someone who'd caused her so much pain and maligned her friend's name. But the journalism world was a small one, and burned bridges were hard to cross.

"Almost didn't recognize you." Five-eight on a good day, like when wind tousled his hair to add an inch and there were lifts in his shoes, Mallory's former boss worked to keep pace with her long strides. "The heels, spiffy outfit. All that hair. What do you women call it, a weave?"

Mallory offered up as much of a smile as she could muster. "Take care."

Sometimes there was no fixing ignorant or asshole, and when someone fit both descriptions, hope was truly lost. Fortunately for her, they reached the room set up for the press conference. It was small, with a rectangular table in front of the room with three chairs behind it and microphones positioned in front of each seat. Extra lighting had been set up, along with a couple rows of folding chairs, twenty in total, already taken by reporters who hadn't received invitations to enter the ballroom-turned-wonderland from which she'd come. She maneuvered through the standing-room-only area in back, partly to get away from Rob and partly to make it to a wall that she could lean against for relief. She was by no means a big girl, but you couldn't tell that to her right toe, the one that had either gone to sleep or straight-up died. She reached the wall and, while pulling a mini recorder from her beaded clutch, shifted her weight and tilted her foot to place the weight on the heel and give her toe a fighting chance at survival. All that did was give room for the sleeping digit to awaken and shoot throbbing pain to the other toes, the ball of her foot, and partway up the shin. She bit back a grimace and opened up notes on her cell phone just as a rush of activity and raised voices signaled that the king had arrived.

Christian entered, and Mallory had to admit it really was as though sunshine had walked into the room. His smile was wide and genuine. He waved, nodded, or spoke to a few of the reporters on his way to the table. The blonde Mallory had seen him with earlier was by his side. Christian sat in the middle, the blonde to his right. The man who'd come from behind her to talk with Christian sat on the other side.

Seconds after they were seated, the blonde pulled the microphone toward her. "Hello, everyone. Thanks for coming. I'm Zoey Girard, publicist for Christian and PR manager for Christian's Kids, among other business ventures. As you all know, and have reported, this has been a hectic and trying week. But Christian's foundation means a lot to him, the kids, and to all of us working with him. Your coverage of this event helps get the word out about what we're doing and what's needed to help Christian's kids have a better life. Even though our time is very limited, we want to answer as many questions as possible."

A barrage of them started immediately.

Christian held up his hands, his smile as relaxed and easy as when he entered the room, the way it had been every time Mallory looked at him, now that she thought of it.

"Maybe I can start by updating you all with what's already been reported. The shoulder. It's a little irritated, a little painful, but I don't have a chip on it."

Laughter rippled through the room. Mallory smiled. The guy had charisma, she'd give him that.

"It was dislocated, but thankfully nothing was torn or

pulled. The specialists, my personal physician, and the team doctor have all examined it, and thankfully it's just a bruise, well, not just a bruise, anytime a six-six, two-hundred-and-fifty-pound troglodyte falls on you, it isn't 'just' anything." He paused, while some laughed, others scribbled down the comment, cameras flashed around the room. "But there's bruising on my AC joint and my rotator cuff that if I continued playing without rest and therapy could worsen. So, I will be sitting out the next few games."

"That's a time frame of . . ." a reporter in the front row asked.

"About a week, Chuck. Hopefully no longer than that."

Another barrage of questions ensued. One rang out over the others. "How is Brandon? The kid you visited in the hospital?"

"Thanks for asking. I'm told he's doing a lot better. Back at home and getting stronger every day."

"What kind of allergic reaction was it, exactly?"

Zoey cut in. "A press release was issued that included all of those details and provided the name of the doctor who treated him. He's the best one for questions involving Brandon's illness."

"Anything to that rumor about attempted suicide?" This from a young reporter at the back of the room, his jeans, black turtleneck, and Navigator knit cap a jarring contrast to the dressy attire worn by most other reporters.

"Anything other than what we've reported is just what you called it, a rumor."

Attempted suicide? Could that be why her boss was given an incentive to publish articles that humanized Graham, because of the potential for bad press?

"And you are?" Mallory asked, directing her question to the man who spoke.

Several turned in her direction, including Christian. Zoey,

too. Mallory could feel both sets of eyes on her, along with others, but she kept hers trained on where her question had been directed.

"Pete Graham, executive director of Christian's Kids."

"Who are you?" Christian asked.

Mallory looked up from typing Pete's name into her phone, met his gaze and felt something shift inside her. "Mallory Knight."

"'Knightly News'?" Pete asked.

Mallory nodded.

"Didn't you win the Prober's Pen?" The guy who'd turned to ask her was only two feet away but coming in a lull between questions, he caught everyone's ear. More eyes turned toward her. Mallory felt warmth creeping up from her chest, crossing her shoulders and reaching her neck. She'd never liked the spotlight and blamed that for the rush of adrenaline that had her blushing. The heat had traveled downward as well, and had started with Christian's question and intent gaze.

"Time for just one or two more questions, guys," Zoey said. "Questions for Christian, not other reporters in the room."

She said it with a playful chuckle and tilt of her head. But her eyes weren't smiling. Mallory saw through the feigned lightheartedness as easy as one could see through glass. She looked at Pete, the executive director. His expression was serious, but his body language was relaxed.

"What are you hoping to get from tonight's gala?"

"A lot of money." Christian's quick, honest answer brought the laughter it intended.

"Why not just use your own?" Mallory didn't realize she had spoken her thought aloud until Christian's eyes found her once again.

"I have, and quite a bit of it," he answered, unbothered, searing her once again with his deliberate gaze. Mallory forced herself to meet his stare. Their eyes locked and held. A challenge of sorts. She read sincerity and confidence in his coffee-colored orbs. And something undefinable that felt dangerous, mysterious, and quickened her pulse.

"A wise one once said it takes a village to raise a child," he continued, his eyes finally shifting from Mallory to take in others in the room. "One child," he emphasized with a long forefinger. "Over a hundred kids come through the foundation's doors on a regular basis. That number doubles during the summer months. Kids who come from unsafe neighborhoods, broken homes, communities where drugs, violence, gangs, you name it, are an everyday thing. The goal of Christian's Kids is to provide a safe haven for these kids, an atmosphere conducive to learning, to growing, heck, sometimes to just being able to be a kid without having to worry about getting a bullet in the back. I know some of y'all paint me as larger than life, but I can't do this alone. I need help." Once again, his eyes drifted to Mallory. "And with your continued support, helping me spread the word, and the generous hearts of my fellow New Yorkers, we'll get it done."

Zoey stood abruptly. "That's all the time we have, guys. Enjoy the rest of the evening."

The trio stood and, led by the small entourage who'd accompanied their entrance, led the way out of the room. Mallory ignored her toe's protest against walking and maneuvered around the other reporters just as Christian and company reached the door.

"Christian."

She said it clearly and quite audibly, but if he heard her, it didn't show. She reached inside her bag for a card and increased her pace. "Christian!"

One of his team turned to block her approach. "No more questions."

"I'm doing a series on the kids," she all but yelled to Christian's back. She executed a pivot and turn to lose her guard that would have made any coach proud, kept her eye on the prize and tried to keep up. "Looking for something besides the canned quotes from your PR team."

Zoey twirled on stilettos with the finesse of a ballerina. "That PR team has another quote for you: The press conference is over. Back off."

In another city that bark may have been enough to intimidate a reporter. Not in New York.

"Zoey, Mallory. I didn't mean to offend you. Just wanting to put the center in a light that New Yorkers haven't already seen. Would love some original material. Here's my card."

It was snatched from her hand. "Got it." Zoey was gone in a flash, but Christian was faster. When Mallory looked up he was nowhere in sight.

Dammit.

She hadn't intended to, but Mallory ended up staying longer than she'd planned. Once seated and able to slide off her heels, she actually enjoyed herself, which she hadn't intended, either. She now had several angles from which to approach Christian Graham and his foundation as the "Knightly News" topic for the next four weeks. What she didn't have was another chance at Christian, surrounded by his entourage and protectors for the rest of the night. Nor did she have a plan B. But on the ride home one began forming, based on the reporter question that Zoey had blocked. The kid. Plan Brandon. Mallory didn't know why, but her gut told her he was the next right move.

10

Christian sat at the head table with one of the richest men in America and tried to appear interested in what he said. Truth was, his mind was on more pressing matters: a dialed-up dick needing to make a call. With the injury and rehab, he hadn't gotten any in over a week. It was time. He was due. A roomful of possibilities awaited. Vivica Khan had certainly caused a stir when she and her party arrived and took a table at the front of the room. She'd gotten his attention the same as all the other men, and half of the women. It had been more than a year since he'd seen her in person, more than three since their well-publicized and slightly exaggerated summer fling. The Bahraini's sultry beauty was as intoxicating as when they'd first been introduced, so much so that he'd actually considered the offer she'd discreetly whispered in his ear while posing for the cameras. But she'd effectively ended any possibilities of further dalliances by mentioning the B-word while vacationing in Turks and Caicos that year. Babies. She thought one created by the two of them would be beautiful. That the thought was anywhere near her mind was enough to shrink his erection. They'd had sex a few more times while there, but even with a condom Christian didn't come inside her. And when he said,

"See you later" at the airport, she'd had no idea that later would be three years from then in a room with five hundred witnesses.

Hers wasn't the only offer. Christian had been given several business cards, some with clear messages that booty calls, not business meetings, were what they had in mind. He wondered about the reporter, Mallory Knight. What was on her mind? He found it hard to believe her claim of knowing nothing about him. How could any New Yorker not know about him, a man always in the press, especially a reporter? He remembered how she'd chased him down after the press conference. Was it really to find out more about the foundation? Or was she like the others, using any excuse to get next to him? Christian decided that it didn't matter. Zoey had warned him to avoid her, and considering the drama swirling around him, she might be right. The last thing he needed was someone who'd earned a degree in how to get in other's business snooping around. Just as he returned his attention to the businessman beside him, a vision of loveliness walked through the ballroom doors. Twins Morgan and Meagan had approached him months ago, with a package deal he couldn't refuse. He had a commitment once the program ended, but after that . . . He reached for his phone and sent a text.

"I think it's great work you're doing here, Christian," the business owner was saying as Christian tuned fully back in. "Have Pete or whomever contact my secretary. We'll send over a check."

Christian held out his hand. "I appreciate that, brother."

The program started shortly after and went off without a hitch. Christian knew that wasn't Pete's doing. His uncle mainly handled financial and legal matters. He was the money man with connections that kept the nonprofit's coffers healthy, the face of the organization after Christian, the star. Carla Whitehead, the assistant director of planning and marketing, and Emma Davis, the assistant director under Pete who handled the day-to-day affairs, were the ones who made everything happen in real time, handling both the day-to-day operation and coordinating tonight's event. As the last person to speak right before the MC—a popular dancer-turned-actor who attributed afterschool programs like those offered at Christian's Kids with keeping her out of trouble and basically saving her life—he made sure they received the public recognition they were due.

Then it was over.

Christian shook a few hands, went around with Zoey for obligatory photos with socialites, philanthropists, moguls, and fans who, between an online auction and tonight's event, had donated more than seven million dollars, twice the annual cost for running Christian's Kids. Yet people like Mallory Knight thought Christian should just write a blank check. He wasn't surprised and only mildly offended. Most people thought professional athletes had pots of gold with no bottom, especially family and friends, which after signing a healthy contract turns out to be almost everyone who knows you. It's why so many professional athletes ended up broke or bankrupt. Christian wouldn't be one of them.

An hour later Christian had returned home, changed clothes, and had a limo pick him up for a night out with the fellas. He loved his uncle, but he'd had enough suit and tie for one night. Now, almost midnight, he wore black jeans, a black-and-white long-sleeved Navigator t-shirt beneath a thick leather jacket and a pair of silver high-tops from his signature sneaker line set for a summer unveiling. He was ready to enjoy a rare Saturday out during the season. Having so many responsibilities for so many years, it was sometimes easy to forget the man wasn't yet thirty. Tonight, he'd help one of his best friends celebrate his birthday. He might even text Vivica on the way home, and party on.

After stopping to pick up DeVaughn, the driver pulled up to a nondescript building in East Harlem, across town from his foundation's building, also located in Harlem near Riverside Drive. A red velvet rope in front of a black metal door was the only hint to the luxuriousness that awaited inside Risqué, a private nightclub reportedly owned by a wealthy ultraconservative's wayward son. It was where the rich and famous, the well connected, the notorious and notable, and beautiful women always gained entry. Where they could party without worrying whether or not a picture would end up in the tabloids. Christian and DeVaughn exited the limo. Christian pulled a keycard from his wallet and slid it into the illuminated lock. The men stepped into a hallway, long and dark, with bodyguards on each side. The pulsating bass of a hip-hop beat seeped through the walls, subdued yet magnetic, inviting them to go farther inside.

"What's up, fellas." Devaughn acknowledged the greeting with a head nod, responding to a text on his phone. Christian turned to the one on his left for a brother's handshake and shoulder bump—the uninjured one, of course—then greeted the man on his right.

"You're the man!"

"What up, C? Sorry 'bout that shoulder, man."

"I appreciate that."

The two continued down the hallway. "That was Big Easy, just now. Wanting to know where we're at."

The automatic door to the main room opened, instantly enveloping them in sound, color, and the subtle smell of weed. Christian gave a nod here and a wave there, acknowledging greetings as he walked along the room's periphery toward the VIP spot on the second floor. There, in one of two circular booths that faced the crowd below, he met the men besides his family that meant the most in his life. The birthday boy, Ethan, better known as Big Easy, sat front and center wearing a black suit, red shirt, bowler hat, and shades. His massive arms were spread across the velvet booth back, a Cuban cigar wedged between pudgy fingers. Upon seeing Christian he broke into a grin.

"'Bout time you got here!"

"What's up? Watch the right, boy, watch the right!" Christian knew a brace wasn't enough protection against his heavy-handed friend's bear hug. He leaned in with his left shoulder. Ethan grabbed him around the waist, lifted him off the floor.

"Glad you made it, man. Didn't have to hurt your shoulder to get out of a game, but way to let a brothah know that you care."

"I'ma care about that cigar smoke in my face." Christian stepped back, smirking at Ethan while accepting a flute of champagne from a scantily clad waitress. "Look at you, the big three-oh. Up here looking like a dark Suge Knight."

Those who heard the dig laughed.

"Fuck you." Ethan slid back into his center position. "You wish you could rock this shit."

"No, I wish I could toss that shit. Right into the nearest Goodwill bin, muthafucka."

Christian had slid into street slang without thought, easily straddling the two worlds he'd grown up in—the proper, elite milieu of his father and the world his mother had adopted and now ruled, and the survival-of-the-fittest community where she'd been raised, and where Christian's cousins still lived. Rebecca Collins Graham could hobnob with the richest and ritziest, but one should not be foolish enough to cross her, because her North Philly roots ran deep. Childhood vacations spent there with his cousins gave Christian the balanced view of the world he'd need growing up as a mixed kid in America, between cultures that were often at odds. He'd eventually grown comfortable in his skin, but being Christian Graham had not always been as easy as it now looked.

Two guys next to Ethan moved over so that long-legged Christian could be on the end. "What up, Treasure? What up, Bink?" He inhaled and wrinkled his nose. "Oh, I see what's up with you. I'm liable to get a contact just sitting next to your weed-head ass. Trade places with him, Trey-Z. Damn!"

The joshing continued as others in the VIP area, including a well-known rapper and his reality-star wife, a Wall Street wonder and his gay lover, a few trust fund titans, and a few actors all came over to pay their respects. Several beauties sashayed past him, flirty, hopeful. The booth to the right of them was filled with beautiful women, including a well-known porn star and a half-dressed socialite openly snorting coke from off the lacquered table. Christian took it all in, switching from champagne to sparkling water after just one flute with no judgment of his fellow imbibers, and chatted it up with the other friends in this close, exclusive circle—Irishman Noah, Harlem Hank, and a bruiser of a guy from a small town in Nebraska that everyone called Cornfed. At one point, Hank gave a nod to Christian and walked down a short hallway next to the upstairs bar. Christian soon followed, entered a small private room, and closed the door.

"You hear anything?" Christian asked him.

Hank nodded. "You probably want to steer clear of this one, money."

"Why?"

Hank took a swig of brown liquor from a tumbler. "Word on the street is that it was a hit; a hired hand took down your dude, or tried to."

Christian rubbed his chin, confused and disturbed at what he was hearing. "I thought Danny was out of the game."

"Wasn't a drug hit."

"Then what?"

Hank shrugged his shoulder. "I don't know."

"Are you sure it was a hit, though, not a random shooting?"

"I got this from someone who knows the guy who done it. The only accident in this situation is that the dude lived."

"So, you know who did this?"

Hank fixed his eyes on Christian. "I know a dude who knows a dude. Dude shot dude, okay? Don't even go there and try to further identify. Snitches get stitches where I'm from so even if I'd asked, bro, he wouldn't have told me. In this type of situation, the less you know, the better. Because folks going around putting hits out on homies aren't the kind you want to do business with."

"You think he'll try again?"

"Hit men don't get paid for almost killing their target. So, if I was dude, I'd leave the hospital and head to a different zip code than the one I had when I went in. You feel me?"

Christian nodded, slowly lifted a fist. "Thanks, man."

Hank executed the fist bump. "You stay out of it, hear?"

"I'll be careful."

"I didn't say be careful. I said steer clear. What's this guy to you?"

"He's a kid's father." *A man who'd wanted to meet with me just before he got shot.*

When Christian and Hank returned to the booth, several beauties had joined the table. Better still, the twins had arrived. Christian signaled one to sit beside him while the other perched on his lap. It was Ethan's thirtieth birthday. Time to get turned up.

He motioned to a waitress, who was instantly by his side. "Bring out that case of bubbly I ordered for the table. Give a round on the house. And crank up the sound!"

As if the DJ heard him, the sound of Wiz Khalifa's "You and Your Friends" filled the room. Downstairs the dance floor filled up. Patrons upstairs started jamming, too. Two waitresses helped fill flutes for everyone at the booth. Two more carried trays of flutes for everyone in the VIP.

"To Big Easy!" Christian yelled.

"Big E!" everyone shouted.

Christian eased Meagan off his lap, placed his hands along her hips and swayed with her as she began to move. Morgan wrapped her arms around him from behind. Tonight belonged to Big Easy and the twins. Tomorrow would be soon enough to try and find out if whatever Danny wanted to tell Christian was news that had almost cost him his life.

11

The sun shone brightly and the air was crisp as Mallory, Sam, and Ava exited the Rodgers Theater and headed down 46th Street

"I can't believe we just saw that," Sam said.

"Right?" Ava gushed. "So amazing!"

"Worth every penny," Mallory chimed.

The ladies laughed, still giddy with their good fortune at getting to see *Hamilton* on Broadway for free.

"What do you have to say now about my trolling, Mallory?"

Mallory's expression changed to one of sincerity. "Bless you, my child."

"Indeed," Sam added. She looked at Ava. "And you met him at the grocery store?"

"Yep, went there to pick up some meat, and boy, did I get a good cut!"

"I still don't get how he got free tickets to a show that's sold out from now till next lifetime."

"Not free," Ava explained. "Those were house seats, which can be purchased by cast members for less than the premium price."

"I thought he gave them to you," Mallory said.

"Who, Aaron?" Sam asked, referencing Ava's meat market find.

"He got them for me," Ava said. "But I paid for them."

"Ava, I thought they were free! Oh my gosh, how much do I owe you?"

"Nothing, Mal," Ava responded. "You either, Sam. I got a great freelancing job this week. Today was my treat."

Mallory linked arms with Ava. "You are the best friend ever."

Hamilton was the topic as the three walked down Fifth Avenue to 50th and headed to a trendy Indian restaurant. Business was booming, as was expected on Sunday, but they managed to snag a corner table farthest away from the door and other customers. They scanned the menu. After getting their drinks and placing their food order, the conversation shifted from the play they'd seen on stage to the drama that continued to unfold in real life.

Ava reached for a strand of Mallory's black, silky hair. "I really like your hair like this."

"Isn't it great?" Sam asked.

"Thanks," Mallory said, self-consciously moving the hair away from her face and tucking it behind her ear.

"You should keep it," Ava said.

"Too much work."

"How'd Christian like it?" Sam asked.

"Yes, tell us all about last night."

"Is he as gorgeous in person?"

Mallory nodded. "He is."

"And as arrogant?"

"It would be hard for being continually worshipped not to go to your head. He's very likable though, so I can see why people adore him, and why Leigh was such a fan."

"Did you get to talk to him?" Sam asked.

"Not privately. His publicist, a woman named Zoey, was

very protective of him. She obviously thought I was just some chick who like all the others was trying to crawl into his bed. We bumped heads initially but I played nice and gave her my card, told her about the series. Hopefully I'll hear from her but I'm not holding my breath."

"What if you don't?" Sam asked.

"I'll keep trying. There's enough info on the web for me to do the first story, which will focus on Graham. Next week I'll reach out to the director at the center."

Ava reached for her drink. "That's part of his foundation, Christian's Kids?"

"Yes."

"Having seen him, what's your gut feeling? Do you think he could have had something to do with Leigh's death?"

"I don't know. If I were to be honest, I can't say that the handsome, charismatic man I saw last night holding an entire press corps spellbound could harm anybody. After I got home, I went through more of her appointment book." Mallory reached for her phone. "There are lots of entries about Christian and the Navs. I took screenshots of a few I found interesting."

She passed her phone to Ava, who read the screen in a voice just loud enough to be heard at the table.

" 'Great game tonight. CG . . . hot! God of the goal. Always flirting. Time to go up." Ava looked at Mallory'. "What does that mean?"

"I tried to make sense of it and still have no clue, but she uses that word throughout the second half of the appointment book, many times with both letters capitalized. Going up. Getting up. Rising up. It's weird, but I don't know that it necessarily means anything."

"CG, up," Ava continued, using her thumb to scroll down. " 'Risqué, 10pm. Then, two days later . . . headed to Hawaii in two weeks! Sometimes secrets are worth keeping.' Hmm."

Ava read the other screenshots and handed Mallory the

phone. "There's nothing incriminating, but clearly he and Leigh hung out."

"Sure looks that way," Mallory said. "And like millions of others in this city and the world, she idolized him. I never heard her say one bad thing about him and if I did, she jumped to his defense."

"What about the other names?" Sam said.

Mallory looked at Ava. "Did you tell her about the accountant?"

"No."

"What accountant?"

"Isaac Bankole, a financial consultant, according to his website. His name was in Leigh's appointment book. The same night I discovered it I saw on the news that he was a person of interest in a murder investigation."

"No way," Sam whispered, taken aback.

"I was shocked," Mallory said. "And immediately did a background check on him. He's a shady character with a variety of charges having been leveled against him from fraud to money laundering to obstruction of justice, the only one that led to a conviction. His brother was involved in some type of scam and once caught, Bankole either withheld or destroyed evidence, or both."

"Did he do any time?" Sam asked.

"He was fined and given probation."

"Who is the woman?"

"Where he's a person of interest?" Mallory asked.

Sam nodded.

Mallory reached for her phone. "Audrey Wilson. Thirty-four years old. Single. Worked as an executive assistant for a consulting firm located in the same building as Bankole's office."

"Hmm. I . . ." Ava saw the server coming with their order.

The food was placed in front of them. No one reached for their fork. "How is he involved?"

"I called up one of my contacts who works in the prosecutor's office and he says that video surveillance shows him talking with Ms. Wilson near the elevators in that building. I guess he was one of the last, if not the last, to see her alive, which is why when it comes to what happened to Leigh I'd suspect him more than Graham, at least for now."

Ava eyed Mallory while slowing stirring her cauliflower soup. "Since Graham is no longer a suspect, could he possibly be a prospect?"

"He is dreamy," Sam said.

"And you're overdue," Ava added. "You've probably got cobwebs by now."

Mallory reached for the perfectly done samosa she'd ordered. "He's not in the clear and I'm not prospecting."

"It has been a while, though," Sam said.

"Not long enough."

As they began eating the conversation shifted from Mallory's nasty breakup the year before with the man Mallory had pegged as "the one," back to the names found in Leigh's appointment book. An hour later, they'd narrowed the list of over a dozen to five that they wanted to investigate further. Mallory took Graham and Bankole. Ava took Randall DuBois, the popular, shrewd politician. Sam was assigned the remaining two—one a musician and one whose relationship to Leigh needed to be figured out.

"Okay ladies," Mallory said as they left the restaurant and prepared to go their separate ways. "Can we meet next weekend for updates?"

"Fine with me," Ava said. "Or sooner if we get something hot."

Mallory headed home, her thoughts on Leigh and what the three of them hadn't discussed. Leigh's unborn baby. Did the person who poured her lethal glass of wine know that she was pregnant? That the poison she ingested would also harm the life inside her? If true, the man who killed so as not to become a father would most definitely kill again to stay out of jail. Mallory's pace increased as she absorbed the potential danger in what she and her friends had undertaken. Her whole body shivered, and not from the cold.

12

Mallory arrived at work earlier than usual, hoping to get a jump on what would be a busy week. After firing up her laptop, she checked emails, pulled up the Christian's Kids website and opened another browser to search online contact information. She'd decided to approach Isaac Bankole as a potential client and needed to set up a meeting with him. She also wanted to make an appointment with Dr. Anaya Kapoor, the obstetrician who ran New Life Medical in Long Island, and whose address had been in Leigh's appointment book.

She'd just found the financial consultant's contact information when Charlie entered the office she shared with another journalist and plopped into a chair.

"So . . . how was it?"

She deftly switched tabs to one on Christian's Kids before swinging her chair around. "Hey, Charlie."

"Whoa, look at you!"

She frowned, then remembered. "Oh. Right. The hair."

"I'll say the hair. Damn, Mal. Now you don't look like a poodle at all."

"Thanks, Charlie Brown."

"I don't think I've ever seen your hair straightened. You should keep it like that."

"Negative, captain. It's a pain in the ass to maintain. In fact, you might want to take a picture, because it'll probably be a while before you see it like this again."

Charlie shook his head. "You should keep it straight. Makes you look . . . I don't know . . . more sophisticated."

"In that case, I'll wash it tonight."

They both laughed.

"You meet Christian?" He walked over to the single chair in front of Mallory's desk, dropped a load of files from it on to the floor, and sat down.

"Not directly. Tried to get close enough to set up an interview but was stopped. Twice. First by a bodyguard and then by his publicist." Charlie's brow rose. "A woman named Zoey Girard who handles his PR. And from the possessive way she shaded him throughout the course of the evening, she may be handling something else. I thought he'd be the asshole but no, she took that title."

"That pleasant, huh?"

"Just peachy. But she wasn't the biggest one there."

"No? Who then?"

"Rob Anderson."

"Your former boss and our current rival. Fun reunion?"

"Would have been if I'd had a weapon sharper than my stiletto. I hate that guy."

"That's a strong word for a man who was just doing his job."

"If that were true, he wouldn't have written those salacious lies and rumors about Leigh. He would have researched to find out the facts before printing bullshit."

"They needed the circulation. That paper was losing subscribers faster than Bolt ran the one hundred."

"So they turn a respectable paper into a tabloid?"

Mallory knew the real reason for her former boss's anger—Leigh's rejection. Rob had come on to her when the three attended the Publishers and Press Awards dinner and Mallory had introduced them. He'd asked Leigh out. She'd said no. He pursued her for weeks—cards, flowers, chocolates. Nothing worked. Leigh finally told him in no uncertain terms that she was not interested. Rob never got over it.

Charlie shrugged. "What about Christian?"

"Professional, charming, arrogant, but aren't all superstar athletes?"

"Do you have enough for a story?"

"There's certainly enough out there to use if it comes to that. But I'm hoping to get an interview in order to offer a fresh, different perspective on the city's favorite son."

"Glad to hear you say that. It means that I won't have to tell you to handle Graham with kid gloves. He's the city's sports salvation, and any negative talk about him will turn into a negative for the paper. With the steady decline in circulation, we need to attract readers, not piss them off. And talking bad about the golden boy will definitely make his fans unhappy."

"Including you?"

Charlie smirked. "You're damn right."

"I'm going to focus on his foundation, Christian's Kids. The organization handles over a hundred kids a day, providing after-school services, tutoring throughout the year, and weekend activities. It's a good use of his money, but I'm not convinced his involvement reaches much farther than his name on the check. Oh, but my bad. I can't write about that."

"He seems involved. There was a story last week about him visiting one of the kids who wound up in the hospital after suffering an allergic reaction."

Or after attempting suicide. Following up on that rumor was another action for her growing to do list, an item she didn't dare share with her boss. Far be it for her to want to smear anything resembling dirt on Christian's spotless image. The less Charlie knew about her real intent, the better. Unless or until she could find solid proof linking Christian to Leigh, the mission was a covert one involving her, Ava, and to a lesser extent, Sam.

"Good photo op if you ask me," she said instead. "But the kids and their stories can carry this series. Bring the type of feel-good stories you want." *And the investigative angle my column needs.* "A couple of them spoke at the fund-raiser. Bright, articulate, with home lives leaving much to be desired. Drugs. Violence. Poverty. The foundation is a light in their dark worlds. It'll be the kind of series you wanted, Charlie, and, yes, highlight Christian and his contributions as well."

Charlie sat back, arms crossed, eyes narrowed.

"What?"

"I thought I knew you pretty well. But you choosing this direction for 'Knightly' surprises me."

"What, you think I don't like kids?"

"No, but I know you don't like fluff. And this kind of feel-good could get fluffy pretty quickly."

"Don't worry about that. I'm not going to use their misfortune in life salaciously, but I'm not going to sugarcoat it, either. They will be honest, balanced stories."

"I'm counting on it. And so is the public. By getting the Pen, you've raised the bar on yourself."

"Lucky me."

"We're the lucky ones, kid." He stood and headed toward the door. "Have something on my desk by Wednesday."

Mallory glanced at her watch. Nine-fifteen. Her colleagues would be coming in at any minute. Back at her desk, she pulled out a card, reached for the office phone, and dialed the number.

"Hello, Zoey. Mallory Knight, *New York News.* We met Saturday night. I apologize for any offense taken to my trying to talk with Christian after the press conference. I assure you my inquiry is legitimate, and I'm not just another floozy trying to get in his pants. I'm doing a four-part series on Christian's Kids and would like the opportunity to interview him for the first article. I'd also like to visit the facility and talk with some of the students. Please give me a call back at your earliest convenience. I really appreciate it, Zoey. Thanks."

She left her contact information, then opened up a search engine. As much as she wanted to speak with Christian, doing so wasn't necessary when it came to writing the four-part series' first piece. There was enough about Graham on the internet to fill up a New York phone book. And while she would have rather gathered firsthand knowledge before resorting to websites, she opened the site for Christian's Kids and found enough additional information. That and what she'd heard Saturday night was enough to flesh out the first article and set the framework for her true focus, the kids. Starting with Brandon, the one Christian had visited in the hospital. The one who may have tried to kill himself. The investigator in Mallory wanted to either refute or confirm the rumor. And if she confirmed it, the next step would be to find out why a young boy would want to die.

A quick search and she found the article on Brandon. There sat Christian in all his handsomeness, leaning close to a young, nice-looking boy with smooth, dark skin, a tremulous smile, and troubled eyes. Mallory peered closer, studied the brooding boy who looked to be somewhere between the ages of ten and thirteen. She tried to read the expression on his face like a novel, tried to figure out that if the rumor was true, why this handsome young man wanted to die.

Opening a Word document, Mallory stared at the screen, waited for inspiration and the catchy first line to begin the article. A few finger drums on the desk and then her fingers began to fly.

Word on the street says that New York Navigator phenom Christian Graham has more than a hundred kids. None biologically, at least that are known by this reporter, but all who've been helped by his largesse through his Harlem-based foundation, Christian's Kids.

Mallory studied her work. Too cheeky? Tabloid-like? *No*, she thought, repositioning her fingers over the keys. It was just the type of sentence that would stop folks in their tracks, especially females for whom he was a fantasy, and make them want to read the rest of the article. Just as she began typing, the office phone rang.

"Mallory Knight."

Perfect timing, Mallory thought, as Zoey Girard announced herself. "A press kit on him would be helpful, but a personal interview—even by phone—would make for a better story."

Mallory listened to Zoey's hesitation while pulling up a search engine to read more about her online.

"A list of questions? Sure, I could do that. What's your email address?"

Zoey gave it to her and was off the call. Brisk but not quite brusque. Professional, without the attitude Mallory felt at the gala. Heck, as far as she knew fending off females might be part of Zoey's job description. Getting to him had to be a common MO for many female requests. They wouldn't have to worry about that when it came to Mallory. She didn't want sex. Just the story, the truth about his relationship with Leigh Jackson. If Leigh was indeed pregnant and if it was Christian's child, that would be a story worthy of an above-the-fold breaking-news headline that even fan Charlie would greenlight. The paper would get the scoop and she'd get a shot at having Leigh's death revisited. With that in mind, Mallory took a break and placed a call. Even though she'd had one just three months prior, it was time for a meeting with Dr. Kapoor and another gynecological exam.

13

The next day, in Upper Manhattan, Christian's penthouse hummed with its usual activity. His personal manager, friend, and former college teammate DeVaughn walked back and forth between the home office and the master suite's huge en suite, getting the boss man's input on renditions for a new company's logo, narrowed down from a dozen possibilities to the final four. Christian sat while his barber gave him a trim and his business manager, Baron, gave him an update on his millions. Pete lounged in the sitting area, constantly surfing the muted flat-screen TV while talking on the phone. Sounds of cooking echoed down the hallway from the kitchen where Christian's personal chef prepared the paleo meal his nutritionist had recommended. A few of his teammates were at the other end of another hall, watching tape on an upcoming opponent in the comfort of a fully equipped theater and library. Christian's personal assistant, Andy, just back from grabbing his laundry and dry cleaning, sat with his laptop updating to-do lists while the home cat, Three-Peat, a rescue so named because he'd lost a paw, lounged from a perch near the living room's wall of windows, unbothered by it all.

The barber finished Christian's haircut and spun him around. Christian turned his head from side to side.

The barber watched him. "Did I take enough off?"

"Yeah. You could have shortened it even more."

"I can, that's no problem."

Christian removed the smock from around himself and stood. "It's cool. I've got to handle some other stuff right now." He walked to a side table, opened a rectangular platinum box, and pulled a bill from a large stack of money inside it. He folded it once and gave it to the barber. "Thanks, man."

"You're welcome, bro. Any time. See you next week or whenever Andy calls me."

"Cool."

Christian stretched, grabbed his phone, and joined Pete in the sitting area. His uncle was still on the phone.

"I agree with you, Zoey. He shouldn't do it."

Christian looked over, a question in his eyes. Pete made a dismissive gesture with his hand.

"Don't think I should do what? Put her on speaker."

Pete sighed but tapped the appropriate button. "You're on speaker, Zoey. Christian's here.

"Don't think I should do what?"

"A personal interview with Mallory Knight, the investigative reporter from *New York News*.

In a photographic mind that catalogued women better than a Victoria's Secret catalog, Mallory's face sprang to the front.

"Why not?"

"Don't worry about it, Christian," Zoey said. "I messengered a customized press kit over and she's emailing a list of questions that I can either fill out or forward over. Either way, it will take up less of your time."

"Less than a conversation over the phone?"

"More controlled," Zoey responded. "I don't trust her."

"Because . . ."

"Because of what I told you the other night. She's not a sports reporter. She investigates murders and the missing. Crime, politics, dirty business. Her column won the Prober's Pen for a series called 'Why They Disappear, Why They Die.' You've done neither. So why the interest?"

Pete chuckled. "You have to ask."

Zoey's voice softened. One could imagine she almost smiled. "You've got a point, Pete. I'm so focused on keeping Christian's name away from that kid's father's attempted murder—"

"His name is Brandon," Christian interjected.

"—that I'd overlooked the obvious."

"Every woman isn't trying to sleep with me, Zee. And if she is, maybe I want to have sex with her."

"You'll fuck anything female. What else is new?"

"I'm not fucking you, am I? Y'all making me out to be a male whore when you know my life is nothing like that. I don't sleep with just anybody. I have high standards."

Pete harrumphed. "Yeah, a shaved pussy. That's about as high as it gets."

"No, uncle, that's you."

"The point is," Zoey continued in a tone that suggested they get back on track, "the invite to last week's gala went to her boss, Charles Callahan. But instead of him, she shows up having done a makeover that, if the pics of her online and what she usually looks like are accurate, had to have taken the better part of a day. Maybe two. Why would an investigative reporter with a serious column go after a celebrity all of a sudden if she didn't have an ulterior motive?"

"Maybe it's not about me. Maybe it's about the foundation, and the kids, and changing their lives. That's a serious topic."

"True, and she did mention wanting a tour of the foundation. I just don't think she needs an interview with you."

"Set it up. I want to talk to her."

"I hope instead of smooth lips you encounter a bush the size of Kaepernick's afro," Pete mumbled.

Zoey chuckled. Christian ignored him. "Give her my cell phone number. Have her call me."

It was after eight before business wrapped up for the day

and Christian was able to chill. Tomorrow the team would head to Chicago and be on the road for the next five days. Many fantasized about the dream life of a ballplayer. Christian knew he was blessed and lived a great life, but he also knew the sacrifices involved and the toll that constant travel, exhaustive physical training and hard, competitive basketball playing had on the body. He grabbed a liter of the alkaline water with chlorophyll that his nutritionist supplied him, requested a light dinner be brought to the theater, then closed himself off in the darkened room with its recessed lighting, projector screen, premium sound and kid leather, reclining seats. After slipping in a game tape, he sat down, reclined his seat and had just taken a long sip of water when his phone buzzed.

He looked to see who was calling, sighed and tapped the speaker button. "Hank."

"Hey, man. What's up?"

"Watching a little game tape trying to relax before hitting the road tomorrow. What's going on?"

"Heard a rumor on the street. Probably shouldn't tell you but I thought you should know."

"About what?"

"The dude who got shot, or his family rather. You know, the kid."

"Brandon?" Christian raised the recliner back and sat up. "He's okay, right? I got a text saying that over the weekend he'd been released."

"Yeah, he's home. Don't know if that's the safest place for him. The guys with the hit on his daddy are pretty upset because dude's heartbeat is holding up their paper. You feel me?"

"You said that the other night."

"What's new is the plan to smoke him out by going after his family. Now, I don't know how true it is or how serious whoever was that made the comment, but I thought you'd want to know so we can, you know, handle that."

"Of course. You know what to do. Call Trey and have security check it out. Tell one of them to post up and find out what's going on. Any word on who's behind the hit?"

"No, man. But whoever it is has some weight behind them because I've hit up my informers and let me tell you, mum's the word."

"Which mean you don't know Danny's whereabouts either."

"He's a ghost, man. Hasn't been back to his house, hasn't been seen on the streets. He probably left town."

"I hope so. Keep me posted and keep security on Danny's family. I'll handle the rest."

Christian ended that call and placed one to Pete. Confident that appropriate actions would be taken to protect the center, Brandon and the family, he pushed play and tried to focus on the Bulls and how to properly defend his man from posting up and making threes. But he couldn't concentrate. Thoughts of Danny, who was after him and why, kept pulling his attention away. He paused the film and reclined his chair, worked to keep relaxed the muscles his therapist had loosened earlier today. He didn't need extra pressure right now. The Navigators were in good shape but everybody knew that the game could change on a dime. The next two months were crucial to entering the playoffs at an advantage. Christian's mind needed to be on the game.

She's not a sports reporter. She investigates murders and the missing. Crime, politics, dirty business.

Christian's eyes fluttered open. Someone with a talent for uncovering hidden information is exactly what he needed right now. He tapped his cellphone screen and placed her name in the search engine. He scanned through the posts with links to her newspaper and read one regarding her Prober's Pen award from the Associated Press. Her stories had led to families being united and criminal arrests? Impressive.

The chef tapped on the door and brought in Christian's light dinner of a huge kale salad with seared chateaubriand, red quinoa and freshly baked bread. He tapped the play button and this time was able to focus on the competition. Later, when he lay down in his customized king-size bed, his thoughts were on the reporter and what she might make of what happened with Danny, the resources that might be available to one connected with a major paper that could help him find Danny and learn what information he'd wanted to share with Christian the night he was shot. Zoey had warned him to steer clear of Mallory. But it was Christian's life and he was behind the wheel. No one could tell him how to drive.

14

Mallory hadn't been able to get an appointment with Dr. Kapoor, but she decided to go by the office anyway. She was surprised to see how secure the facility was—they definitely valued client privacy. Which is why she'd returned home, fired up a search engine, and entered three words: *avoid security cameras*. The results were both shocking and satisfying. There was a noble cause behind the crime she hoped to commit, but what about true criminals out to scam and steal? She put the worry behind her and after ordering a Faraday case, an LED-strung baseball cap, and studying how to obscure one's facial features through an art called CV dazzle, Mallory felt that if given the opportunity, or being able to create one, she could obtain Leigh's medical records without being identified. Unless she got caught. And providing Leigh's medical records were even there. Now all she needed to do was become an expert at breaking and entering, an act that could carry some serious jail time. She typed *how to burglarize a business* into the search engine. When several links came up, Mallory could only shake her head. And read. And take notes. One way or the other, she was going to find out what was in the doctor's files. Whichever way it took . . . she'd be ready.

Mallory took off her criminal hat, focused on her day job, and called Christian's Kids. No one answered. She left a message for the director. The next day the assistant director, Emma Davis, called her back and scheduled an appointment for three o'clock.

Christian's Kids was located in Harlem, housed in a colorfully painted building that appeared to take up half a block. Mallory walked up to a set of double doors painted bright red, a perfect contrast to the mustard-colored cement blocks and blue window trim. She turned the knob. The door was locked, but an intercom box was to her right. She pushed it, and after announcing herself she heard a loud click as the door unlocked. She stepped into an interior even brighter and more colorful than the building's façade. A wide blue line divided walls that were painted bright yellow on top and black on the bottom—the Navigators' team colors. Posters with positive messages lined the short hallway. The man in one of them was instantly familiar. Christian. Handsome and smiling. Casually dressed and holding a basketball as he leaned against a wall, his eyes seemed to follow Mallory as she passed by. *If you can dream it, you can do it. That's what I did. You can, too.*

A door stood open at the end of the hall. She entered what appeared to be an administrative office. The wall color went from yellow to sky blue and was covered in more inspirational posters. A row of colorful wooden chairs lined one side of the room, opposite a wall unit filled with books, board games, and electronic gadgets. A desk was anchored against the far wall where a young woman typed on a laptop, bobbing her head to a softly playing tune. The woman looked up, noticed her, and smiled.

"Good afternoon. Welcome to Christian's Kids."

Mallory walked toward her. "Hi. Good afternoon."

"How may I help you today?"

"I'm Mallory Knight with the *New York News*."

"Hello, Ms. Knight. The assistant director, Ms. Davis, is expecting you." The worker dialed an office phone, once again moving to the jazzy sounding music coming from small, discreet speakers Mallory now noticed recessed in the ceiling tile.

"Ms. Knight with the *New York News* is here. Should I send her back or . . ." The woman smiled at Mallory as she listened. "Okay, will do."

She hung up the phone. "Ms. Davis is just wrapping up a conference call. She'll be out shortly. Can I get you something to drink while you wait?"

"No, I'm fine."

"It shouldn't be that long. You're welcome to have a seat until she comes out."

"Okay, thanks."

Mallory pulled out her tablet and studied the questions she'd prepared for Emma, a professional, well-put-together woman who looked nothing like her name. In Mallory's mind, the name Emma was an old-fashioned one—and given that her own moniker dated back to the eighth century she could judge—so she was surprised to go online and discover that not only was the center's assistant director young and beautiful but also a highly educated mother of two with commendations and awards to her credit. She'd been instrumental in formulating a curriculum of tutoring that focused on math and science but was balanced with critical thinking and the arts. Her credentials impressive, but Mallory wanted a variety of opinions regarding the foundation from people who were involved with it. The young woman in front of her, Mallory deduced after looking up once again, was a good place to start.

"Excuse me, what's your name?"

"Lisa."

"Lisa, I know you're working, but do you mind if I ask you a couple questions?"

She turned away from her computer with a smile. Short, natural do. Bright eyes. Pretty girl.

From what all she'd seen of the women around Christian, beauty seemed to be a prerequisite. Mallory walked over to her desk.

"You like working here, obviously."

"I love it."

"Do you mind if I ask why, and record your answer? I may use it in an upcoming article."

"I don't mind." Lisa rested her chin in her hand as she thought. "Many reasons, actually. First of all, I love kids. I have a little boy that's two years old. I can't wait to bring him here. It's a really positive environment. Everyone is so friendly, so helpful, like family. The kids are great. Working here make you feel valuable, like you can actually make a difference in someone's life. I go home feeling . . . good. Yeah, that's it."

The door behind them opened, one that blended in so well with the colorful stripes and bright posters that Mallory hadn't even noticed. She immediately recognized Emma from the pics on the web.

"Hello, Mallory." She continued toward her arm outstretched. "Emma Davis."

"Hi, Emma. So nice to meet you."

"Likewise." She turned to Lisa. "If he calls, find me."

"Absolutely, Ms. Davis."

"Thanks." She turned to Mallory. "Sorry to keep you waiting. I was on the phone with the director, Pete, who sends his apologies for not being able to meet you himself."

"I believe he left me in good hands."

Emma smiled. "The tour won't take long."

"Sure, one moment." Mallory reached into her bag and turned to Lisa. "I wanted to give you my business card. Do you have one?"

"Yes." Lisa opened her desk and gave one to Mallory.

"Thanks."

"Am I going to be in your column?" Lisa asked.

Mallory smiled. "Probably." Mallory followed Emma out of the office. "I hope it was okay to speak with her."

"Lisa's a sweet girl with a bright future. Hopefully she provided you with some good material."

"She gave the foundation glowing reviews."

"Everyone loves it here. Christian is kind, honest, respectful of others, compassionate . . ."

"Wait, are we talking about Christian Don't-Give-a-Damn Graham? No offense, but—"

"None taken. Christian can come across a bit rudely at times. Arrogant at others. What the average person doesn't understand is the pressure he's under, and the lengths some go to try and meet him. There's a reason Biggie said more money, more problems. Yes, being a pro athlete is lucrative, the lifestyle, glamourous. But it's not as easy as it looks, and not for the faint of heart."

"Duly noted." Then, remembering Charlie's concern for a pro-positive approach, she added, "That he has a foundation like this speaks to the character beneath the bravado."

"I'm glad you recognize that. He truly loves these kids."

"Where are the students?"

"On the second level, where our after-school program is housed."

"It would be great to speak with them. I promised Christian to use only first names, or keep them totally anonymous if that's preferred."

"Depends on who's here." Emma offered a brief smile. "We'll see."

They walked down a long hall with what Mallory assumed were offices on either side and through a set of double doors, a large, open space with tall ceilings and rows of windows set high enough to let sunlight flow in unobstructed. On one side of the room were several rows of rectangular tables—blue, green, yellow, red, and multicolored chairs around them. A glass-paneled room on the back wall showed rows of computers. A video camera set on a tripod in the corner. On the other wall was a stage with microphones and what looked like props from a theatrical performance.

"Is this the auditorium?"

"This is the main assembly area. The kids put on concerts here. Theatrical performances. This is where they gather when speakers are invited. Basically, anything that involves everyone takes place here. When set up for assembly this room can hold three hundred people."

"And along the back wall, a computer lab?"

"Yes. Fully loaded laptops with the latest programs and accessories. Scanners. Printers. Everything needed for our students to be proficient in the technology and also a few that are dedicated to those who want to write their own programs or design games, which we highly encourage. We also have fully equipped studios for filmmaking and music production."

"Wow, that's way more than can be found in most schools, and partially answers my question for how a center for kids would spend seven million dollars."

Emma fixed her with a look that conveyed understanding of Mallory's question inside a question. "We are very thankful for the many donors and supporters who help us run one of the best foundations of this kind in the nation."

She motioned toward a hallway opposite where they walked. "Down there is the cafeteria and cooking lab for those interested in the culinary arts. That section also houses the gym, with rooms for yoga, meditation, and tai chi. Classrooms are upstairs. We'll go there now."

They continued through the room to a set of stairs on the other side. It was only then that Mallory realized the building was much bigger than it appeared.

"Classrooms? So is there an accredited academic side to the center?"

"Not yet fully accredited but that's our goal. Currently we work with the New York school district to provide summer school classes for kids who have fallen behind, need extra tutoring or assistance, or who would not be promoted to the next grade without it. Every child learns differently. Part of my job is determining what type of learning works best for each student. Some do well with books. Others learn faster with a hands-on approach. Some kids are smart but aren't good test takers. The better we understand how each child learns, the better we can teach."

A din of voices drifted toward them as they climbed the stairs. Mallory's ears perked up. *Kids!*

"What room is that? Can we go inside?"

Emma looked inside the class. "Sure. This is the math and science lab."

They stepped inside. Mallory was immediately struck with a mural that had been "tagged" on the back wall. It showed boys and girls in typical teen gear and poses against a gritty yet colorful city brick backdrop. Above them a banner: Nerd Nation.

"I really love that wall." Mallory dug into her bag for the paper's high-powered digital camera, which she'd brought along. "Mind if I take a picture?"

"Not at all. That mural was painted by one of our students."

"The juxtaposition sends a great message. That kids can be both smart and cool."

They continued over to where a group of kids surrounded one of several islands in the room, each one equipped with working space, a sink, and several drawers for storage. They looked up, smiling and speaking at once.

"Hey, Ms. D!"

"Auntie Em!"

"What's up, Ms. Em?"

"Students, this is Ms. Knight, a reporter with *New York News*. She's doing a series for the foundation and would like to ask a few questions."

"I can do it!" A young woman eagerly replied.

"We're going to be in the paper?" another inquired.

A tall, lanky kid pushed the others aside. "I'm the one you want to speak with," he said, crossing his arms in an authoritative manner. "What would you like to know, Ms. Knight?"

"Your name, for starters," Mallory said as she pulled out her phone and engaged a recording app.

"Justin Bailey."

She conducted a brief interview with Justin and the kids surrounding her. As they turned to leave, Mallory noticed a young girl at another island. The student had several small clay pots lined up, a bag of potting soil, and several of what looked to be packs of seeds lying on the counter.

"What's she doing?"

"Harmony is our resident horticulturist," Emma explained. "She loves gardening, has a dream of starting one on the rooftops of all the high-rises in her neighborhood."

"I'd like to speak with her."

She watched Emma's expression change to one of compassion. "Another time, perhaps. She's dealing with a few challenges right now. I think the gardening is therapeutic and helping her heal."

Emma's phone rang.

"Excuse me. Yes, Lisa?" She paused to listen. "Tell him I'm on my way."

As she ended the call, a young man bounded up the stairs. "Akil, perfect timing. This is Mallory Knight from the *New York News*. I was just wrapping up a tour with her but have to attend to another matter. Can you show her the media center and wrap up the tour?"

"Sure, Ms. Davis."

"Thank you." And to Mallory: "Sorry to cut this short. It's been a pleasure. Please call if you have further questions. I look forward to reading this week's column."

"I look forward to writing it. Thanks so much for your time."

She watched Emma hurry down the stairs.

"Mallory, right?"

"Yes, and your name is Akil?"

He nodded. "The media center is down here."

They began walking. "This is such a wonderful program."

"More than that, really. It's an extended family."

"I can see that. Even when faced with challenges, the students still come. Like Harmony, for instance."

"Yeah," Akil agreed with a sigh. "Your father getting shot and brother almost dying in one week is hard to take."

Mallory stopped midstride. At Akil's questioning glance she began walking again. Her heart had already skipped several beats. "Right, her brother Brandon."

"You interviewed him?"

"No, but I'd like to."

"I don't know how likely that is to happen. He may come back here eventually, but it's going to take a while."

"What's his dad's name?"

"They call him D-Man but I think his real name is Danny."

"And his last name?"

Akil shrugged. "Brandon's last name is Walker, but I think that's his mother's name. Here we are. The media center where students create magic."

Mallory listened as Akil took her around the media room and completed the tour. She barely heard his explanations of films being made and beats produced. Much more interesting to her was learning that Brandon's dad had been shot shortly before the boy was admitted to the hospital for what had officially been described as an allergic reaction but was rumored to have been an attempted suicide. Why would a twelve-year old boy try and kill himself? Could he have been distraught over almost losing his father? She remembered how quickly Zoey had cut off the reporter who'd asked about it. Did Christian's camp know more than they'd let on, and should any of that matter to Mallory? One mystery on her plate was enough, but that didn't stop the investigator in her from wanting more information. So many questions without any answers . . . yet.

15

Sam had a sick baby and couldn't meet her at Newsroom but Ava did, and after hearing the details of Mallory's week, she said, "Damn, detective. You've been busy! I feel like a slacker."

"I thought you said the doctor was out of town."

"She was but I still went there. I told them I was in the neighborhood and wanted to confirm my appointment. It gave me a chance to do recon." Mallory took a bite of spicy grilled salmon and missed Ava's look.

"Recon. Listen at you. Jumped from *Sherlock* to *NCIS* in a heartbeat. I can't keep up. That was a joke, Mal."

"I know, listen." She looked around, lowered her voice. "I noticed a file room. We've got to find a way to get in there and see if there are any records on Leigh."

"The whole world has gone digital. Do hospitals still keep paper records?"

"I saw stacks of files on the receptionist's desk. But you're right. Everything is stored electronically now." She thought for a moment, thin worry lines marring her forehead. "It may net me nothing but we've got to try."

"I said I'd help you get answers and I will, but breaking into buildings is where I draw the line."

Mallory offered a quick headshake. "Hope it won't come to that. They've got video surveillance."

"Oh, because they've got cameras. Not because to do so is a felony!"

"There's got to be a way. I thought about whether or not the office has a cleaning crew and maybe bribing one for a shift, but still . . . those damn cameras."

"I don't see anything working, short of becoming an employee."

Mallory's head snapped up. "That's it!"

"Okay, Mal. I'm starting to worry."

"No, really. If I could somehow find a way . . . shoot . . . too problematic. I guess you're right. What about the politician? The one Leigh met for lunch several times and briefly dated. Anything there?"

"Randall DuBois? You know who he is, right?"

"I pulled a few images online but other than him being a politician and easy on the eyes, I don't know a lot about him."

"He's a member of the House of Representatives. Conservative. Successful. Pretty boy good-looking, as you know since you've seen his picture. He's happily married, at least that's how it appears from pictures of him and his wife."

"That doesn't mean anything. Or it could mean everything. Getting someone pregnant while having an affair is not a good look for Capitol Hill."

"Not at all, especially for someone who aspires to the highest office in the land."

"He plans to run for president?"

"Not quite yet. His short-term goal is to be the next Majority Leader, perhaps even Speaker of the House. But he's being carefully watched and secretly groomed for the long-term goal—to possibly be the Republican Party's Obama in about eight years."

"Hmm, interesting indeed."

"There's more," Ava said, her eyes containing a conspiratorial sparkle. "A few years ago, the insider rumor mill was all abuzz about a supposed affair between him and an attorney he worked closely with on several bills. My source says this wasn't his first affair. What made this one different, however, is that she was the first one who made his wife feel threatened. The attorney was smart, beautiful, cultured, all of that. So the wife demanded that he end the affair and cut off all contact."

"That sounds serious."

"According to my contact the missus was not having it and since they've been married for twenty or twenty-five years, she probably had enough to throw him under the bus, the train and the subway, okay?"

Mallory and Ava cracked up.

"So what happened?"

"One day she was there, and one day she wasn't. The assumption is that she was paid off but neither that nor the affair was ever confirmed."

"Good work, detective! So he stays on the list?"

"Definitely."

"What about the high-rise where you thought the musician lived? Did you get a chance to check it out for a resident directory?"

Ava shook her head, checking her phone. "I'm mired in the Rump scandals, which unfortunately show no end in sight. Sorry I can't help more."

"You would if you could."

"I read your column last night."

"Yeah? What did you think?"

"Good stuff. You mentioned him without genuflecting and then painted a picture for what happens inside. I mean, horticulture? For real?"

"I was pretty impressed. Really want to talk to her."

"About her brother."

"That and . . . herbs."

"You're such a bullshitter."

"Hey, I need help trying to grow them on my window sill. It's like I'm swimming in a pool of questions, conjecture, and circumstantial possibilities so that that I can't see a thing."

"Maybe that's because you're too deep in the water. You know, that whole thing about forests and trees. Works in water, too. Get out of the pool. Relax. Change your perspective."

"You might be right."

"I know I am. Focus on the center and what's happening with the kids. I know you went in it with an ulterior motive but at the end of the day it's pretty amazing what's happening over there. And with so much negative media about kids from those neighborhoods, the success stories are ones that need to be told."

Christian had been on the road for five straight days. Today's practice would be light, and there was a home game tomorrow before having Saturday off and getting back on the road. The NBA schedule was the most grueling of all sports, and coming off an injury made it feel that much worse. The average person looked at the money they made without taking into account the toll that playing a sport professionally took on every aspect of a player's life. Or that the average career span for a basketball player was less than five years. Was he complaining? No. Would he do everything he'd done to get here all over again? Absolutely. But there was a price to getting rich this way. Right now, his body was paying it.

He pulled his pricey sports car in front of a brick building that stretched the length of a block in Port Washington, New York, where the Navigators practiced and where several lived. Boutiques and other customer-oriented businesses occupied the lower levels of the two-story building. The top floor was a series of offices, which was where Christian headed, his long legs allowing him to easily take the stairs two at a time. He entered the last door on the right, facing the hall, bypassed an empty receptionist desk, and entered the office behind it. Pete sat in one of two chairs, gave Christian a somber nod as he walked in.

"Hey, fellas." Christian returned the nod and stretched his hand toward the man sitting behind the desk. "Hello, Nick."

"Christian. Ready for the game on Saturday night?"

Nick Bianchi, a private investigator, was a nice-looking man in a street-tough kind of way with a compact frame and intense black eyes. Christian knew that he and Pete had been friends for years.

"Getting ready." He looked at his watch. "Practice is in an hour. Pete says you have news?"

"I do. From one of my guys with connections in Queens. He knows a lot of people. All levels. Gets a lot of intel from there, and it's credible."

"And he got news on Danny, why he was shot?"

Nick steepled his fingers as he leveled his eyes on Christian. "Drug deal gone wrong. Danny wasn't the target. He was just in the wrong place at the wrong time."

"That's not what I heard. Someone I know who's probably closer to those streets and the drug game than your man's man said it was an attempted execution. Was sure of it."

"He was shot in the back of the head. An easy assumption to make."

"Not just that. Danny had kicked the drugs and was out of the game."

"He was gunned down on the street, Christian," Pete said. "In that area, the wrong guy gets shot every other day of the week."

"My guy's info seemed fairly solid," Nick said. "I believe him."

"I want to. Either way, getting shot is a bad situation, but drugs were involved, then at least we'd know why. Were you able to track him down?"

"Not yet. The guy has relatives all over the country. He could be just about anywhere, and if he's laying low it'll take that much longer to find him."

"Keep looking."

"Why?" Pete asked.

"Just want to talk to him, see for myself that he's all right."

Christian stood, reached over to Nick for a handshake as he stood. "Thanks, man. We can always depend on you to find out the truth."

"We sure can." Pete stood up, too. He placed a hand on Christopher's shoulder. "Which is why there is someone else I had him check out."

"Who, DeVaughn?"

Christian never understood Pete's discomfort and dislike of a best friend he'd known since middle school. He'd never tried to figure it out, either, mainly because the feelings were mutual. DeVaughn felt that Pete used the organization to gain a high profile and impress the ladies. For the most part, they each stayed out of the other's way.

He chuckled and strolled toward the door. "I know you've never liked him. But I don't think trying to pin Danny's murder attempt on him is going to stick."

"Not thinking about him, but there's an idea." If Pete was joking, his face didn't show it. "No, it's Knight."

Christian had reached for the knob but turned around at Pete's answer. "The reporter? Why?"

"Because I believe there's something up in why she switched from investigating murders to investigating you. I don't buy her interest in the foundation or the kids for a second. Not with her background. And Nick agrees."

"So you've already checked her out?"

"Just a simple background check so far," Nick replied.

"Seriously, Pete?"

"Why not? Just about everything to know about you is at the fingertips of anyone with the internet. It's only fair that we know as much about her."

"So you've conducted background checks on every reporter who's ever interviewed me?"

"Haven't had to. Those other reporters were known sportscasters. They covered sports, not murder investigations. Something about her I don't like, that I don't trust."

"Whatever, man. Do whatever you feel you have to do. I'm going to take my own advice and head to the gym."

It was just after seven when Christian headed home. Two and a half hours of practice, another one watching film, and two spent in therapy had his body feeling better and his mind ready for Saturday's game. He tapped his Bluetooth icon, glanced at missed calls, and dialed the first one back.

"Hey, Emma."

"Hello, Christian."

"I missed your call?"

"Yes."

"Everything all right?"

"Fine. We met today on the expansion you wanted to do in both the math/science and media labs. A detailed report is being worked up to send over next week."

"What about the musical instruments?"

"I have a friend who graduated from Juilliard who's agreed to be a consultant. He's requires a fee, but nothing crazy."

"A Julliard graduate's knowledge is well worth the price. Go ahead and schedule that for sure." Thinking of his earlier conversation with Pete, he changed directions. "How'd the tour go with Mallory?"

"You didn't read her column?"

"No, haven't had time."

"You should. It's excellent. She's a very skilled writer. As for the tour, it went very well. She met some of the kids and wrote their stories in a way that elevated it beyond the 'hood makes good' narrative often touted in papers. She highlighted their strengths and achievements while painting a backdrop with their background that made the things they'd accomplished an even greater feat. I'll send you the link."

"Cool."

They talked a bit more, until Christian's personal assistant, Andy, interrupted the call. He returned a couple more calls after that, including one to his mother confirming a luncheon date for them next week to make up for not seeing her sooner. When his indicator pinged, he tapped the message icon and clicked on the newspaper article link. Emma was right. Christian immediately liked her writing style. Direct. Engaging. He was the hook, but her focus was on the center and the difference a positive, nurturing environment made in the children's lives. The way the article was written made it seem that she genuinely cared about their future, the same as he did. It made him think about last week and feel bad for setting up an appointment and then being a no-show. Then her being afraid or either too classy to call him out on his shit. He tapped on images. There were only a few. Zoey was right. She looked different at the gala than she did in these shots, with curly hair and no makeup. One showed her in jeans with a baggy sweater covering up all that deliciousness on display the other night.

Even as the warnings about her from Zoey and Pete sounded in his mind, Christian scrolled to her number. Zoey may have misjudged the reporter's motives. Pete might be off the mark, too. It was time to finally return her calls and draw his own conclusion.

16

When Mallory saw Christian's number pop up on her phone, she almost didn't answer. The article on him had been written and published. The remainder of the series would focus on the center and the children it served.

She was a reporter, though. She was doing an article on his foundation. And looking for evidence to open Leigh's case, maybe even catch her killer. Christian might have that evidence, hell, may *be* the evidence. Dammit, she hated when reason prevailed and she couldn't justify acting as though she were two.

"Mallory Knight."

"That was a good article."

"Thank you."

A span of silence followed. Mallory began counting in her mind, and much like the child who threatens to hold their breath until they die, she was holding.

"I apologize for not returning your earlier phone calls. I've been on the road."

Your cell phone doesn't work in those cities? "No worries. As you know from reading the article, I was able to pull together the info I needed."

"You did, and very well." He paused. Mallory waited. "When is the last time you attended one of our games?"

"I haven't."

A longer pause. "Never?"

Mallory chuckled. "Nothing personal. I'm not a huge sports fan."

"Then I'd like to invite you to our next game."

"Why? Not that I don't appreciate the gesture," she hurriedly added, realizing how her reaction may have sounded. "But it's not necessary for the series I'm writing on you and the foundation. There's plenty of writers reporting on your basketball. The focus of my series is on what happens off the field."

"Court."

"Right. Court."

Christian laughed out loud. "You really need to come to a game. At the very least you can learn the basics of the sport that funds the foundation at the heart of your series, whether you write about what you've learned or not."

Mallory couldn't argue. He had a point. "Put that way, I guess it would be a good idea."

"Thursday night. In Philly. I'll have a ticket left for you at will call."

"As in Pennsylvania? I'm not flying to Philadelphia for a basketball game."

"Don't worry about your flight, hotel, and whatnot. I'm handling all that."

"What makes you think I'd drop everything to come watch you play?"

"Because I have some information. What do you reporters call it . . . a scoop?"

"About?"

"Me, of course."

"Of course."

"So are you coming or what?"

Mallory was hesitant to accept his invitation. She really wanted to, and that worried her. For the first time since he'd come into her crosshairs, she understood Leigh's attraction to him, and the fan's adoration. His personality was magnetic and at the moment, she felt like steel.

"This Thursday?"

"Tomorrow. You'll fly back on Friday. So that's a yes, right?"

"Sure, I'll come see you play."

"My assistant will call you to schedule your flight. His name is Andy. You're welcome."

"Thank you," she answered.

He'd already hung up. Mallory sat stunned, both at Christian's effortless manipulation and her easy acquiescence. In hindsight, she recognized an assurance in his demeanor. An almost certainty that she'd say yes. *And why not?* It had probably been that way with every woman he'd ever met

She walked over to the mantel, picked up the jigsaw puzzle piece, and contemplated how best to use this golden opportunity, possibly the one and only chance for a conversation away from cameras or other mics, or Zoey. Sending a group text to Sam and Ava, Mallory headed upstairs to her walk-in closet. What did one wear to a pro ball game? And the next day. The meeting. How should she dress then? Never much of a clotheshorse, she knew from conversations with Leigh that her appearance was important. Christian loved beautiful women, and while she'd never use that label to describe herself, she'd come as close as possible. She'd use every available weapon to disarm, charm and find out if Christian was Leigh's secret friend.

It seemed she'd hardly made it up the stairs before her doorbell rang. "What'd you guys do, hail a taxi?"

"No," Sam sweetly began as she entered, stomping snow-covered boots on the foyer's rubber rug. "I just jumped on the back of Ava's broom."

"Sam!" Mallory looked at her, then Ava.

Ave shrugged. "She's just mad because I called her out on her bullshit."

"Happily ever after isn't bull," Sam retorted, tapping her shoes while pulling off her coat and hanging it on a rack nearby. "Just because you're jaded about the existence of true love doesn't mean the rest of the world has to live with that cold, pessimistic point of view." She turned to Mallory. "I told her that something heating up between you and Christian was not outside the realm of possibilities."

"On the other side of probabilities, though." She followed her friends into the living room.

"This is cool."

Mallory looked over to where Sam held the jigsaw puzzle piece. "That was in the bag of stuff that belonged to Leigh."

"Let me see it." Ava ran her hands over the smooth metal. "Is it real gold?"

Mallory shrugged. "I doubt it, but with the circles that Leigh liked to travel in, you never know."

Sam placed the puzzle piece back on the mantel. "Come on, guys. What are we doing? Fritz can't handle baby duty for more than an hour."

"You guys are helping me dress for a game. Let's go upstairs." On the way, she relayed her conversation with Christian.

"A round-trip flight. Hotel. Ticket at will call. Wow, all of that because you're not a fan?"

"I don't know, Sam," Ava said. "This trip might win her over. I may have discounted your romantic musings too quickly,"

"Knock it off, you two. This is work. And I never mix business with pleasure."

Sam walked over to a pile of clothes on the bed. "This is nice." She turned to Mallory and held up a black jumpsuit.

"I like it but thought that it looked too plain."

Ava walked into Mallory's closet. "Where are your accessories?"

"In that jewelry box on the top shelf."

Ava pulled down a small, rectangular shaped box and
opened it. "This is it?"

"Afraid so."

Sam joined her in the closet. She saw a duffel bag on the
floor, opened it, and pulled out a bright scarf. "Now we're
talking!" she exclaimed and walked out of the closet. "This is
gorgeous and provides the pop of color you need. Ooh, and
look at this purse! Doesn't look like your style at all, Mal, but I
love it."

"All of that belonged to Leigh."

Sam walked over to the bed and upended the bag. "Oh. My
God." She held up a pair of thigh-high boots. "You've got to
wear these, Mal."

"Where, to the funeral? Because a few steps in those stilts
and I'd surely break my neck."

"Those are funky," Ava said, walking over to inspect the
treasures found in Leigh's bag. "Live a little. Try them on."

Mallory looked at the boots and knew that she shouldn't,
but in for a penny, in for a pound. She slipped them on, and
after several attempts, Mallory gripped the footboard and
stood up. Her mind told her legs to walk, but they were afraid
to move. This had to have been what trying to walk felt like at
ten months old. She did a tippy-toe waddle over to the mirror
and . . . hot damn! She looked like a . . . well . . . she looked
like a fool, to put it quite nicely. On Leigh, Mallory was sure
the boots looked sexy. On her they looked like a bad idea. An
unfortunate photo op waiting to happen. She could see the
tabloid headline accompanying the picture. "Reporter Falls for
Basketball Star." Literally.

"Okay, here's what you're doing." Ava held up a gorgeous
burgundy cropped fur coat. "This, for sure."

"That's real mink," Sam answered, shaking her head. "Totally incorrect."

"You're meeting Christian, not PETA. If someone asks, lie and tell them it's fake. Wear it with the boots, a black turtleneck, and some skinny jeans."

"The top and jeans I can live with, but me and the boots are an unnegotiable no-go. Thanks, guys."

"You're welcome." Sam began putting items back in the oversized bag.

"Leigh had great taste." She held up small cream-colored purse with an adjustable strap. "Ava, feel the leather. This wasn't bought at a discount store."

"Too small for me," Ava said.

Mallory looked around. "Do you want it?"

"Seriously?"

"Sure. It's not something I'd use."

"I love it. Thanks." Sam slipped the strap over her shoulder and opened the purse. There was something inside it. "What's this?"

Mallory walked over. Sam gave her the light blue envelope. Mallory looked at Sam and Ava, then sat on the bed. Sam and Ava leaned in. Mallory raised the flap and pulled out a card. When she opened it, two pictures fell out. One was with a smiling Leigh posed between two men. The other was her cuddled up with just one—Christian Graham.

Sam gasped.

Ava exclaimed. "Damn!"

Mallory whispered, "Oh. My. God."

Ava sat next to Mallory who now held the card. The front read, *Thinking of You.*

Her hand shook as she opened it. Inside said simply . . . *Always.*

"Until next time," was scribbled beneath the word, along with what looked like a name.

Mallory handed the card to Ava. "Can you read that?'

Ava studied the signature, slowly shaking her head. "Me . . . Mr . . ."

"Are you sure that's an M?" Sam asked, peering at the card from over Ava's shoulder.

Mallory picked up the picture of Christian and Leigh. "This picture doesn't need decoding. I always thought there was more going on between them than friendship. This proves it."

Ava picked up the other picture. "Who is this guy?"

"The director of Christian's Kids, the foundation. He was at the press conference that was held the night of the fundraiser."

"These were taken the same night," Sam said, pointing to the pictures. "It's the same outfit."

Mallory frowned. "And?"

"Just making an observation."

"You think Mallory's rushing to judgment?" Ava reached for the pics and studied them side by side.

"They look pretty cozy, but that in itself doesn't mean anything."

"Or it could mean everything." Mallory took the pictures and stood. "One way or another, I'll find out."

Thirty minutes later, Sam and Ava left. So did the boots. They looked great on Ava, and what was even better was that she could walk in them. Mallory fired up her laptop, sent Charlie an email and a rough of Friday's column. While doing so, a new email popped into her work in box. She clicked on it absentmindedly, thinking about her glam squad's parting words about a trip to the hair salon and the spa.

She opened the email. What she read stood her hair on end.

I thought you were a better investigator, Ms. Knight. But after reading your column, one thing is clear. You've drunk the Graham the god Kool-Aid just like all the others. And that's a damn shame.

Mallory immediately replied to the email. She asked for the writer's identity and contact information, requested an interview and included her cell number. No reply came in the next few minutes. None was expected. But to say her interest was piqued was an understatement. The rumor about the kid. His publicist's standoffishness. And now this anonymous letter? *What's going on?*

Contrary to what the anonymous writer thought, Mallory was under no delusions about Christian's grandeur. She was on a whole other mission. Mallory signed off her work email and fell into a restless sleep, dreaming that she'd come face to face with the bogeyman who'd caused Leigh's nightmarish murder.

17

The next morning, after being flat-ironed to within an inch of her scalp, Mallory returned home, placed her toiletries and jewelry in the carry-on bag, and finished a quick meal just in time for her Uber pickup. Airport traffic was fairly light. Security was a breeze. Two hours after entering JFK, Mallory arrived in Philadelphia just after one o'clock, and per Andy's emailed instructions she headed down to ground transportation to look for her name. Her driver was easier to spot than her name, a six-foot something, three-hundred-pound, bald-headed, shade-wearing mountain in a room of molehills. He had tree limbs for legs and a physique that suggested he was more muscle than fat. In a collision with a car the size of her Toyota, the car might sustain more damage. He gripped a tablet reading "KNIGHT" with fingers the size of jumbo franks. She schooled her features into an expression masking her thought of *damn, buddy, you're huge!* and walked over.

"Hi, I'm Mallory."

"Hey, Mallory. Thomas." He offered his bear paw. "Everybody call me Treetop."

Of course they did. He was tall enough to be related to the old sequoias in Yosemite National Park that she'd heard you could drive a car through. She shook his hand.

"Nice meeting you, Thomas." Somehow calling a grown-ass man Treetop, even one who resembled it, seemed incorrect.

"You got more luggage?"

"Nope, this is it."

"All right, then. Car's right out front."

Really? How'd that happen? At Kennedy drivers could barely drop off or pick up passengers before traffic cops were demanding they move it along. They stepped outside to brilliant sunshine. It was warmer here than in New York. Mallory tucked the gloves she'd pulled out of her bag into a side pouch. She walked to the rear, where Thomas held a door open, entered the Jaguar SUV with tinted windows that was waiting curbside, and looked into the eyes of why the car was allowed to idle there without being towed.

"Christian!"

"Why the frown? I'm the reason you're here."

"No, sorry, I just wasn't expecting anyone in here."

"Rolling with me is always full of surprises." He stared at her unflinchingly as she settled inside the roomy back seat. "What's up?"

Was it her, or did Christian inhale all the air in the car? She shook his hand and felt the kind of jolt written about in the romance novels that Sam read. His lips curled into a smile. Hers, the ones that Christian couldn't see, applauded the move. Her body's reaction surprised her. Unless she got it together, and quickly, this was going to be a very long ride.

She realized she hadn't answered Christian's question of a greeting. "Thanks for the ticket," she blurted. "I could get used to first class."

Mallory heard the words as they left her mouth, saw Christian's smile, and could imagine an annoyed Leigh rolling her eyes. One of the rules, she remembered, was to experience their wealth and seem unaffected, as though their pampered world was your own. It would take focus for her to maintain the control she'd maintained in her mental scenario. But she had to admit, Christian left her off balance. She hadn't felt so flustered since the age of thirteen when she saw her first real live penis, the one Wally Chancellor flashed during recess. Then, her reaction had been one of curiosity framed by disgust. The guy beside her now stirred up a whole other set of emotions. She donned mental armor and a professional veneer. She was thirty-one, not thirteen; this was Christian, not Wally; and they were not on a playground. This was work. And recon. Mallory needed to keep her head in the game.

The melodious sound of a tenor saxophone caught her ear.

"Wait, is that Tivon Pennicott?"

Christian's brow shot up. "Yeah. How'd you know?"

Mallory smiled. Her shoulders relaxed. "I'm a jazz fan, especially horns."

"No shit. I'm surprised."

"Me too. It's the last sound I expected to hear while hanging with you."

"What'd you expect? Hip-hop?"

She shook her head. "Rock."

"Ha!"

"Definitely hip-hop, something self-absorbed, maybe."

"Damn, shorty! You don't think much of me, do you?"

"Outside of the work being done for this series, I don't think *about* you."

Christian's face turned serious. Mallory held his stare. A second passed. And another. Then he burst out laughing.

"I like you, Mallory. You don't brown-nose. You don't bullshit. You probably have no idea how rare a reaction that is to someone like me."

"I can imagine."

The energy shifted a bit. Mallory didn't know whether to be less nervous because they had something in common or more so because her body was responding in a way she hadn't wanted.

Christian's vibrating phone pierced the silence. He reached for it and began to text. "Where'd you learn to love jazz?"

"My dad. What about you?"

"Same. He's had one heck of a collection since I can remember. Used to sneak into it and grab classics to sample with hip-hop beats." Mallory nodded. "Your dad a collector?"

"Musician."

"Oh, yeah? What does he play?"

"Sax."

Christian nodded slowly. "Cool. Do you play?"

"No. Do you?"

"I dabble."

"Interesting."

"Interesting good or interesting bad?"

"I don't know. Depends on how you play."

"Ha!"

"What's here in Philadelphia that was so important you flew me over? And met me at the airport? You guys don't practice on game day, or have some other routine?"

Christian finished texting and settled himself more comfortably in the soft leather seats, his long legs having room in the back seat only because the car had been customized. The car's interior was navy outlined in yellow gold.

"Are you always in reporter mode? Firing off questions, thinking about your column and what to write?"

"When it comes to obtaining information, most reporters take advantage of every opportunity presented."

"I can understand that." They both took a minute to gaze out the window. Christian finished off a water and casually tossed the bottle on the automobile floor.

"Read your article again. With a second look that first line sounded cheesy."

"About you having a hundred kids? Why? I made it clear

that the reference was to the children who attended your center, not your personal brood."

"Ha! Gee, thanks a lot."

"I'm not saying you have a ton of children, though you guys are known for generously spreading your seed around."

"There you go again with another negative comment."

She shrugged. "I wasn't trying to offend you. Just making a statement based on—"

"On assumptions and stereotypes."

"No—"

"Yes, you are. I have my share of women. Won't lie about that and won't feel badly. Grown folk choose to do what grown folk do. But it's not like I'm wilding out twenty-four seven. I'm a man with discerning taste."

Mallory pulled out her laptop. "Mind if I quote you on that?"

"Go right ahead."

She felt his eyes on her but continued to type.

"The first time I saw you I thought you were either Hispanic or had people in the Middle East. But with all that attitude you're bringing, I suspect you're a sister."

"Black women aren't the only ones with attitudes."

"I should have guessed from your pics online, all that curly hair."

"Been checking me out, huh?"

"I figure turnabout is fair play."

"What, you thought I was Latina?"

"Or Indian, or Middle Eastern." He reached over and grabbed a lock of her hair.

"Hey! Don't touch my hair!"

Christian snatched his hand back. "Yeah, you're a sister. That's definitely black."

"Ha!" Mallory relaxed again, only now realizing that she'd gotten uptight.

"So your mother's Black?"

Mallory shook her head. "My dad. Mom is originally from a small town in a small state. Vermont."

"Ah, that's the bit of an accent I hear. New England. Is that where you grew up?"

"I spent a lot of time there. But I was born in Saint Louis, Missouri. Lived there until my parents divorced when I was seven. Then I moved with my mom to Omaha, Nebraska, my stepfather's hometown."

"Omaha, huh?" She nodded. "Never been there. What was that like?"

"Okay, I guess. Some days better than others. I wasn't always the easiest kid to raise. Had a lot of insecurities, resentments. Thought Mom was trying to keep me from my dad."

"But she wasn't?"

"In her mind, she was protecting me. Giving me a better life. Dad struggled as a musician, bounced from job to job while chasing his dream. Mom wouldn't let me visit him, and he was allergic to Nebraska. I felt isolated. Obviously different. Mixed kid in a household of blue-eyed blondes. Growing up is hard enough, even harder when you and your family don't feel like a fit."

"I can relate."

"You can?"

"Why do you act surprised? You didn't know I'm biracial?"

"You're the product of an interracial marriage, but you seem pretty comfortable in your skin."

"I am now. Getting here was a process. It's why I can relate to the kids that I mentor, because I can see myself in their shoes. Wanting to help them is one reason why I majored in psychology. Minored in education. Most of these kids out here aren't bad. They're hurting and hungry and want better for their lives."

The statement set Mallory back in the seat, fingers flying across the keys to capture the statement. Earnest. Profound.

"So that's why a foundation appealed to you. As a path toward a sound education."

"A good education and a great life. We have business professionals, teachers, other athletes who volunteer as mentors for our core kids. Those are the ones who are actually enrolled in our program and come every day, five or six days a week."

"What percentage is that?"

"About forty. The others either come for a couple hours after school or whenever they get the opportunity to escape where they're at."

Mallory looked up and realized they'd left the highway and the nice part of town, and were an area that vaguely resembled parts of Bed-Stuy.

"Where are we?"

"North Philly."

"But you didn't grow up here, correct?"

"Did you hear that, Tree? The queen of Google acting as though she doesn't know where I was raised."

Treetop turned down the music that had switched from Pennicott to classic Coltrane. "What'd you say, Dee?"

"Never mind."

"According to your online bio, you were raised in upstate New York, which is why I asked. Why are we here?"

"Because what isn't printed in those carefully crafted PR pieces is the amount of time I spent here as a kid, hanging with cousins on my mother's side. Here, in the hood, with all it has to offer. Many a fool in the streets has made the mistake that I don't know how to get down. You aren't the only who's acted presumptively. Most see my style, my degree, my life, and think I walk with a silver spoon up my ass. I live a blessed life, but am not enshrined behind a castle wall or over a moat or some shit."

Mallory typed, Christian too. Her on a tablet, him on his constantly buzzing phone. Treetop Thomas pulled to the curb in front of a multi-storied corner brick building that had seen better days. It was during work hours with temps dropping, yet a group of young men hung out near the building's entrance. Poster children for what the media and politicians defined as thugs—sagging pants, expensive jewelry, tattoos. One of them, a tall, handsome, dark-skinned man with short dreadlocks and a bright white smile strolled over to the car just as Christian got out.

"Player!" He greeted Christian with a shoulder bump hug and unique handshake.

"What up, Dex? How's life?"

"Comes and goes, bro, you know the drill. How's that shoulder, man? You ready to rock and roll in the rock and roll?"

"Always ready to Navigate. Cleveland had better be ready for us." He turned and opened the door on Mallory's side. "Come on out," he told her. "There's something I want to show you and some friends I want you to meet."

Mallory placed her tablet inside its case, grabbed her purse and got out.

"Mallory, this is Dexter Payne. He's going to be an assistant director for our first CK satellite campus." He nodded at the structure from which three guys watched them converse and a fourth headed over to join them.

"Nice to meet you," Mallory offered, as she watched the second young man feign a punch and a headshake fake to Christian before coming in for a hug.

"What's going on, Curtis? Staying out of trouble?"

"Hard to do when you are the trouble," Dexter teased.

"This your girl, man," Curtis asked Christian, giving a blatant once-over with big, brown eyes that contained a playful gleam.

"This is Mallory Knight, a reporter for the *New York News*."

"Ah, hell, let me bounce," Curtis said. "I'm trying to stay out of the limelight."

"Don't let these guys and their saggin'-braggin' fool you. This spring Curtis will graduate from the Community College of Philadelphia with an associate's degree in facility management. He'll head to Philadelphia University in the fall to get his BS."

"He don't need Temple for that," Curtis said. "He's already full of BS."

"Whatever," Dexter responded, totally unfazed. "Just be ready to hold down your spot when the program starts."

"His spot," Christian said to Mallory, "is AD for our computer science program. Little cuz can build a computer from scratch and program it with his eyes closed. And that's after smoking a blunt." The guys laughed as Christian reached for Mallory's elbow. "Come on, let's go inside so I can show you the future."

Mallory followed, rather dumbfounded at what was occurring. Whatever she'd imagined would happen today, this was not it. A satellite school? Employing kids who looked like gang bangers to build computers and upgrade buildings? No wonder kids looked up to him, their eyes filled with unabashed admiration. If she wasn't careful, she noted, catching a whiff of Christian's alluring cologne as they and the other guys entered the building with Treetop close behind, she might look at him that way, too.

"I started coming here and hanging with my cousins when I was around five," Christian shared easily as they navigated the wide, worn halls. "Would come down for holidays, a month or so in the summer. By then this was an office building. In here,"—he turned and stepped into a large room near the entrance—"was a neighborhood grocery and deli."

Christian continued the tour, as comfortable in the dilapidated building being brought back to life as he was in the Jaguar or the other night in the press conference. As they walked through the building she understood the dress code. The building was old and dusty with construction materials all over the place. At various times Christian would place a gentle yet firm hand on her arm, silently directing her around or away from the potential disaster of a loose floorboard, broken glass, or exposed nail. Caught up in the excitement of Christian and the guys about the first satellite center, Mallory found herself listening not just as a reporter but as a person hearing how much was possible when one person decided to help another, to reach down and lend a hand.

They left the building and headed back to the car. Christian liked to arrive at the arena three hours early. That was the direction Treetop Thomas pointed the car. A couple blocks from the building Treetop Thomas turned right onto a block that had seen better days. Like fifty or so years ago. Crumbling row houses, windows shattered or shot out long ago, covered with gang graffiti–stamped slabs of wood. Overgrown lots. Grass tired of being green, or even alive, sprouting through side-walks unevenly. In pieces. People hurried along on their way to nowhere. Heads down, expressions drawn, their body language that of "you mind your business, I'll mind mine." Mallory looked at them, and the area around them, opened her tablet, and typed one sentence.

Poverty had a feeling . . . and a face.

"This was our block back in the day," Christian said, pulling Mallory from her thoughts, the first article in the series being mentally rewritten with every moment she spent with the man. "My cousins stayed right there." He pointed to a building doing a mean gangster lean, two men with red eyes and brown bags lounging on the steps. "Curtis is his son."

"So when you said little cuz . . ."

"It wasn't gang lingo."

Mallory leaned against the door and stared at him. "I finally get why people worship you."

"You don't, but you will," Christian said, not looking up from his cell phone screen. "Tonight. The arena. That's when God arrives."

A devilish smile showed that he was teasing. Later, his words almost proved to be true. Christian was a god in a religion called basketball. Mallory enjoyed being a part of the congregation. Watching Christian lead his team was nothing short of magic. The tour of Christian's life in North Philly was a valuable eye-opener, letting Mallory finally see the man in 3-D. They hadn't talked about Brandon, and she'd not mentioned Leigh's name as she'd planned to gauge his reaction. But she left Philadelphia with what she considered a jackpot. She retrieved and pocketed Christian's used water bottle. She had proof that, if it had to be used, would not lie—Christian "Don't-Give-a-Damn" Graham's DNA.

18

Once back in Brooklyn, Mallory headed straight to the office. She ditched the article she'd written for next week's post and started over from scratch with what Christian had shared about himself and the vision for Christian's Kids, the true connection he had with impoverished youth who reminded him of himself at that age. His desire to make a difference in the world. To improve lives. She scanned the notes she'd made on the plane, took a breath, and began typing.

All of Christian Graham's children don't live in New York.

Mallory left work at five and after getting a text from Ava headed over to midtown for dinner and drinks. The Newsroom was her favorite bar and eating hangout, but Ava wanted different, so she'd chosen a popular spot for the young professional, Bar Sixty-Five. When Mallory reached the floor for which the place had been named she spotted Ava's curly locks in a sea of heads and headed to a window-side table.

"Haven't been here in forever," Mallory said, once they'd hugged and sat down. "Forgot the beauty of this view."

"It's one of my favorites."

"Used to be Jack's and my favorite place, too. When we first broke up, I couldn't eat here."

"I'm glad you got over that, and him. Gosh, I'm starving. What should I eat?"

After deciding on dinner and ordering drinks, Ava got down to business. "What happened?"

Mallory told her about the visit to Philadelphia, the neighborhood where Christian spent time as a child, and the building he'd purchased for the first satellite campus for Christian's Kids.

"It started out a bit rough. Both of us defensive. But we connected over jazz and eventually I saw the side of him that draws in crowds, and I believe he's serious about his foundation."

"No longer think it's just a tax write-off?"

"Any man with money benefits from a nonprofit. But I think he's more hands on than I believed."

"Like visiting that boy in the hospital?" Mallory nodded. "Did you find out what that was about?"

"No, but I'm working on that next week. While at the airport in Philadelphia I sent an email to Emma Davis, who runs Christian's Kids. Told her I wanted to interview Harmony Walker and she agreed. Harmony is Brandon's sister."

"Oh, okay. Good luck with that. Hopefully one mystery solved."

"Yes, and I have what's needed to possibly solve another mystery, too. If Leigh was indeed pregnant, I can find out if he's the father."

"What could possibly do that besides his DNA?"

"Which is what I've got."

"You slept with him?"

"No!" she said so forcibly that those around them turned.

"Don't look so mortified! If that happened, bagging a condom would be a no-brainer."

"It was much easier than that. He littered the town car floor with a water bottle. I decided to recycle. The bottle is wrapped and in my freezer. I have a contact in Baltimore who can run the tests."

"Interesting that happened, because I've got some news, too."

"You look serious. What?"

"Sam and I felt bad about not doing our part to get justice for Leigh. Although you two were besties, we knew her, too. So she took on the task of IDing the guy in the Manhattan high-rise, and I did a little digging around the family planning center."

"Dr. Kapoor's office?"

"Yes."

"You got Leigh's records?"

"I said dig, not pilfer. Saw a cleaning crew go into the building. When they came out I inquired about work. Said if they had an opening in the evenings, I knew someone who might need a job."

"Who?"

"You! I don't do windows or floors."

Mallory's brow furrowed, and her fingers rapped the table as she considered pulling off the role. "If the file room isn't locked I can pull it off. This is genius, Ava. When do I start?"

"I didn't get that far. You need to call them, and quickly."

"Be right back." Mallory pulled out her cell phone and headed out to the street.

The following Tuesday Mallory sat parked around the corner from New Life Medical, wearing baggy black jeans and a black tee as the employer requested. A straight brown wig with blonde highlights and bangs covered her curls, with an LED cap perched on top. Inside her pants pocket was an LED flashlight, burner phone, screwdriver, nail clipper, and a bump key, should she need to pick a lock. Mallory hoped that wouldn't happen. A ten-minute YouTube video on how to quickly and easily open any lock wasn't the best guarantee against a) being successful b) ending up in jail or c) both. Her cell phone was at home in Brooklyn, providing a cell-tower alibi if the need for one ever came up. Her legal ID was in the glove compartment. A fake driver's license with a common name was in her pocket with the phone. Using the computer vision dazzle she'd re-searched online, makeup had been applied to reshape her nose and thin out her lips. Her big brown eyes were partially hidden behind thick round glasses that along with the carefully ap-plied makeup would offset her angular face. With a last check-off of the mental list she envisioned, she reached for her keys and the car door handle.

"You're on, Knight. Come with me, Leigh. We can do this."

While walking to the door, her nerves were so frayed she thought she'd throw up. She'd filled out the paperwork online, but the woman she'd talk to on Friday and again yesterday seemed like a hard-ass rule-follower who toed the line. But a few seconds in the presence of a distracted assistant super named Anna, in an ongoing argument with her boyfriend or whoever was on the other end of the Bluetooth, Mallory re-laxed. Maybe Leigh really had sway wherever she was, because the distraction would make her job easy. After pointing out the various rooms, the super gave Mallory the task of emptying all of the trash cans and cleaning the bathrooms. Jobs obviously for the low man on the totem pole, she reasoned, but if the file room had a trash can her job, the main one she'd entered the building to handle, would get done.

Mallory cleaned the bathrooms first, taking the time to calm down and go over the plan in her head. How to comb through the files quickly. Praying that the files contained actual patient records. With so many hospitals going digital, that might not be the case. What to do if the cabinets were locked. What to say if she got caught. She put on latex gloves and then, grabbing a circular trash can on wheels, Mallory started in the reception area, dumping the contents of smaller trash cans into the round receptacle. She kept her head down, remembering that she'd seen a camera in the waiting room. It made sense that at least one was outside by the entrance and that one would be in the file room, too. Now and then the super could be heard either laughing or cursing, but with Mallory's limited Spanglish it was really anyone's guess. The other woman working with Anna and her ran a vacuum, making meticulous lines on the carpeted floors. Mallory hoped the whirring sound would cover up any noise she'd have to make if the file cabinets were locked.

She reached the main hallway. There were four doors, all closed. Even with the mental preparation, her heartbeat increased as her hand touched the knob on the first door on the left. She turned the knob slightly. Easy. Unlocked. She entered an administrative office with two desks facing each other. Within the seconds it took to empty the trash cans her investigative eye took in pictures of a family on one desk and those of girlfriends and dogs on the other. A married woman and single chick. She believed given five minutes she could have written their lives.

She quickly checked the next room and emptied the trash, but when she turned the knob to the third door, it was locked. Her mind wobbled with one question after another. Should she find the super and ask what was behind door number three? Try and pick the lock? Check the other rooms first and then come back? She looked at her watch. She tried the final door in the hallway. It was locked, too. *Crap!* One she figured belonged to the doctor. But which one? And how much time and luck did she have to find out? They were to be finished in an hour. With refocused intention, she turned the corner that led to another short hall and the examination rooms that

Mallory remembered from her prior visit. There were two more rooms down this hall, a supply room and a kitchen with a table for breaks. Taking a deep breath, she returned to the short hallway, and after listening for the vacuum's location and taking a quick look around, she pulled out the set of bump keys. She wasn't big on religion, but she prayed anyway. *Please, work quickly. Please be the file room.* Her hands shook as she reached for the one resembling most office keys and slid it into the chamber. No go. She quickly reached for a similar one and tried it. *Bingo!* Holding the key with her right hand and turning it slightly, she tapped with her left, working quickly and a bit too efficiently for someone's first time. A burglar in another life, perhaps?

Come on!

Click.

Without hesitation Mallory pushed open the door and walked right into . . . Dr. Kapoor's office.

Shit!

She headed toward the basket beneath the desk and then remembered she wasn't supposed to be in there. After a quick check of the hallway she closed the door, checked the knob to make sure it was locked, and then pushed the large trash container beyond the other locked door to the hallway leading to the bathroom. She still held the key that had worked on Dr. Kapoor's door and quickly slid it into the chamber and began tapping and twisting. She'd hammered twice, maybe three times before realizing what was wrong with the picture. She could hear the sound way too loudly.

The vacuum cleaner had stopped.

Where was the other cleaning lady?

Right behind you, Paranoia answered in her head.

Get the fuck out! Fear screamed.

And then another voice, this one a calm whisper. *Go on. Hurry.*

Mallory tapped twice more, as quietly as she could. The

lock turned. She slipped inside, her heart beating louder than the sound of the screwdriver tapping the key. She leaned back against the door, took a couple seconds to quell her heart's pounding. It would have worked except the vacuum cleaner started up again.

Right behind her. Right outside the door.

Did the cleaning crew have a key to the file room? More importantly, would they be using it anytime soon? *Like while I'm in here trying to steal shit?*

The thought spurred Mallory to action. She turned on the baseball cap's LED lights, which according to the internet description would make her head disappear behind a ball of white light. The lights definitely lit up the room, so much so that she didn't need the mini flashlight to navigate it. There was a row of vertical filing cabinets against the back wall. A large, horizontal one was on the right wall along with a rolling cabinet. Shelving covered the other wall above a rectangular table containing file folders and other supplies. She walked to the tall cabinets at the back of the room and pulled on the first drawer. It was locked. A good sign for Mallory. Probably contained patient files. She retrieved the nail clipper from her pocket, pulled out the file part of it, and hoped the lock on these files was as easy to pick as hers had been the night before.

It was. One push, one turn. *Click.*

She eased open the file drawer, reached toward the middle, and pulled out one file at random.

Bates.

She moved to the last drawer in the cabinet. It contained a different set of folders altogether. Gray instead of manila. *What does that mean?* Pulling out her mini flashlight she knelt down and thumbed through the first couple files. She ran into names beginning with A. She opened the file and scanned the first page's contents. *Children's files?* Not what she needed. She quickly moved to the second cabinet. The lock was more challenging than the first but opened after ten seconds of jimmying it with the file.

How long have I been in here? Mallory didn't know but something told her, *Hurry.*

She reached inside the first drawer. *Franklin.*

She scanned its contents. An adult. Female. Pregnant. *Closer.*

Closer. She reached into the back of the drawer. *Izsak.*

Oh. My. God.

She closed the first drawer and opened the second one. She pulled out a folder near the front. *Jaber.* Mallory screamed on the inside. *Yes!* With urgency she raced through the folders. Then a thought paralyzed her.

What if Leigh had used a fake name?

Mallory searched even more frantically. *Jaccard. Jace.* And finally, *Jackson.*

There were a lot of them.

She focused on the first names, looking for L. *Lacy. Lisa. Lillian. Lori.* And others. No Leigh.

"Grace!"

Mallory flipped through the L's again, focused on each name. The one she wanted to see wasn't there.

"Grace!"

Mallory heard the name, and her heart stopped beating. Anna was calling her! She couldn't respond. She couldn't leave now, so close to the truth. She'd stay there all night if she had to, deal with the consequences in the morning. She looked for a place to hide, slid closer to the rectangular table and gripped it while checking out the space beneath and what could be used to conceal her. Crouched on the floor, her hand came in contact with something dangling off the table. She snatched her hand away, pulling it with her. She stashed it in her pocket and crept back to the files.

"Grace! Where are you?"

The other cleaning woman. The quiet one. Yelling.

"Think, Mallory!" she hissed to herself between gritted teeth. *Elizabeth.*

From out of nowhere came Leigh's middle name. Mallory flipped back to the E's. L. Elizabeth Jackson. DOB: 07/31/1984. Height: 5'7". Weight: 125. Hair: Black. Eyes: Brown. She'd found it. The file of her friend, Leigh Elizabeth Jackson.

Swallowing a wave of emotion and another of fear, Mallory whipped out the burner phone and began snapping photos. She took several angles of the file—entire pages and the blocks contained in them. No time to read. She just snapped and hoped that the truth was somewhere in the photographs.

Voices came near the door. Mallory snapped off the flashlight and turned the LED cap away from the door.

"Where is she?" Anna asked.

"I don't know. Her trash can is by the bathroom, but she isn't in there."

Nothing on Mallory moved, not even her breath. The conversation continued down the hall. The file was a small one. Mallory captured everything in it on the phone, then checked to make sure the images were there and that they were time-stamped. Satisfied that she'd gotten as much as she could, she replaced the file and closed the drawer. There was no time to try and lock it with the file. She placed the nail file, flashlight, and phone in her pockets and felt what she'd pushed down seconds before, what had swiped across her hand when by the table. Instinctively, she put it on, tiptoed to the door, and pressed her ear against it.

Silence.

Taking a deep breath, she cracked the door, then eased it open. She slid out from behind it, closed the door. She took a tentative step, and then another, headed toward where she'd left the trash container.

"Grace!"

Her whole body seized up for at least two seconds. She turned, slowly pulling an earbud from beneath the wig's long, straight hair.

Holding the earbud as evidence, she said, "I'm sorry. I guess my music was turned up too loud."

"Where were you?"

"I was . . ." Mallory swung her arm in a general direction. "Cleaning. Like you told me."

"Where? You weren't in this office when I checked a few minutes ago. And the bathrooms still aren't clean."

"I did go outside to take a call in private. But just for a second." The lie wasn't much, but it was all she had.

Anna's eyes narrowed as her hand found a hip. "You know what? I don't think this is going to work out for us. We have a lot of offices to clean, and the last thing I need to spend my time doing is going behind somebody who doesn't want to work. Consider this first day your last one"

"I'm sorry." Mallory had to work to keep the smile off her face and the joy out of her tone. Getting fired was the best thing that could have happened right now. It saved her from another lie later.

"Do you want me to leave right now?"

"Yes. Right now. And don't expect to get paid for the whole shift when you only worked an hour."

"But, Anna, I—"

"Leave."

"Okay."

Mallory held her composure until back in her car and on the way to Brooklyn. Once on the highway she let out a scream of victory and relief. Back home she uploaded the pictures from the phone to her laptop, where they could be enlarged and read quickly. Her eyes stayed glued to the screen as some of the answers she'd searched for slapped her in the face.

Leigh was pregnant at the time she died.

19

The mystery consumed her. Who fathered Leigh's baby? Who ended her life? Early on Mallory had honed in on Christian, but the more she got to know him the less likely he seemed. In Philadelphia, she'd watched his easy interaction with friends and fans, making them feel special just by being around him. His passion for the foundation and the communities it served seemed genuine. Why would a man who obviously loved children not want one of his own? Was it Isaac Bankole, the shady accountant with a record, named as a person of interest in another murder case? Randall DuBois, the ambitious politician who seemed to have the most to lose? The musician, whom she now knew was named Josh Weir? The last guy on the list who continued to elude them? What if the answer was none of the above?

Mallory spent the weekend at home, online, revisiting websites, reviewing the information she'd compiled for the umpteenth time. That's when she saw it—Anthony Wang.

The only officer who wasn't convinced Leigh's death was suicide.

The force of the memory stood Mallory straight up. She raced to her file cabinet and the accordion folder filled with every business card she'd received for the past few years. Her fingers flew across the tabs and came to rest on W. Collecting the cards scattered haphazardly in the pocket, Mallory remembered the short, intense man who'd approached her on the sidewalk outside Leigh's apartment, moments after she'd seen her best friend naked and dead.

"Detective Wang," he'd said, almost brusquely while handing her his card. "Call me."

Mallory had been in shock then, but a month or so later, she'd called the number on the card. It went to voicemail. She'd left a message. He'd never called back. Mallory immediately called the number. She got voicemail again.

"Hi, Detective Wang, this is Mallory Knight. We met a while ago at a crime scene. You gave me your card. The victim was Leigh Jackson. Her death was ruled a suicide. I think she was murdered. Maybe you do, too. Either way, please call me." Mallory left her cell number. Now she'd have to wait.

Meanwhile, she put Bankole's name in the search engine, learned that he'd been questioned and cleared. Sam was on mommy duty, but Mallory called Ava, who joined her to commiserate. They believed that if they figured out who Leigh was seeing and who fathered the baby, they'd know who killed her.

Mallory rose on Monday with the dawn, determined to gather enough evidence to turn over to police and force them to reopen the case they'd closed. To add pressure, she planned to present the same evidence to Charlie and do a column on Leigh—the beautiful woman, loyal friend, excellent reporter—and her untimely demise, to keep her name in the news, her face in the public eye. For any of that to happen, she needed facts. So she donned latex gloves, removed the water bottle from the freezer, and carefully cut it in half. She trusted Johnny, her Baltimore connection with access to DNA labs and more, but she didn't want to take any chances on losing the only potential link she had between Leigh and Christian.

She left for work, but before going to the office she stopped to have the package overnighted, then walked the four blocks to her office in order to make some calls. The first one was to Baltimore.

"Hey, Johnny. Mallory. Remember what I asked you awhile back about having something tested for DNA? Well, I just overnighted you a package. How quickly can you get it back to me?"

Mallory winced at the answer. "A month? Why so long?"

She smiled at Johnny's answer. A month was a very quick turnaround. Testing routinely took six months or more. Further, unless the DNA belonged to someone already in the system, there was no way the identity of said person could be confirmed. This wasn't news to Mallory. She already knew that without probable cause one could not be made to submit their DNA to the authorities. With Christian's money he likely had the MVP of law firms already. Getting him to provide a sample in connection with a pregnancy terminated by murder would be no easy feat. But nothing about this situation had been easy. So far, somehow, Mallory had made a way.

It was hard to focus on work, so after two unproductive hours and being annoyed by the presence of the other two reporters who shared the office, Mallory gathered her things, hit the street, and called Charlie. She got voicemail and left a message.

"Hey, boss. I have an appointment at Christian's Kids for the last column in this series. Headed out to Harlem, and after that I would like to work from home. If that's a problem, please call me back. Also have ideas for the coming months that I'd like to run past you. Will be back in tomorrow. Thanks."

Mallory hopped down the subway stairs and took the train to Harlem. For the fourth and final column on Christian's Kids she wanted to interview Brandon's sister, Harmony. As she neared the stairs to exit the subway, a lone figure with a familiar face traipsed down them.

"Harmony?"

The girl looked up but said nothing. She didn't smile, either.

"You're Harmony, right?"

"Who are you?" Harmony continued down the stairs.

Mallory followed. She reached for her business card in the side pocket of her purse. "I'm Mallory Knight, with *New York News*. I've been writing articles about the center and interviewing people who work there and students like you in their after-school and summer programs. Last week's article was about the math and science component of the program. I interviewed Justin. You know him?"

"Yeah."

"He's a whiz at math and science, which I think is really cool. Not what you always think of when you see a young man like him."

Harmony looked as though she couldn't have cared less.

Mallory looked at her watch. "Why aren't you in school?"

"I wasn't feeling well."

"So you were headed home?" Harmony nodded. "That's a shame. I was headed to the center to ask where I could find you."

"Me? Why?"

"Because Emma told me you were into horticulture, and that you were really good at it."

A sparkle of interest, at least direct eye contact. Good. *Progress!*

"I bought a planter for my windowsill one time. The only thing I grew was mud."

A smile. Mallory had an idea she knew how Christian felt when he scored a three-pointer.

"So I was hoping to interview you, maybe even get you to help me grow something. Would you like that?"

"I guess."

"Perhaps I can take the train with you and speak with your mother, see if it would be okay to interview you, maybe go grab a burger and talk."

"Mama's at work."

"And you're not feeling well."

"I feel okay. Just bored at school."

Not a good reason to lie, but Mallory chose not to die on that hill. She stayed focused on what mattered the most to her right now.

"Do you think she'd mind you speaking with me?" Harmony shrugged. "Do you want to talk with me? Look, I'd really like to find out your secrets for planting a seed and actually having something come up, but I don't want to force it. There are other kids that I can talk to, so . . ."

"I can help you."

"Are you sure?" Another nod. "Great, but first I need to get your mom's permission. What's her name?"

"Karen."

"Can you call her?"

Karen was obviously busy. The conversation was brief, but she gave Mallory the okay to interview Harmony.

"I know a great burger place. A hole in the wall that is one of Harlem's most well-kept secrets."

Twenty minutes later, Mallory and Harmony sat in a booth at an old-school diner with burgers served on paper placed in red plastic bowls. A large order of fries sat on the table between them with separate miniature ketchup cups for dipping beside each plate.

"You ever eaten here before?"

Harmony shook her head as she took a big bite.

"Was I kidding about it being the best burger ever?"

"No." Harmony licked her fingers before reaching toward a silver holder for a couple of napkins. "It's really good."

"It's my favorite. I'm glad you like it." Mallory pulled out her recorder. "Instead of asking you a series of questions, we can just keep talking like this, natural, and I'll pull out the good stuff. Okay?"

Harmony nodded.

"You don't talk much, huh?"

"I talk, but . . . not a lot, I guess."

"Probably doesn't help that I'm a stranger. I promise, I don't bite. I can't imagine there are a lot of gardens in your neighborhood, so how did you become interested in growing your own food?"

"I saw this show on TV where they used an egg carton as a planter to grow stuff. They put a couple seeds in each of the pockets, you know, where the eggs go?" Mallory nodded. "And then they showed the results from a month or so later and the seeds had sprouted. I ran to my mom and asked if I could do it and she said yes."

Mallory had no problems getting Harmony to talk after that. Immersed in her world of germination and harvest, the girl's personality came through. There was pride mixed with awe as she spoke of the rooftop garden she'd started in her building and the plans for others. She became animated and lively, and gave Mallory more than enough to put together a great article likening the children to those seeds. When planted in good soil, they will grow.

A great article, however, wasn't her main reason for speaking with Harmony. Mallory wanted to know more about Brandon. But she had to be careful and let a conversation about him unfold organically. To do that, Mallory needed more time. As they finished their meal and headed back to the subway, she moved on to part two of her plan.

"You've got me ready to try my windowsill garden again. But I don't have a green thumb like you."

"Anybody can plant a garden."

"Girl, the last plant I had was plastic and I killed it, okay? I'm really bad." The comments got the laughter Mallory hoped for. "Perhaps we could visit a garden store together. You could help me choose the right materials for making my windowsill garden grow."

"Sure."

"What about this Saturday? Or will you be at the center?"

"I can go."

"Tell you what. To make it easier, I'll pick you up at your home and take you back. If you give me a phone number I'll also clear this with your mom."

"Okay."

Mallory woke up on Saturday and dubbed it "Leigh's Day." It began in Queens at the Bankole's office. Something about him rubbed her the wrong way immediately. His small, beady eyes and inflated ego. The comment he made when she mentioned Leigh's death. "A shame all of that beauty is now covered with dirt." Not that Mallory would dismiss the possibility that she was being overly sensitive. When it came to those around her at the time of her death, and who hastened her to it, their status was guilty until proven innocent.

Rather than respond to his tasteless comment she asked, "How long was she your client?"

"I don't discuss client business. That's confidential."

"Of course. I wasn't asking for specifics, just curious. She mentioned you a time or two."

His eyes narrowed. Mallory held her breath. The comment was totally bogus, an attempt to try and get him to open up.

"She is the reason why I called your office."

"Then let's discuss your financial planning needs and how I can help."

The visit was totally fruitless, not even a cup in sight that she could pilfer to check DNA. Mallory left his office without any evidence to either confirm or eliminate the financial consultant in Leigh's murder. But if first impressions meant anything, Bankole looked like a man who could kill or at the very least, order the hit.

Harmony's family lived in Jamaica, Queens, about fifteen minutes by car from his office. Mallory pulled up in front of a brick high-rise that took up the block. Not sure where Harmony would exit, Malory pulled up to an entrance with a number and texted it to her. More than ten minutes passed before Harmony strolled up to where Mallory sat parked and surfing the web. The animated Harmony that she'd left at the subway platform was gone. The quieter, more introspective child had returned.

"Everything okay?"

"Yeah."

Mallory wasn't sure about that. She eased into a line of questions to find out more. "Was your mom home?"

"No."

"I was hoping to meet her. I'd imagine she works a lot. New York is expensive, especially if she is a single mother."

Harmony looked out the window.

So much for finding out if there was a dad in the house. "Do you have brothers and sisters, or is it just you?"

"A brother."

"Older or younger?"

"Younger."

"Does he attend the center also? I may have talked with him."

"He does but . . . not lately."

"Oh, okay."

Mallory knew from the carefully crafted answers that there'd be no getting information about Brandon from Harmony. So for the next two hours she took off her investigative journalist hat and put on the big sister role. They arrived at a large home and garden store. The livelier kid returned, and among other tidbits Mallory learned that Harmony's favorite celebrity was Rihanna, her favorite color was blue, and Mallory's first offering, the hamburger, was her favorite food. After a gentle inquiry about Brandon, Harmony revealed that her brother had been sick, but was better. When asked about her father Harmony became quiet, then said simply, "He's out of town."

It was just after five o'clock when they pulled back up in front of Harmony's building.

"Harmony, I've got a big favor to ask you."

"What?"

"Can I use your restroom? I don't know why I didn't before leaving the house, and I'm not sure I can make it back."

"Um, yeah, okay."

"Thank you!"

Mallory pulled into a space about a half a block down. Though early evening it was almost dark, and the streets were fairly empty. As she looked around, the block reminded her of the one Christian's satellite building was on in North Philly. The people had the same energy, too. Head aimed downward. Eyes alert but no eye contact. Everyone minding their business, alone in a city of millions.

They entered the building and took an elevator to the fifth floor. Harmony pulled out a key as they neared a door midway down the hall.

"Our house is a little dirty, but . . ."

"It's okay. As long as you have a toilet, I'm good!"

They went inside. Mallory had hoped to see Brandon, and she was not disappointed. He half sat, half lay on a couch in the living room watching TV.

"Hi, Brandon."

His mumbled response was barely audible. Having come in on the ruse of having to pee, she let it be and turned to Harmony.

"Where's your bathroom?"

"I'll show you."

They headed down a short hallway. The bathroom was to the left. Mallory made quick work of a forced pee, wiped her hands on her jeans with no hand towel present, and headed out of the bathroom for a second attempt with Brandon. What she saw in the room across the hall from the bathroom pushed that thought right out of her mind. Hanging on the wall was a gold metal sculpture in the shape of a jigsaw puzzle . . . with one missing piece.

20

The vision knocked Mallory against the wall and then pulled her forward like a magnet. *Am I really seeing what I think I'm seeing?* Her eyes never left the sculpture as she walked forward. It was the only thing she saw in the room. She stood before it, staring at the space for the missing piece and tried to visualize the one on her fireplace mantel. *There's no way that piece fit into this puzzle. Was there?* She took a step closer, placed a finger on the gold metal, and traced the empty space. Smooth. Cool. Just like the piece that belonged to Leigh.

Take a picture.

She hurriedly pulled out her cell phone and snapped several pictures from different angles. Leaning in, she worked to get as clear a picture as she could of the space where a missing piece would go. *Just a little more to the left.*

"What are you doing?"

If she hadn't already gone only moments before, Mallory would have peed her pants. Instead she jumped, almost out of her skin. Her phone fell out of her hand and skidded across the carpet, stopping at the feet of a woman who looked none too pleased.

She picked up Mallory's phone and marched over. "Who the hell are you, and why are you in my room?"

"I'm so sorry." Mallory struggled to pull out her business card holder. "You must be Karen. I'm Mallory Knight with *New York News.*" Karen took the card, but her eyes remained on Mallory. "We talked, earlier this week. I'm doing the piece on Harmony and her urban gardens."

"Ain't no damn garden in here, in my Got damn bedroom!"

"I had to use the bathroom, and Harmony was kind enough to let me come in. I was headed out when I saw this piece." She motioned toward the sculpture. "I love unique stuff like that and . . . I wasn't even thinking. It just drew me in. I took a couple pictures of it to try and find one for myself online. You can check my phone. The only pictures I took are of the sculpture." For the first time, Mallory glanced around the room and saw the disarray. Clothing, jewelry, magazines, and more were strewn across an unmade catchall bed. Opened closet doors revealed clothes haphazardly placed on hangers, piled in overflowing baskets and across the floor. The nightstand beside the bed was equally overloaded, with a partially opened pizza box perched between it and the bed. Mallory was suddenly embarrassed to have entered the woman's bedroom. She had totally overstepped her bounds.

"Ms. Walker, Karen . . . I am so sorry. I wasn't even thinking. I just saw the piece and . . ."

"Look, I got it. I saw the pictures you took. But that's not cool. Walk around in the wrong house and you might get taken out in a body bag. Coming in your room and finding a stranger can have a bad ending in this neighborhood."

Karen walked out of the room. Mallory hurriedly and gratefully followed behind her into the living room. She couldn't wait to get out of that house. She needed space and time to think. What had just happened? What had she just seen? Could her running across the jigsaw puzzle sculpture be a mega coincidence? Mallory didn't think so, but something didn't add up. The sculpture was completely out of place. Leigh being involved with this family was even stranger. She had questions for Karen but knew that now was not the time. Instead of coming here and getting answers, more and more questions filled her mind.

Mallory reached the door. She turned to Karen. "Thanks for letting me use your restroom. That was a lifesaver. And again, my apologies for trespassing." She turned to Harmony. "Thanks for going shopping with me and helping me get the items for my windowsill garden. I'll take pictures if anything grows."

"Just remember to keep the soil moist. Use the sprayer every day."

"I will. Bye, Harmony."

"Bye."

Mallory forced herself not to break into a flat-out run down the hall, bypassing the elevator and taking the stairs. She punched the down button and waited, pulling out her phone and sending a text just as a ding announced the car's arrival.

You two free tonight? If not, phone chat at seven? The plot thickens.

Once home, the girls touched base by phone. Sam and Ava had other commitments that night but promised to meet at Mallory's house the following evening for an investigative powwow. Mallory changed into a comfy fleece sweat suit, and after grabbing a throw and the gold puzzle piece she settled into the couch. She fired up her laptop and opened the email where she'd forwarded the picture of Karen's art piece. She clicked on the attachment and after enlarging it, placed the piece she held in her hand above the screen. The piece she held matched the shape of what was missing in the art on Karen's wall. Coincidence? Or the artist's intention? And if the latter, how did Leigh come to possess it? She opened a search engine and used various words to try and find the artwork online.

The next evening after work, Mallory ordered pasta takeout from her favorite neighborhood restaurant and then went to the corner for a bottle of wine. By the time Ava arrived shortly before their agreed-upon meeting time, Mallory had found a white poster board and rounded up Sharpies. She wanted to put what they'd gathered so far in writing. Somehow words became clear for her when written down.

Ava's questions began before her coat hit the couch. "Did you see the accountant?"

"The financial consultant, Bankole? I did."

Mallory drew a rough chart and placed his name on the first line, followed by Graham, DuBois, Weir and a question mark.

"Did you learn anything?"

"Nothing, really. He was tight-lipped, cautious, like a man with something to hide."

"I could have told you that. Much like with an attorney, client privilege is protected by law."

"I knew that, but was hoping that by presenting myself as the best friend come to him on Leigh's high recommendation he'd let down his guard."

"So he's a dead end? Sorry, I could have probably found a better choice of words."

"Because of his history and the bad vibe I got, he seems capable of doing really bad things. But I have zero proof that he was anything other than Leigh's consultant. Which means . . ."

Mallory drew a line through his name.

"One down, four to go. Is that all you found out?"

"Not hardly."

The doorbell rang. Ava stood. "I'll get it."

Sam entered rambling about a sick baby and a husband who had been called out of town. Rarely harried, the normal epitome of peace didn't pick up on Ava's disinterested expression or that Mallory had barely acknowledged her and kept writing on the board.

"Leigh was pregnant."

". . . and then my mother-in-law came here and—What?"

The comment turned Ava's head as well. "Pregnant?"

Sam plopped into one of the dining room chairs. "How do you know?"

"I saw the records, and have the copies to prove it."

"You took the cleaning job?" Ava asked, shocked. "And didn't tell me? Or Sam? Anybody?"

"All of this just happened in the past few days. I wanted to share it when we were all together, like now."

Sam looked from Ava to Mallory. "Cleaning job? What are you guys talking about?"

Mallory filled her in. "When Anna fired me, I almost gave her a hug. Couldn't have written a better ending."

"I can't believe you risked your career like that," Sam said. "You could have been caught, arrested, and charged with a felony."

"But I wasn't, so calm down."

"I will not calm down!"

"You really should," Ava suggested. "Or else you'll have a heart attack when you find out about Christian, and how she got his DNA."

Mallory quickly brought Sam up to speed and told them both about the puzzle in the bedroom at Harmony's house. "That's why I'm not so focused on Joseph anymore," she finished.

"The financial consultant," Ava said, answering the question on Sam's face.

"Here's what we have so far."

She went back to the white board, and spoke as she wrote.

"I have nothing on Bankole so for now have crossed him off. When it comes to Graham, there are several connections."

"Leigh. Navigator fan."

"Graham. Navigator, founder of Christian's Kids."

"Puzzle found in home of CK student."

"Matching piece—Leigh. Oh, and I did a search online.

Couldn't find an exact replica of that sculpture anywhere. So however it was obtained, it's not mass-produced."

"You should have the piece tested," Ava offered. "See if it's real gold."

"Good idea." Mallory wrote the suggestion on the board.

Sam leaned forward. "Maybe to Christian she was more than a fan. The picture we found makes that a definite possibility. But wouldn't she have told you, Mal?"

Mallory shook her head. "When it came to matters of the heart, Leigh was really private. She was seeing someone for about a year before she died. Someone wealthy." She joined her girls at the table. "Honestly, I thought the guy might have been married and that's why she kept him a secret. But if it was Christian, I can see her being quiet as well. Keep what was developing out of the spotlight until they were officially dating."

"Why?" Ava asked. "I'd think she'd want to flaunt that man for the world to see."

"Not initially. She would have never wanted to be considered just one of his many flings, as a thought. Leigh was proud that way, and very aware of her image. Then there's her staunchly religious parents who, given his reputation with the ladies, would surely have disapproved. As rocky as their relationship was, she always tried to please them."

"What about the kid?" Sam asked. "The one Christian visited. At one time, you thought there was something there, too."

"Yes, and now I'm even more convinced."

Mallory returned to the table and jiggled the mouse. Her laptop screen came to life, fastened on a picture of the puzzle sculpture taken in Karen Walker's bedroom.

"This is why I called you two last night."

Ava leaned forward. "What is that?"

Mallory walked over to the mantel, retrieved the puzzle piece, and returned to the table. She set it next to the laptop screen, sat down and crossed her arms.

The room grew quiet as all three stared at the screen.

"That piece fits in the puzzle?" Ava finally asked.

"Testing it is the only way to be sure for certain, but given how it appears the shapes align, it's a pretty close match."

Sam looked over. "Where'd you get the photo?"

"I took it, this past weekend." Mallory paused for effect. "At Brandon's house."

Ava cursed. "Wait a minute. Hold everything. Now I am totally confused. How could that boy have anything to do with Leigh's murder, or with Leigh, for that matter?"

"I don't know," Mallory said. "But this was in Leigh's belongings." Mallory held up the puzzle piece. "And this artwork, from which it appears the piece was taken, is in the home of a boy whose father was shot and has since disappeared."

"That can't be mere coincidence. I can't imagine what connection Leigh would have with this family. But I'll keep searching until I find out."

21

In between basketball and bed bouts with various women, Christian was surprised at how often Mallory Knight popped up in his mind. Like now, for instance. He'd put in two hours at the Navigators' training facility in Port Washington—almost three hours of practice followed by physical therapy and watching film—and while getting into his car he thought of her. He pulled out of the lot and headed home, checking voice-mails that included messages left by seven different women, all requesting the pleasure of his company. Christian checked in with DeVaughn and Zoey but decided the other calls could wait. Tonight, he was only in the mood for a big meal and a good night's sleep. Shortly after the chef had prepared his paleo meal, Christian released him from the duty that usually included a healthy snack around eleven p.m. and a full, hearty breakfast the following the morning. From high school on, Christian almost always had a crowd around him. He enjoyed it for the most part. But tonight he wanted to be alone.

His solitude lasted a full fifteen minutes, long enough to enjoy the delicious meal of glazed salmon over wild rice and a mountain of veggies while listening to an audiobook. Any other woman calling would have gotten the red reject button, but he'd always take this call.

"Good evening, Mother."

"Good evening, son."

"Haven't talked with you all week. What's up?"

"Your schedule, busy man. I called a couple days ago but didn't leave a message. But I've kept tabs on your whereabouts somewhat through your father. How's the shoulder?"

"Fine. Totally healed."

"Good. I'm going to come watch you on Friday."

"Nice!"

His mother's melodious laughter warmed his heart. "I thought you'd be pleased. While I'm not as able to attend as many games as your dad, please have no doubt that I'm as proud of you as both he and Pete combined. In fact, I've invited a few of my friends to join me tomorrow so they can see for themselves what I've bragged about. Do you think you could secure a total of four tickets for me and a few of my friends?"

Christian's brow raised as he looked at the phone. While his mother had always supported his athletic and educational efforts, she wasn't big into sports and rarely attended a game. He couldn't remember the last time she'd requested extra tickets.

"Of course. No problem at all. I'll have DeVaughn make sure they're at the will call window."

"Thanks, Christian."

"Who's coming with you? Anyone I know?"

"Well, dear, funny you should ask."

Oh, no. Here we go.

"You remember the Gateses, don't you? The next-door neighbors to our Hawaiian vacation home, at least during your high school years?"

The better question would have been how could he ever forget? Heather Gates. Tall. Light. Brown hair and green eyes. She was a junior when he was a freshman. The woman who introduced him to oral copulation. Rocked his world and blew his mind. For the rest of their stay that year and the next, he followed her around like a puppy dog. Of course, neither set of parents ever had a clue. Christian hoped it would stay that way.

"Sure, I remember the Gateses. Didn't know you were still in touch with them. How's Heather?"

"So you remember her as well?"

"I rarely forget a pretty face."

"If you thought that way then, you should see her now. Absolutely stunning, Christian. She graduated Vassar, you know, with a degree in business administration. Not that she'll ever need it, except for managing her own estate. Her grandparents died and left her a fortune. That, on top of her father's wealth and social standing as one of California's premiere surgeons and her mom's philanthropic efforts, makes her quite the catch for both the man lucky enough to win her heart and the families as well."

"Wasn't she engaged to a doctor?"

"Yes, but that's over. Susan, Heather's mother, hired a private investigator who uncovered that the young man had left out a few critical details about his life, and had outright lied about other matters. At any rate Heather and Susan are in town for one of her sorority sisters' engagement party. She asked about you, and when I learned your game was here tomorrow, I thought it would be a nice way for us to catch up."

"I don't mind getting tickets for you, but I won't be available this weekend."

Rebecca chuckled. "I didn't mean for that 'us' to include you, Christian. Susan, Heather, and I, and one of her friends, will have dinner somewhere near the arena and then come watch you play. I also wanted to give Heather your number so that the two of you could chat in the future."

"I don't mind talking to her, but I'm not looking to date anyone seriously right now, and I'm definitely not looking for a wife."

"Men never are, darling," Rebecca murmured. "But I thought you'd enjoy speaking with someone on your level socially, financially, and intellectually. For a change."

Christian knew where this conversation was heading. He didn't want to go there. So after agreeing to meet his mother one day next week, he ended the call.

Moments later he lay in bed scrolling through his cell phone, recalling the day. He placed Heather's name in the search engine. Several images appeared, mostly related to either social or charitable efforts. His mom hadn't lied. Heather was even more beautiful than he remembered. Maybe hooking up with her wouldn't be so bad. He mentally went through the list of women who'd left messages, examined the role they played in his life. While he wasn't one of those athletes with hook-ups in every city, Christian had had his share of sexual partners. He felt that since both participants were grown, knew the rules, and wanted it, why not? Three of the seven who'd called were just that. Sexual hook-ups. Of those three, one was a celebrity, the latest pop sensation. A lot of fun and cool Hollywood-style perks, but not the material for a serious relationship. He didn't judge divas, but he didn't date them long-term. He didn't date women like Vivica, either, his video vixen. He knew the summer fling with her was all they'd ever have. She was funny, smart, and one of the most beautiful women he'd ever known. But she'd been with too many men that he knew. A double standard, perhaps, but the truth. Plus, she was beginning to catch feelings and want something more than a casual friendship. *No bueno.* Two of the women who'd phoned him were friends who'd become lovers. Friends with benefits. One he'd known since college, the other since the earliest of his pro playing days. Successful, smart, beautiful, independent, almost too strong. He was sure some of his female executive and entrepreneur friends would disagree with him, but at the end of the day, no man wanted a woman whose dick was bigger than his. Then there was Zoey. His publicist. Someone he'd grown up with, played with as a child. Pete had tried to warn him about taking the relationship to another level. He had said she'd never be able to keep the personal and professional lines straight. He'd been right. Christian knew that now. Not that Zoey said so directly. She was too smart, too classy for that. But Christian knew she wanted more than he could give her. Then there was Mallory, the jazz lover, the professional, who showed no interest in a personal connection. He smiled to himself and wondered how long it would take for that to change.

Switching over to a search engine, he typed in the name of her column, "Knightly News," and clicked on the latest article. He liked the second one even better than he had the first, especially how she'd involved the students and expounded on his program's highlighting subjects not emphasized in many urban school curriculums, subjects like computer technology, science, and math. He smiled when reading about Harmony's horticulture projects, remembering how the quiet girl had come to life and grown in social ability along with her plants. He loved that her dream was to see urban gardens on every block to provide healthy eating options for the families living there. Christian made a mental note to speak with Emma and the board about helping this happen. Too many kids in poor neighborhoods limited their dreams to music and sports. Honorable work when you could get it, but the road to riches had several lanes. He wanted to be a catalyst in highlighting more of them to the kids his foundation served.

"Pretty good stuff, Mallory Knight," he mumbled, even as the warnings from Zoey and Pete niggled at the back of his mind. Still, he tapped the phone's face and dialed her number, ready to do some investigating of his own. He placed the call on speaker and settled himself comfortably against the headboard.

"Mallory Knight."

"Mallory, it's Christian. How are you?"

"Hello, Christian. I was just thinking about you."

He nestled further into the feathery pillows behind him. "All good, I hope."

"Mostly, yes."

"Mostly? Which parts weren't good?"

Mallory laughed, a sound that caused Christian to smile and want to make it happen more often. "Are you pouting? None were bad, really, at least not personally so. I interviewed some of the kids for this week's article."

"I read it."

"Really?"

"Yes, that's partly why I called. When you first reached out, the team was leery of your intentions, but so far your articles have been on point."

"Thank you. Covering your foundation is very different from the columns I usually write."

"That's what my team said, and why they were suspicious."

"Your team as in the Navigators?"

"No, as in the people I have around me to keep me safe."

"From . . ."

"Predatory reporters who'll do anything to get a story."

"Are you talking about me specifically now?"

"You are an investigative reporter, right?"

"A reporter, not a predator."

"Yeah, they warned me about you." Christian's low chuckle was met with silence.

"I'm not laughing."

"I apologize."

"Who are these people warning you about me?"

"See, there you go again. Trying to get the scoop."

"Let me guess. One is your uncle, the one you call Pete."

"Yep."

"Even though he's your uncle. The other is the pretty blonde glued to your side at the gala. Your girlfriend, I guess. Or one of them."

"You don't miss much."

"One would have had to be blind to miss that."

Christian chuckled. "That was Zoey, the one who helped you set up the first interview. She handles my PR."

"I can assure you both you and your team, Christian, that there is nothing to worry about. A couple more articles and this series will be over. And I will be out of your life."

"Don't sound so happy about it. I might want to prolong your stay. In fact, that's why I called."

"Okay." The long, drawn out way she said the word conveyed her wariness.

"Dang, woman. Are you this suspicious of all men? Don't answer that question because, honestly, I don't give a damn. I'm not them. Anyway, we're having a home game tomorrow. I want you to come."

"Why? I told you I'm not a fan."

"That's part of the reason. I want to make you one."

"Can I take the ticket and give it to my boss? He's someone who would really appreciate it."

"Maybe next time. I want tomorrow to be about me and you."

"Wait, is this a date?"

"Is that a problem?"

"Yes. I don't date people I write about."

"All right, just friends then. The game, dinner and drinks." No response. "You do eat, right?"

"Occasionally."

They both laughed at that.

"Tomorrow night. I'll leave the tickets at will call along with a pass so that after the game you can wait inside while I change to go out." More silence. "You coming or what?"

"I guess so."

"Cool."

"See you tomorrow night."

22

On Friday night, a fresh-faced, curly-haired Mallory joined twenty thousand fans who cheered the Navigators to a nail-biting three-point victory over one of their biggest rivals, the Cleveland Cavaliers. The pregame show was an event in itself. New York's own Mary J. Blige sang the national anthem. Stars were everywhere, the biggest ones on the court. The game was exhilarating. The atmosphere was electric, no more so than the section where she sat. It was filled with the players' families, friends, and according to Chatty Cathy sitting beside her, many of their mistresses, or side pieces, as Chatty said they were called. At halftime, Mallory pulled out her phone to record a few observations she wanted to remember and to check her emails. While various women around her had given her the side-eye, then whispered and giggled as though they were twelve, she hadn't expected any bold enough to approach. That opinion changed when one sat down beside her.

"Who are you?"

"Who's asking?"

"Don't worry about who I am. Are you here for Christian?"

"I'm here for the same reason you are, to watch the game."

"Ah, yeah. You must be a newbie to think anybody would

believe that shit. Just know that you're not ready for this level, baby. He can throw tickets at bitch for a game now and then, but I'm not going anywhere. I've been with him before you and all those other hoes, and I'll be the last one standing. Believe that."

Just as the average New Yorker would not run from a fight, neither would Mallory. Especially a verbal one she felt sure to win.

"It would appear to me that you're the one who needs to believe it. Because this unfortunate show of your ignorance and insecurity suggests that your status, if not in jeopardy, is at the very least in doubt."

"Really, bitch? You going to talk shit like that me? You don't know who you're fucking with?"

"You're right, but not because I didn't try to ascertain that information. I'll try once again. Who are you?"

"Keep fucking with Christian, and you're going to find out."

Mallory watched the woman traipse back to her seat three rows above hers, shooting daggers while offering the friend beside her what Mallory assumed was play-by-play.

Looks like the publicist has some competition, she thought, having continued her assumption that she and the ballplayer were fucking. If forced to choose which woman would take the win, Mallory's money wouldn't go on the loudmouth who'd just accosted her, but on Zoey.

After the game Mallory passed on lounging in the bleachers with friends, fam, and fans waiting for the players and headed to the town car to wait with Treetop. Christian joined them forty-five minutes later, slid into the back seat and leaned over for a hug.

Mallory acted as though she was part of Big Joe's Terror Squad and leaned back. "What are you doing?"

"What, no love for the winners? I played my heart out for you out there."

"Oh, just for me, huh." Mallory allowed the embrace but kept it short. He felt too good and smelled too lovely to chance more than a second or two. This was all for Leigh, she reminded herself. The only reason she'd agreed to this date was to find answers and get justice for her friend.

Christian hit the back of the seat. "Let's roll, partner."

Treetop entered the traffic and headed uptown.

"Where are we going?"

"I'm taking you to a place where the chef is a personal friend of mine."

They rode to the Upper East Side and arrived at a restaurant with a private room. The award-winning chef whose face Mallory recognized greeted them personally before seating them in a discreet corner booth.

Christian studied Mallory a moment. "I didn't say anything earlier, but you look nice."

"Thank you."

"You're welcome. When it comes to little black dresses, I've probably seen a thousand. But that colorful scarf and the bangles,"—he nodded and leaned back to peer beneath the table—"even those ankle boots. Nice touch."

"I'm glad you approve, although it would be perfectly fine if you didn't."

"I'm sure. But no matter. I like your style—simple, practical, but with a little flair. But the coat. Is that real fur?" Mallory nodded. "That threw me."

"It's not my style nor my coat. Belonged to a friend who is no longer with us."

"I'm sorry."

"Me too. You might know her. Leigh Jackson?" Mallory watched his reaction closely for any signs of recognition when she mentioned the name. "She loved basketball and was a huge fan. I think she may have met you."

"The name doesn't sound familiar, but I meet a lot of people."

The chef interrupted them with the night's menu. Conversation shifted after that to Christian's childhood and the balancing act of having one foot in the exclusive, upstate Clifford Park neighborhood where he lived and the other in areas like North Philly where his cousins resided. They exchanged stories of a reality familiar to many in the biracial world. The dilemma of being too white for one culture and too black for the other. A friendship began developing on this common ground.

Amid succulent appetizers and exquisite entrees, Christian reminisced about being an outcast in his early years and how that changed the day his cousin's uncle put a basketball in his hands. His natural skill gave him confidence, and something in common with the relatives who had no interest in the Dow that he discussed with his father or the love for astronomy he shared with his uncle Pete. She asked about his apparent closeness to Brandon and learned that in the boy Christian saw his younger self.

"Understandable, then, why you'd get so offended at someone suggesting he tried to commit suicide."

She watched eyes fixed on her for most of the evening now try and avoid her.

"That is what happened, isn't it?"

"You asking as a reporter or as a friend?"

"It can be off the record if you'd like."

"That's the only way I'll answer. If you promise that what I share won't end up in print."

"It won't."

Christian took a deep breath as his eyes met hers once again. "The rumor's true."

Mallory nodded, her only reaction. "I'm sorry. That had to have been a terrible thing to find out."

"It was horrible. Couldn't imagine a worse feeling had it been my own kid."

"Why would he do that? Was he bullied, or is there a mental condition?"

"No. None of that. His father got shot."

"Oh, no."

"They'd only recently reconnected. The parents divorced years ago, and Danny left town for a while. Brandon was torn up over that pretty bad, according to his mother."

"Karen."

"How do you know her?"

"I met her after my interview with Harmony."

"Oh, right."

"Strong woman."

"Got to be. Anyway, when Danny came back to New York a few years ago, Brandon became his shadow. He stopped fighting and getting into trouble. His grades improved. They grew very close. Then Danny got shot, and Brandon couldn't take it. Thought he'd lost him again. This time forever."

"But the dad, Danny, survived."

"Thank goodness."

"But he's not back with Karen."

"Have you turned reporter, or is this still the friend asking? I heard that murder and mayhem is your thing, but I don't want this in the papers. Am I clear?"

Mallory took note of Christian's tone, how it had grown dark, almost threatening.

"There's really no line between who I am and what I do. But I'm not a liar. I said I wouldn't write on this. And I won't. But I'm curious. Why would someone want to kill Brandon's father?"

"I don't know."

"Where is he now?"

"Don't know that, either." Christian's eyes narrowed. "Been looking for him to ask about some things, make sure he's all right. Maybe as an investigative reporter, that is something you can find out."

"What's his last name?"

Christian told her.

Mallory typed it into her cell phone's memo section. "Won't make any promises but I'll give it a shot."

Conversation shifted again, to jazz this time. Mallory finally told him about the woman who'd confronted her at the game. Christian laughed it off, said it came with the territory. He then shared a war story or two about dodging determined groupies and borderline stalkers. Mallory didn't know it, but by the time dessert arrived she knew more about him than women he'd slept with, even dated, for months at a time.

What Christian didn't know is that he'd given Mallory a shovel full of information that should he have anything to do with Leigh's murder might help her dig his grave.

23

The next day, Saturday, before the sun went down, Mallory knew everything on public record regarding Danny Groves. Everything but his current whereabouts. She was more than a little frustrated, so when Ava's face showed up on her cell phone she was ready for a break.

"Hey, girl."

"Don't 'hey, girl' me. Why am I finding out about you and Christian online instead of by phone, like before, during and after the game?"

"What's online?"

"Google yourself and find out."

Mallory opened a search engine and typed in her name. Up popped a picture of her and Christian from last night, taken on the side street next to Vaucluse as he helped her from the town car. The camera's angle made it appear that she was looking into his eyes adoringly, a big smile on her face. The truth was she'd almost tripped, he'd grabbed her arm, and they'd shared a good laugh. But the look on his face and the way her body leaned in to his told a different story. So did the caption.

"From Knight Writing to High Rolling."

And the subtitle, in case one verbal punch to the gut simply wasn't enough. *Looks like New York's Golden Boy has a New Boo.*

Mallory knew she shouldn't read the article, but she couldn't help herself.

After bringing his team from behind once again, and trouncing the Cleveland Cavaliers, New York Navigator and the night's MVP, Christian Graham, was seen getting cozy with his latest love interest just outside of Vaucluse, one of several upscale, private restaurants owned by the James Beard Award–winning chef Michael White. The lucky lady is investigative journalist and New York News *columnist Mallory Knight, whose latest series highlights the basketball player and the foundation that bears his name.*

"Mal? You still there?"

"Yeah, I'm here. Reading this nonsense."

"That's what you get for hanging with a superstar. Welcome to their world. The story's actually pretty accurate. It could have been much worse."

"The story is bullshit. I'm not Christian's love interest, and we weren't getting cozy. I went to the game and to dinner afterwards. After that I came home. End of story."

"Don't get mad at me because the evening ended early. That you didn't get in a round of horizontal aerobics with his fine ass is entirely your fault."

Mallory scrolled down the page, clicked different links. "I hope this doesn't dilute the strength of the series and have readers think I wrote from a biased perspective. Christian's Kids is an excellent center with an aggressive educational component that pushes those kids to greatness. I'd hate for that to be second-guessed because he and I shared a meal."

"It's not me you'll have to convince. It's any reporter who sticks a mike in your face angling for a story."

Mallory wasn't much worried about that. This was New York, and these were New Yorkers. Jaded. Unbothered. Minded their own business. By the time she went to work on Monday, this story would be two days old. Virtually forgotten. A good thing, too, because after the research she'd done on Brandon's father, Danny Groves, Mallory had more important things on her mind.

Except, not really, a fact she discovered Monday morning when she turned the corner of the building where she worked.

"Mallory!"

"Ms. Knight!"

"Is it true about you and Christian?"

"Are you dating Christian Graham!"

Mallory reacted instinctively, put her head down, pasted a don't-fuck-with-me-frown on her face as she barreled her way through more than a dozen reporters. One thing about New Yorkers, though, including reporters: They were tenacious, and when going after a story, relentless, too. The questions continued, pounding her back as she slipped past the angel of a security guard who halted their progress as she continued to the elevator that would ferry her away.

She reached the *New York News* offices, and after a quick side trip to the bathroom to collect herself, she marched directly into Charlie's office armed for battle and ready for war.

"Hey, Charlie. Got a minute?" She turned and closed the door. She reached into her satchel, walked over and plopped down a manila folder on his desk.

"What's that, your resignation?"

"Why would you think that?"

"Because of this."

He tossed a newspaper on top of her folder. A collage of pictures from Friday night. A shot of Christian scoring a three-pointer. One of her smiling and clapping, one readers would assume was her cheering him on. Truthfully, she probably was. *Dammit.*

"Yeah, about all that, Charlie. It's not how it looks."

"How is it?"

"Christian and I are not hooked up. I went to a game, just like twenty-something thousand other people. We were all cheering."

"Yeah, but you don't like basketball. So I'm left to assume that your cheering was for a player, not the game." Charlie smiled and wriggled his brows as he sat back and chewed on an unlit cigarette.

Rather than comment, Mallory swiped the newspaper to the floor and pushed the folder toward him.

"What's that?" he said.

"Evidence. Take a look."

"Evidence of what?" Instead of responding, Mallory removed her hat and coat and threw them over a pile of papers stacked in the corner before sitting down.

He opened the folder and just as quickly slammed it shut. "Oh, no, Mal. Not this again."

"Just hear me out, okay? Look at what's in front of you. Real proof that points to the conclusion she was murdered. Just take a look. Please."

Silence as he opened the folder and skimmed the file's contents.

"She was pregnant?"

"Yep. Whoever killed her murdered two people."

"Or the father didn't want her or the baby, so she killed herself."

Mallory bit down rage and chewed on patience. It was an angle she hadn't considered. Leigh had shared dreams of marrying wealthy, international travel, and becoming a socialite, but had never painted a picture that included babies, a dog, and a white picket fence.

"That picture is of a unique jigsaw puzzle sculpture. The

one behind it, yeah, that one, is of what appears to be the sculpture's missing piece. That sculpture hangs in the home of one of Christian's kids. The missing piece belonged to Leigh."

Charlie held a picture in each hand, looked back and forth. "That's interesting. But still, doesn't prove much. For all we know there are hundreds of sculptures and pieces out there."

"Negative. It took a great deal of searching but I finally found the piece online. It's a limited edition, made almost entirely of gold. Limited because the young, up-and-coming artist was tragically killed after just five were made, which significantly increased its value."

"To what?"

"About half a million dollars."

Charlie whistled, picked up the picture to study it more closely. "Hardly looks like it would be worth that much." He placed the pic back inside the folder and slid the folder across the desk.

"I'd like to title the month's piece either 'March Murders' or 'March Memories,' a play on March Madness, which will bridge February's focus on Christian and basketball with this new piece."

"I don't see the connection, and even with the pregnancy information, which, since confidential, was probably illegally obtained and therefore impossible to print for fear of a lawsuit, I don't see much new in the way of Leigh's death."

"Just the title," Mallory calmly replied. "March Murders. March Madness. I know, a stretch, but one that segues back into the types of stories that those who read my column have come to expect."

"Yes, and it was ruled a suicide."

She placed her palms on the desk and leaned forward. "Leigh did not kill herself, Charlie. I would bet my life on that. She was murdered, and the fact that she was pregnant offers a possible motive as to why. The news of her pregnancy can easily be attributed to an anonymous source but if pushed to defend the content, I have solid proof. Sharing this information with the public might put enough pressure on the NYPD that they reopen her case and go after her killer."

"If you feel that strongly, take what you have to the police. That's where what you've uncovered belongs, not in this paper. I'm fine with you returning to what you do best, but you're going to have to find a subject other than Leigh Jackson. I know she was your friend, but she's dead. And so is this topic. I know that's tough, kid, but that is the hard, cold fact. Don't bring it up again, all right? I won't change my mind."

Mallory left Charlie's office and headed for the exit. Paparazzi or no, she needed fresh air. She was angry, spent, her mind was in turmoil. Bypassing the elevators, she took the stairs, thinking so hard she felt her brain might explode. She'd always thought Leigh killing herself was impossible. But was it? What if Charlie was right? What if the father had rejected the baby and ended the relationship? Leigh was a hopeless romantic who'd been excited and happy about her secret love. She'd even alluded to having caught a big fish. Had she thought a baby big enough bait to reel him in? Had she been wrong? Could he have ended their affair and sent her into a downward spiral that resulted in suicide?

She exited the building through a side door, ignored the frigid temperatures and the fact that she'd left her coat in Charlie's office, and walked up one block and down the other. No way could she go to the police. She'd watched them in action. Been at the scene of Leigh's death, one that for them pointed to suicide but to Mallory screamed foul play. By the time she returned to the front of the building her head was clear and her mind was made up. Leigh was capable of doing some crazy shit, but suicide wasn't one of them. Charlie said there was no place for the story in *New York News*. There were other papers. Mallory was going to write the story and see if anyone would print it. She wasn't going to stop until somebody listened.

She walked back into the office calm and collected. Only then did she notice the coworkers she passed. The nudges to each other, subtle glances and smirks. She went to the break room for a bottle of water. Conversation stopped when she entered. Knowing looks. Ignoring them all, she went to her desk. There was a story to write. She reached it to discover a present left on her chair. A Christian Graham bobble head had been placed on her seat with a typed note taped to its crotch. *Mallory's new prober's pen.*

Haters.

She changed her mind about writing the story on office property or on company time and instead focused on the new subject for the March series that would launch on Friday. It was about another single professional, female, who'd disappeared on her birthday after a night at the bar. She channeled her anger into a mad creative flow, and titled the series "March Mystery." She worked on the piece for the rest of the day and that night. The next day she went into the office early, planning to get in a few hours before her coworkers arrived and tried to chill her creative juices the way they had the day before. It was just after eight, but when she arrived both George and Lima were already there. Even though they'd been nasty, Mallory took the high road and spoke as she entered, carrying a large latte with three espresso shots in one hand and a bagel in another.

George snorted. Lima gave Mallory her back and began typing on her computer. Mallory shrugged and kept it moving. She didn't have time for petty office politics. As much as she liked her colleagues, they could go the rest of all their lives without speaking to her and she wouldn't lose any sleep.

"Heard you're working on some big story." George spoke without addressing her by name. "That that's why you've been spending so much time away from the office."

"Always working on a big one, George."

"A big dick maybe," Lima muttered under her breath.

"Excuse me? I don't think I caught that."

She said it in a tone that suggested that not only had she heard it but that if the comment were repeated, things might get ugly.

"Never mind," Lima replied coyly, turning around to give Mallory a sickeningly sweet fake grin and exchange a look with George. The two laughed. Mallory bit her tongue to remain quiet. She could hear Leigh telling her to not let the haters see her sweat. Leigh never did. Even her closest friends, like Mallory, never knew if or when anything was amiss. Had that not been the case, she may still be alive.

Mallory looked at the clock. Five after nine. She settled into her seat and pounded out back-to-back articles on subjects she knew well, had written about before, and wanted to update. Women who were loved and missed by their friends and families the same way that Mallory missed her friend Leigh. She felt good about the series, like she was providing a service for the families that was harder for them to do by themselves. She was keeping their loved one alive in the paper, and hopefully fanning the flames of justice into a fire. She worked hard for *New York News,* and before leaving she sent the rough draft of that week's column over to Charlie. Then she left, walked to a coffee shop two blocks away and wrote another column. An article about another murder mystery, for another paper, one that she knew firsthand tripped over ethics to grab high circulation. Mallory opened a new document, came up with a name, and began writing an op-ed piece that she hoped would make it over a bridge that she'd almost burned. The piece was short, word count less than a thousand. Yet it took Mallory longer to write it than others twice as long. Every word counted. Every sentence mattered. She read it, reread it, walked around the block and then read it again. When she pressed send she was satisfied that the truth had been written. Now all she could do was watch and wait.

24

The next day Mallory stopped at the corner and purchased the rival paper to the *New York News*, the *New York Reporter*. It was the paper she'd left after her boss printed a piece that maligned her dead friend's name, and the one she hoped would now help clear it and catch the man who killed her. She leaned against a pole and went straight to the op-ed page, looking for her article, hoping it got printed. Usually writers were contacted when what they submitted was chosen, but that hadn't happened. She'd used a pseudonym with false contact information.

It wasn't there. The next day either. By Friday she figured it wouldn't get printed, for that scumbag Rob Anderson to print evidence of a murder on a subject he suggested had committed suicide was an act too decent for him to commit.

She didn't purchase a paper that morning. She put on her earbuds and got lost in jazz. That night when the train came she flopped into a seat and pulled out her phone to play a game. When it came to reviving interest in Leigh's murder, Mallory had tried and failed. She was back to square one, out of options, and felt her passion slipping, too. She shifted when the woman beside her opened her paper and crowded Mallory's very limited space. Agitated, she gave her a look and began to rise. That's when she saw it. An article at the top of the op-ed page with a name that she recognized: the pseudonym she'd used on the article about Leigh's murder—Z. D. Woods. Mallory jumped off the train at the next stop, rushed up the stairs, and bought a paper from the first kiosk she saw. Two doors down was a fast food joint. She grabbed the first chair at the first available table and opened up the paper. The title she'd chosen leaped from the page:

Suicide by Murder—A Mystery Unsolved

Last January, broadcast journalist Leigh Jackson was found dead with an empty pill bottle and two wine glasses near her naked body. Two wine glasses and an empty bottle of opioids in the home of a woman who'd balk at even taking an aspirin and was so conscious of her appearance that she'd never strip nude knowing that her body may be found by strangers. Yet in less than a week the death was ruled a suicide and her case was closed. More than one year later, the question still being asked is why? Why such a rush to close out the case? Why no inquiries into her love life, her professional life, into the possibility of enemies made along the way? Jackson was known to socialize with an A-list crowd. Movie premieres. Front row for concerts. Floor seats to watch her favorite New York Navigators. Could it be that her love for the high life clashed with her job of uncovering facts and delivering news? Could she have been on to a breaking news story so explosive that it cost her life? Her killer knows.

Mallory finished the article and sat back, satisfied. The truth as she knew it, as she'd researched and investigated it, was out, done in a way in which no one was named or exposed directly but so an astute New Yorker could connect the dots. *Yes! Finally, Leigh's death will get a second look.* It had to. After what she'd written, the public would demand it. She felt like celebrating. She sent a text to her girls, then headed out into the cool night air. Halfway to the subway station her message indicator beeped once, then again. She paused to check them before going below. There were a lot of options where she was on Third Street. Maybe her friends would want to meet there.

The first one was from Ava. She tapped to open it.

Celebrate? Call ASAP. You must not have read Rob's Op-Ed yet.

Rob's Op-Ed? He wrote one? Frowning, Mallory tapped the message icon again. The second one was from Sam and sounded even more troubled.

Good Lord, Mallory. What have you done?

Mallory trudged down the subway steps, instead of skipping the way she thought she would just seconds ago. The train arrived when she did. She entered the car, steadied herself against a pole, and turned back to the page that she'd marked with a crease. A title beneath the article she'd written and read immediately caught her eye, and held it—"A Dark and Lonely Knight" by Rob Anderson.

How had it happened that she'd missed it before? Mallory didn't know, and anyway it didn't matter. Even before reading the first word of the piece, her blood ran cold.

A Dark and Lonely Knight

The other day the *New York Reporter* received an op-ed piece from a writer named Z. D. Woods. Even though the contact information appeared to be falsified, we decided to print the piece, which was titled,

'Suicide by Murder." We felt reasonably sure that the name Woods was possibly a pseudonym meant to protect the true identity of the writer and also, that the perspective offered regarding one of New York's own might be of interest to our readers.

Writers choose anonymity for several reasons. Perhaps he or she works for a competitive newspaper who refused to run the story. Or maybe they'd recently won an award, the Prober's Pen for instance, and didn't want to be tied to a tabloid-style article. Or maybe the writer didn't want to be sued by high-profile celebrities, people like Christian Graham, at least allegedly.

She closed the paper and found a seat, stunned by a move she never saw coming. Her ex-boss had stabbed her professionally again. This time, it might be lethal.

Mallory reached Brooklyn but instead of her brownstone, she knocked on Ava's door.

"Get in here," Ava urged after using the peephole, grabbing Mallory's arm to bring her in faster. "I've been waiting for your call!"

Mallory walked in like a zombie and fell on the couch. "I thought I'd dotted every i and crossed every t. But I jumped in a cesspool with a shark, and he bit me in the ass."

Ava returned from with the kitchen with two glasses. Mallory didn't even ask what it was, just turned it up and swallowed.

Ava sat down beside her, the boisterousness of her greeting now subdued and quiet. "What happened?"

Mallory told her about the meeting with Charlie, how she'd gotten upset and come up with what she thought was a foolproof alternative. "I thought my tracks were covered, and that even if Rob detected my writing he wouldn't print the piece if he disagreed. I never thought he'd print it and then go after me publicly. I should have known."

"Hell, Mal, you did know."

"You're right. I let my emotions get in the way of common sense and sound journalism. Now it's out there in the atmosphere, and there is nothing I can do."

"Do you think Charlie has seen it yet?"

"No. I'll probably get a call the second he does. Saying I've been fired and to come get my shit on Monday."

"I wish I could disagree with you, but giving a story to a rival paper, one he told you not to write? That's a hard hurdle to jump over, Mal. Damn, I wish you'd run it past me or Sam before sending it over."

"Sad to say, I do too now. Hindsight is a bitch."

Mallory sat up suddenly and jumped off the couch. "You know what? I take that back. I don't want to lose my job at the *News*, but I'm not sad about writing that article. I don't feel bad that it got printed. Every word in what was printed can be backed up, and even so, all of the possible theories were 'alleged.' More than that, it's not an article but an op-ed piece. My thoughts. My opinion. Freedom of speech is mine by right. No one can take that away from me.

"Charlie told me not to write about Leigh in my column. He didn't say anything about writing it for someone else, especially published under a pseudo. It's not my fault that my name got connected to Z. D. Woods. Rob Anderson did that." Mallory began pacing. "I'm going to talk to a lawyer. Sue his ass. He had no right to expose me like that."

"Like you, he used the word 'alleged.'"

"Got damn, Ava, whose side are you on?"

"Yours, which is why, good, bad, or ugly, I'm going to tell you the truth. And the truth is . . . you've fucked up."

As if to prove her point, Mallory's phone rang. Charlie. She didn't want to take the call. But ignoring the scandal brewing wouldn't make it go away. Mallory looked at Ava and answered the call. She put it on speaker, expecting bad news, and giving Ava a front row seat to the execution.

"Hi, Charlie. I can explain."

"Are you fucking kidding me, Mal? You go against my direct orders not to write about Jackson and then screw me in the ass by taking the story to our biggest competition. The one who dug your friend's grave and now has one to put you in?"

"Rob had no right to do what he did and connect me to an article written by Z. D. Woods."

"Save the bullshit, Mallory. I know what I read. That piece has your style all over it. And your passion. Contains the information you tried to shove down my throat."

"All circumstantial. There's nothing to prove that article came from me. When my attorney is done with Rob, he's going to understand that."

"Oh, so you're a got damn attorney now? On top of being an investigator and an honorary member of the NYPD? Do you know what kind of firestorm you've caused with the execs, the kind of shit raining down on my head from your obsession? I won't even start with the repercussions you'll face from Graham's camp, let alone the millions who worship him!"

"I never mentioned Graham."

"Mention him? You sent a got damn picture of the guy!"

"As proof that the two knew each other. I never thought he'd print it." Mallory took a breath. "I'm sorry, Charlie. I never meant to get you involved."

"You didn't, but I am, up to my got damn ears. And I can assure you that he is, too! I have some news for you, though. You won't have to worry about involving me again, because as of this moment, you're fired."

"Charlie, wait!"

"Come by on Monday to get your things. Security will be ready to escort you in and out of the building. I took a chance on you. Believed in you. You had everything in here, could write your future. Because of this obsession you've thrown it away. Hope it's worth it, kid. Goodbye."

"Charlie, wait—"

He didn't. The line went dead. Silence screamed in the room. Ava walked over, pulled Mallory into a hug. "That was brutal. I'm sorry."

"I deserved it." Mallory broke the embrace and crossed the room. "I betrayed a trust. Acted like a rogue journalist. I deserved to be fired."

"What are you going to do?"

Mallory crossed her arms and looked out the window. "I have no idea."

Her phone beeped again. "It's Christian. Fuck."

"Don't answer it."

Mallory pushed talk and the speaker button. "Mallory Knight."

"You have the nerve to answer after the shit you pulled? Asking if I knew somebody when you had a picture of the two of us together? And thinking she might have had something on me, something bad enough for me to have her killed?"

"I didn't mention your name. Your anger should be toward Rob Anderson. He's the one who called you out. Not me."

"You can't be that dumb. Neither is the reading public. A blind person could have looked through the thin veil you used to cover your ass and know that I was one of the people you wrote about. And what about the picture?"

"It was sent over as evidence, not to get printed. I reported the truth as I knew it, in a way I felt shielded the parties allegedly involved. The *Reporter's* editor picked apart my story and outed whom he thought I meant. I understand your anger, but if you read the article objectively, the one I wrote, you'll see that it could have been any number of athletes. Still, I'm sorry for any problems that I've caused you because of it."

"You're sorry, all right. But not nearly as sorry as you're going to be. You fucked with the wrong player. And now it's too late to back out of the game."

He ended the call. Mallory put the phone in her purse. "Well, that went better than I expected."

"He just threatened you, Mallory. Don't make light of it."

"He's just angry. He'll calm down."

"You'd better hope so. He's got money, fame, and power. That's a no-joke triple threat."

An hour later, Mallory left Ava's and headed home. When she reached the block where she lived, shit got real. She scoped the scene in two seconds and crouched behind a trash can to avoid being seen. Two media trucks were illegally parked in front of her house. She counted at least six reporters and one photographer invading her stoop. Sam's question played like a loop in her head.

What have you done, Mallory? What in the hell have you done?

She eased around the corner retracing her steps, pulled out her phone, and called Ava.

"I'm on my way back there."

"Why, what's wrong?"

"My place is crawling with reporters. I can't go home."

Mallory lowered her head and hurried toward refuge. For the first time since walking in on Leigh's crime scene she was confused, unsure of what to do. The cover she thought the blog provided had been blown. Because of Rob's response to her op-ed piece, everyone in New York, and around the world for that matter, knew that Z. D. Woods was a pseudonym and

Mallory Knight was the author behind "Suicide by Murder." She was fully exposed and being hounded. Being on the other side of the story sucked. She felt empathy for those she'd relentlessly followed. Now she knew how it felt.

Mallory spent the night at Ava's house, then sent her on a scouting mission to check out her house. When she returned, Ava asked a question. "How many reporters were out there yesterday?"

"About half a dozen."

"Then sorry, *chica*. I don't have good news. There's twice as many out there today.

Turning on a national news channel, they found out why. The story had gained traction and was a national headline story. Mallory hadn't considered it earlier; it was easy to see why. It was the down-home stretch of the basketball season. The Navigators were heading into the regional playoffs before the NBA Finals. Had Mallory stopped for a moment and thought things through, she might have made the connection. Had she stopped, calmed down, and let logic rule, the article would have been different, too. Maybe not even written. Maybe there would have been another button pushed when she finished writing. Like delete, instead of send.

By Saturday evening Mallory had had enough of hiding. She was ready to go home.

"Want me to go with you?"

Mallory shook her head. "It's enough of a circus as it is. Let me be the only clown."

"Hold on a minute." Ava walked into her bedroom and came out with wide-brimmed straw hat and Jackie O glasses. She shushed Mallory's objections and placed them on her. "Now you're ready for your close-up.

"Thank you."

They hugged.

"Holler if you need me."

Mallory feigned a scream and walked out the door, down a few blocks and into madness. The reporters weren't the worst of it. Her face was mostly hidden behind the floppy hat and oversized shades. No, it's what happened once inside her brownstone, with her blinds pulled tight and her lights on dim. After she opened her laptop and logged into her work email. That's where the public poured out their scorn, hatred, vitriol, and death threats. Mallory already regretted the op-ed piece getting published. Not even twenty-four hours later and it had cost her a job. Now, it might cost her life.

Suddenly the problem became too big to handle. She retrieved her phone, walked upstairs, and crawled into bed. There she dialed the one person who'd been with her from the beginning, the one who despite their rocky relationship always sent her love.

"Hey, Mom."

"Mallory! Hi! How are you, darling?"

Obviously, her mother Jan hadn't seen the news. "Fine."

Without thought or warning, she started to cry, proof that she was anything but.

"Mallory! What's the matter? Oh my God, did something happen? Are you all right?"

Mallory gave an abbreviated version of the past few days. "I wanted the story to shake things up. But with Leigh's murder and the NYPD. Not my job and definitely not my life!

"Hell, then again, given how angry I was at the time I probably would have written it anyway. I want justice, Mom, for the system put in place for that specific reason to function in a way that forces those involved to do the right thing!"

"You can't think about any of that now, Mallory. You have to think of yourself, and your safety. What are you going to do?"

"I don't know."

"Is there somewhere you can go for the night? A hotel, maybe. Or do you want to come here?"

"Maybe, or I could use the break and go see Dad. I haven't seen him in forever, like five or six years. I have a half brother I barely know. Feel bad about it, really."

"Oh, dear."

"What is it, Mom?"

"It isn't good, honey, and with what you're already dealing with . . ."

"Tell me, Mom. What's wrong with Dad?"

"It's, well, it's cancer, honey. I just found out not too long ago myself."

"And you didn't tell me?"

"I thought that was something he should share. Gave him your number and encouraged him to do so. Obviously, he didn't."

"Is he dying?"

"The last we talked, he's doing better. He had surgery and chemo and is now on the mend. I'm sorry you didn't know, hon. But I didn't want to suggest you come here instead and not give you a reason."

"Maybe I won't go anywhere. I'm not going to let anyone run me out of this city."

"Then don't wait for them to run you out. Leave on your own. Tonight. Right now!"

"People really serious about committing a crime rarely post about it. Easier to sound tough and bluff behind the anonymity of a computer screen. They're probably all cowards who I won't hear from again."

"I certainly hope so, hon. But it only takes one who isn't bluffing. And then instead of solving one tragedy, we'd have another. Oh, Mallory. I'm genuinely afraid."

"Don't worry, Mom. I'll be fine."

Mallory spent a few more moments convincing her mom

that she was safe and would be okay. But after reading messages that came in while talking with her, it was Mallory who needed to believe it.

Then, just before turning off the computer two more emails came in.

The first one contained only one word. *Congrats.*

The second one held two. *You're dead.*

25

Christian sat at the head of his dining room table slowly maneuvering a pair of platinum Baoding balls in his hand over and over again. He'd read the article by Z. D. Woods, aka Mallory, and the one by the editor of the *New York Reporter*. He'd endured Pete's "I told you so" rant and listened to Zoey. He sat there and tried to be rational and logical, tried to understand why someone he'd genuinely befriended would stab him in the back. He'd thought the girl who laughed easily was a straight shooter and loved jazz. Over the years he'd learned to read people well, and being a bullshitter didn't fit her anywhere.

And he hadn't mentioned him, at least not directly. Yes, one could assume he was the pot of gold at the end of Leigh Jackson's rainbow, but the article didn't mention his name. That correlation was made by Rob Anderson in his response to what Mallory had written. That was the problem. If the *New York Reporter* was to be believed, Mallory had written the piece. Now the whole fucking world had him under scrutiny for possible murder of a bitch he couldn't even remember meeting, let alone taken out on a date. He stopped twirling the balls and began to squeeze them, imagining Mallory's neck.

Pete returned to the dining room, ending a call. "That was Matt," he said to the room in general. "He's on his way over."

"Matt who?" Zoey asked.

"Hernandez. One of the finest defamation attorneys there is. He's read the articles and has a plan of action he wants to discuss." Pete sat down and rubbed his hands together. "We're going to crucify that bitch."

"I'm not so sure," Zoey said. "When you look at each article on its own, hers only implies, it doesn't specify. Knight's piece starts a flame for sure. But the *New York Reporter*'s editor pours on gasoline."

"And then there's the picture," Christian added. "Of me and that girl. Once I saw it I remembered her. But I swear she and I never had sex. I go through a lot of ladies but I remember them all. Pete, do you remember that girl, Leigh Jackson?"

Pete shook his head. "I remember the place, though. That picture was taken at Club RSVP after a charity basketball game, along with probably dozens of others."

Zoey picked up the picture she'd had printed and enlarged. "She's a pretty girl. Journalist, like Mallory, and according to the articles written about her for the 'Knightly News' column a talented one. Single. Thirty-two when she died. Dated a few guys here and there but none seriously, at least that I could find."

"You should get Nick to check her out too, Pete."

"Why in the hell would I have him research a dead girl? Everybody knows where she is." He laughed at his attempt to make a joke. He was the only one.

"Not funny, Pete," Zoey chastised him.

"Zoey's right," Christian said. "No matter that we didn't know her. That was someone's daughter, maybe someone's sister, and at least one person's best friend."

"Or lover," Pete mused, rubbing his chin. "Maybe I will

have Nick check her out. Find out the real reason behind Mallory's obsession and attempt to smear your name in the process. That's all right. She fucked with the wrong team. When he gets done with this Mallory chick, she'll be 'Knightly News' all right. She'll say good night to her column and her entire got damn career!"

"This is probably my fault," Zoey said, pulling a hand through tangled tresses. "I should have worked harder to protect you from her, cut her off at the gate."

"You tried to," Christian said, his voice dangerously calm. Seductively soft. "You warned me about her. Both of you did. Don't blame yourself. You either, Pete. I'm a grown man. Striking up a friendship with her was my decision alone. If anyone, I created this problem. And just like I created it, I'm going to take care of it. Watch."

"Negative, Christian." Pete's voice was as stern as Christian's was calm. "Mallory Knight has tried to fuck up your life, but you're not going to do anything. Not to her. As of this moment, this second, Mallory Knight is invisible to you. Don't mention her name directly or indirectly. No tweets. No posts. No reaction. Your words to the press are 'no comment.' Every reporter, every time. And for God's sake, don't contact her or take her call."

"Or text," Zoey added.

"None of that. Phone, social media, fucking stool pigeon. Nothing. Let us handle this pile of shit for you. Keep you clean and smelling fresh, and ready to win championship number five. We're on the back stretch to making history. I wouldn't put it past one of your rivals to have dreamed up this shit. History, winning another championship, not this hyped-up drama, has to be your one and only focus."

Christian met his uncle's eyes, just as determined as his own. His gaze slid up and away from him as once again he twirled the balls.

Pete placed a hand on Christian's forearm. "You trust me, Christian?"

Christian nodded. "With my life."

"Then believe me when I say I'll take care of this. Can you do that?"

"I want my name cleared. And I want her . . . actions . . . to have consequences."

Pete eased back in the chair, a satisfied look on his face. "We want the same thing, Christian. I'll take care of it."

26

Mallory handled the online harassment, but after a crazed-looking stranger pounding on her door at two o'clock in the morning, she removed the briefcase of evidence hidden in her closet behind a fake wall and left the brownstone the following morning and decided to visit her Mom in Omaha. It had taken two extra days to strategize with the girls and pull it all together, but the second Tuesday in March, four days after the world blew up, a woman wearing an oversized nylon jacket over jeans and a tee, with long black braids, an apple cap and big round shades, though it was just after seven in the morning, stepped out of a Brooklyn apartment and after a quick look around for paparazzi or hit men, slung a backpack over her shoulder and joined the morning traffic headed to wherever. Yesterday the woman's name was Mallory Knight but today, thanks to the handiwork of her Bronx fake ID connection, it was Pamela Johnson headed to Penn Station to catch an Amtrak train. She walked fast and kept her head down, looking just like many others she passed. At an intersection, she'd look around for oncoming traffic or Christian Graham fans with an ax to grind, one of the authors of more than a thousand "go fuck yourself" type reactions to Rob's outing her or a face (and fist) behind a dozen death threats she'd received. Fortunately, it was a typical morning like most of the others she'd experienced while bopping down the street to catch the 2 or the 3, the B or the D. Man, she missed Brooklyn already.

Once at Penn Station, she became blissfully lost in a sea of travelers. Ava had purchased her ticket online and had assured Mallory there'd be no problems with the fake ID. It's why she'd decided to travel by train. Security wasn't as strict. No sophisticated scanners or astute TSA agents. Still, her heartbeat increased as she found her train and got on it. She felt as though at any minute security would come up, demand several forms of ID, and once the fraud was discovered remove her in handcuffs. None of that happened. To the other passengers and the conductor who punched her ticket she was one in a sea of passengers headed to Omaha by way of DC and Chicago.

After getting her ticket punched, Mallory sat back and truly relaxed for the first time since Friday. She'd been up all night, but her mind was too busy and body still too wired to think about sleep. There were several unchecked items on her to-do list, ones she couldn't handle until they arrived in DC and she gained a modicum of privacy in a sleeper car. So she found a comfortable position in her window seat and mentally replayed the past seventy-two hours.

On Sunday night, Sam had come over. Calm, rational. Ava developed the overall plan. Sam found ways to execute it. Mallory drank wine, listened, and hoped to wake up.

After they'd decided that she'd head to Omaha to stay with her mom, it was Ava who determined there needed to be a way to not leave a paper trail. She'd taken the death threats more seriously than Mallory's mom had. Mallory tried to play it off, but she was shook up, too. Every step was built around the fake ID. Everything except the first order of business when the three got together. Sam had opened a new bank account. Mallory wrote a check to Ava, who had a contact in a Tribeca accounting firm that was actually a high-end cover for a multi-billion-dollar money laundering operation. She cashed the check. Sam deposited the money and from there set up train tickets and rental cars, bought a couple burner phones and paid an African braiding whiz heading back to the Motherland five hundred dollars to hook up her hair and keep her mouth shut about it. Somewhere between that thought and the one about Sam suggesting a similar style for her white husband, Mallory fell asleep.

They arrived at Washington, D.C.'s Union station. After a three-hour layover, a harried and paranoid Mallory entered her sleeper car and exhaled. After the conductor came around and punched her ticket, she felt it safe to get to work. First up was a call to Karen Walker. It wouldn't be easy so rather than think about it, Mallory pulled up the number and punched it in.

It was a new, unfamiliar number. She totally expected voicemail and was taken aback when Karen answered the phone.

"Karen, hi, Mallory Knight."

"Who?"

"Mallory, the reporter who interviewed Harmony."

"Oh, you."

"So you saw the news."

"I saw it. Why are you calling me?"

"Not about the article that got me fired." Mallory attempted a laugh. Karen didn't join her.

"A whole lot of people hate you right now, girlfriend."

"I hope you're not one of them."

"Hmph. I don't give a damn about you one way or another."

Spoken like a true New Yorker. She was rough around the edges, but Mallory liked this girl. "You know what, Karen. I'm not going to keep you on the phone. And I'm not going to bullshit you. Honestly, that was the way I'd planned to go, but you're intelligent, street smart, and would see right through it. So I'm going to be real with you. I need your help."

A second of silence. Then two. Three.

"I don't know how I can help you."

"I'm not sure you can." Mallory took a deep breath and plunged off the dive. "It's about the sculpture on your wall, the one I was admiring when you caught me in your bedroom."

"What about it?"

"I really did love it. So much so that I went online and tried to find where I could buy one for myself. Turns out it's not very common. Where'd you get it?"

"I didn't buy it. It was a gift."

"Do you mind telling me from who?"

"That's really none of your business. Look, you'll have to find somebody else to help you with your art search. I gotta go—"

"It's also about who shot Danny."

Mallory couldn't see that she'd gotten Karen's attention. But she could feel it. "Who shot him?"

"That's what I'm trying to find out. Karen, I'll be honest. You were right that people hate me. I've decided to leave town. I need to find answers to the questions posed in the article I wrote. I believe some of them are wrapped up in that gold artwork in your room."

"Gold? That thing isn't gold."

Mallory allowed her to believe that for now.

"What does that jigsaw puzzle have to do with me and who shot Danny?"

"Because the person I wrote about in the article, the one who was murdered, was a friend of mine. My best friend. Recently, her mother gave me a bag of some of her things. In the bag was a puzzle piece, one that looks like a perfect fit for the missing spot in the one you have hanging in your bedroom. I believe if placed inside it would be a perfect fit and complete the puzzle. That's why the sculpture drew me into the room. That's why I was so taken aback, Karen, and so intrigued. I believe that whoever gave you that artwork somehow knew my friend."

"Look, Danny didn't kill nobody."

"I don't think he did."

"Somebody gave Danny that thing. He didn't have anywhere to hang it so he gave it to me."

Ah. Progress.

"Here's the thing, Karen. That piece is most definitely gold."

"No, it's not."

"Worth at least a hundred thousand dollars, maybe more."

"What the hell?"

"Don't take my word for it. Get it appraised. Not in some neighborhood pawn shop. By a reputable art collector or dealer in gold. Then ask yourself who would give away a piece that valuable, and why? As a birthday present? A thank-you gift? I don't think so."

Karen didn't say anything. Fine. That meant Mallory had her attention.

"Do you know where Danny is?"

"No."

She said it way too fast. "It's okay if you don't want to tell me. But I believe you know. And I believe that whoever shot Danny is somehow connected to whoever killed my friend. The common thread is the artwork, so finding out where it came from would put me one step closer to who killed my friend and who tried to kill your husband."

"Don't you worry about that. The streets have their own brand of justice."

"I know. And their own code, which most often doesn't involve law enforcement. I understand why. Heck, sometimes I even agree. Too many have trusted the justice system and gotten shafted. But my friend, Leigh Jackson, she wasn't out there hustling. There's no way I can get justice for her murder out on the streets. The system, as biased and corrupt and broken as it is, is my only option. The only card I can play."

"Look, I gotta go."

"Okay. I hear you. Thank you for taking the time to listen. And please remember what I said. You have something very valuable in your house. Hopefully me, you, and the person who bought it are the only ones who know its value. Don't take it to just anyone to have it appraised. And think about taking it down off your wall. Putting it somewhere for safekeeping. At least for now."

"Okay."

"One more thing. Did my number come up on your phone when I called?"

"Yes."

"Could you do me a favor and save it, but not under my name. Save it under Goldie. That way you'll remember. And after you've thought about all I've said, and found out what I've told you about the art is true, think about giving Danny my number. It is really important that I talk with him, maybe a matter of life or death. Bye for now."

Between D.C. and Chicago, the next stop on the journey to Omaha, Mallory had plenty of time to think—about the conversation with Karen, Leigh, Christian, her life. She gave her Mom an update and finally nodded off for some much-needed sleep. She took her meals in her room and enjoyed some downtime. When she looked in the mirror she saw a chick named Pamela.

An hour into the second leg of her journey, Mallory felt more like herself than she had in days. Less paranoid, too. And in need of a shower. She locked her carry-on, grabbed her toiletries, a couple towels and her purse, and headed down the hall. When she got back in the room, her phone vibrated. Mallory thought she would have heard the phone ring, even in the shower. *Was the ringer not on?*

She tapped the screen awake. There were two messages. The first was a text that she'd missed. From Karen.

Here's D's #. He said call. About that other stuff, thanks.

Mallory's heart felt light as she dialed the number. He didn't answer, but that was okay. She left a message, and thirty minutes later, he returned her call. It was a short conversation that called for a change in plans. A flurry of text messages later, the last leg of Mallory's trip had been switched from Omaha to St. Louis. In a twist that she totally didn't see coming, and a coincidence she liked to view as a wink from Leigh, Mallory wasn't going to stay with her mother. She was headed to the city that would allow her to bond with her dad.

The second was a voicemail from Detective Anthony Wang. Mallory listened to the short message and redialed the number.

"Detective, it's Mallory."

"Hey there, Knight. I see you've been busy."

"You could say that. In a bit of hot water."

"I'd say boiling."

"No doubt. But it's worth it."

"Why?"

"Because I believe Leigh Jackson was murdered."

"Convince me."

Mallory was on the phone for an hour. By the time the call ended, the detective was an ally and Mallory felt she was one step closer to getting justice for her friend.

27

After speaking with her father, Melvin, on the way to St. Louis, Mallory canceled the rental car reservation and instead took a taxi from the St. Louis Lambert Airport to where her father, his wife, Trudy, and Mallory's half brother lived in an area known as Tower Grove East. Thinking over the past few days of her father's mortality had drastically changed her perspective and, quite frankly, made her feel bad for not being a more involved daughter over the years. Growing up, her mother had constantly reassured Mallory that they didn't need her father, that they were much better on their own and, following her mother's second marriage, better off with her stepdad. It suddenly bothered Mallory that for all intents and purposes she didn't know her half brother from her dad's second marriage. He was a young man around eleven or twelve years old, one who might have benefitted from being one of Christian's kids . . . before she believed he was a murderer.

Twenty minutes later, and the car stopped in front of a square brick building that looked to have been turned into duplexes. Rechecking the address, she noted that her father's house was the one on the right. She paid the driver, grabbed her luggage, and went to the door.

Seconds after ringing the doorbell she heard heavy footsteps running down the stairs. The door opened, and instead of looking down on the head of a young boy, she stood eye to eye with a young man who must have looked more like his mother, because nowhere in him did she see her dad.

"Are you my sister, Mallory?"

She nodded. "That's me. You must be Tyson."

He stood back to let her enter. "You're tall."

"I was just thinking the same thing about you."

He nodded. "You're pretty, too. Come on up."

"Tyson! Grab her bag."

His expression showed slight embarrassment as he wordlessly took her carry-on. They continued up the steps to the main living area on the second floor. There, in a recliner by the window, sat Melvin Hill, the father she hadn't seen in almost ten years, three years longer than she'd guessed during the conversation with her mom, Jan. He seemed smaller than she remembered, a bald head replacing the locs he'd sported when last they met.

An unexpected lump arose in her throat as she walked over. "Hey, Dad." She leaned over and hugged him.

"Hi, Mallory." He stared for what seemed an eternity when really only seconds passed.

"How are you?"

"Not bad for an old man. Have a seat. Ty, take her bag and put it in the spare room."

"Oh, no. That's okay. I booked a room not too far from here. Downtown. Technically this is a business trip, so . . ." She shrugged, as there was no reason to put at the end of that sentence.

"I understand. Are you hungry?"

"Not really." It was then Mallory noted the smells in the air and heard the sound of stirrings in what she assumed was the kitchen. "I could eat a little."

A short time later Melvin's wife, Trudy, entered the living room. "It's good to see you, Mallory," she said warmly and gave her a hug. "Your dad talks about you all the time. Said you were a jazz buff, even when you were little."

"She sure was. I used to bet my friends on the knowledge she retained, facts stored in that computer of a brain she had. Would ask her a question. She'd rattle off the answer in no seconds flat. You still got it like that, baby girl?"

"Not those facts. Wow, I'd forgotten about those early days. Your friends used to come over and practice in the garage."

"Yep. We'd practice all day and play all night. I had a singular focus back then. It was all about the music. Didn't leave much time for family. I'm sorry about that."

"Singular focus, huh. So that's where I got it. No worries, Dad. You did what you could at the time. Hey, do you have a copy of the recording you did, *Up the Hill* or something like that?"

Tyson entered the room. "Daddy, you made a CD?"

"I made an album, son. *Top of the Hill*. Distributed it on vinyl and cassettes."

Tyson scrunched up his face. "Vinyl? Cassette? What's that?"

The music was the bonding agent. Over a down-home meal of smothered steak and gravy, green beans and rice, the family talked about jazz and Mallory's early years. Memories she'd long forgotten. They listened to Melvin's album and Tyson's rap. Mallory learned that in the time since she'd seen them, Trudy had become a registered nurse. It was her skills and excellent insurance that afforded her father a middle-class lifestyle. Trudy was warm yet no-nonsense, and she loved Melvin to pieces. Mallory had no doubt about that. In the taxi ride over, her mind had been mostly on Danny. After seeing her father, she knew that could wait. Time enough to get on the investigative grind tomorrow. Tonight, she was Mallory Anne,

Melvin's daughter. The one who knew more than a thing or two about jazz.

Two days later, Mallory wheeled a nondescript white Ford Taurus she'd bought yesterday for seventeen hundred cash into a nightclub parking lot in East St. Louis, as Danny had instructed. It was a Friday night, and the lot was crowded. She found a space near the club's back entrance, put the car in park, and kept the motor running. She wasn't one to stereotype or label all urban areas dangerous, but this spot looked like one familiar with screeching tires and fast getaways. Taking a breath, she scanned the local stations for one with jazz and landed on 90.7, KWMU. She immediately recognized Freddie Hubbard's trumpet as even through cheap speakers the notes oozed out and coated her nerves. She pushed back the seat, stretched her legs, and took several deep breaths in an attempt to further relax as she waited for a black Nissan driven by an average-looking brother wearing a Rams ball cap, as Danny had described himself. She killed the engine to further blend in. An idling car in a parking lot could draw unwanted attention.

A black car pulled in. Mallory tried to be inconspicuous as she checked out the make and the occupants. It was a Honda filled with girls who looked dressed for the club. Another black car showed up ten minutes later. A dude. Mallory straightened and peered through the darkness. She couldn't tell the make of the car, but the guy who got out was not wearing a ball cap. Several more minutes went by. Mallory's mind began to race. If her facts were right, Danny and Christian were connected, maybe even partners in crime. She'd taken Danny at his word, but what if this was a setup? What if there was a price on her head and Danny needed money? What if Danny hadn't agreed to meet in order to help her but to shut her up for good?

Mallory didn't know, but she wasn't going to wait to find out. She fired up the engine, put the car in drive and—

Knock, knock, knock.

Hard knuckles on the passenger window. To Mallory's paranoid ears they sounded like gunshots. She almost passed out. Her head jerked around to find a man dressed in black and wearing a Rams ball cap peering into the car. He tapped again, more lightly this time, offered a brief smile and said, "You gonna let me in?"

Mallory pushed the button to unlock the door. Danny slid in and openly checked her out. Mallory sized him up, too, a sweeping look from head to toe. If pulled from the car and handed over to a sketch artist, Mallory could have described him to a tee.

"What happened to you arriving in a black sedan? You scared the hell out of me just now."

"It's always better to have the element of surprise on your side. I don't know you. Karen just met you. How do I know you are who you say you are?"

Mallory made a move toward her purse. Danny's reaction was a hand disappearing into his jacket.

"Whoa, wait a minute. I was just reaching for my cell phone."

"Do yourself a favor and never make a move again like that anywhere around these parts, you hear me? Folks are liable to shoot first and ask questions later."

"Got it. So listen up. I'm going for my phone," she said with an exaggerated enunciation that made Danny smile. "After this past week, I can't believe you don't know about me, but it's easy enough to prove. I'm all over the web."

"I know. Karen told me."

"Then what are you talking about, not knowing who I am?"

"I'm not into computers. And I don't watch the news."

"Then you've probably never heard of Christian Graham."

"Come on, now," Danny responded. His offense was evident in the side-eye given. "I'm a New Yorker. Everybody anywhere knows Don't-Give-a-Damn Graham."

Mallory typed her name into a search engine, tapped on images and held the phone up next to her face." Is it a match?"

"All right, then."

"Cool. What else did she tell you?"

"She told me a bunch of shit that didn't make sense." His eyes narrowed as he gave her the side-eye. "That I don't believe."

"What I told her about the artwork is true. Did she take it to have it appraised?"

"I told her that until I get back don't take that muthafucka out the house. That shit's under clothes and floorboards and all other whatnot. Hell, even roaches would have a hard time finding that shit. Still don't know if I believe you, though."

"I have proof to back up everything I'm saying." Mallory looked around. "But I don't feel comfortable sharing it in this parking lot. In fact, I don't feel comfortable in this parking lot at all."

"I feel you. East St. Louis ain't for everybody. But it gets a bad rap."

"Are you from here?"

"Spent enough time to know my way around. Tell you what. I'll go get my car, my black sedan, and pull around. You can follow me to a spot where you can feel safer and we can talk."

The safer spot ended up being a neighborhood pool hall where everybody in there looked like they were packing heat. But they all seemed to know Danny, which provided some comfort. Mallory was given slow smiles and long stares. Another time and place and she might have been offended. Tonight it made her feel as though she belonged.

They found a rickety table near the back.

"You want something to drink?"

"No," Mallory said, waving her hand. "Nothing for me."

"All right, then. I'll be back."

Danny going to get a drink was a ten-minute situation, laughing and chatting with the same men they'd just passed. A comment or two about her, given the stares. Mallory knew it wouldn't do any good to try and hurry along the evening. She repositioned her purse, which sat on the table, deftly turning on the recorder hidden under the strap. Given the information he might have to share, Danny was a whale of a fish she was catching. She intended to take her time, put her foot on the rail, and slowly reel him in.

He returned with two drinks in plastic cups. "I know you said you didn't want nothing, but you might get thirsty. Gin and ginger ale. They don't serve no girly drinks up in here."

"Thanks."

She pulled the drink toward her, placed her lips to the rim, and pretended a sip. Her throat almost closed up at just the thought of drinking something from a cup that a near stranger had brought her, poured by another somebody she didn't know in a part of town where everyone carried a gun. *Um, thank you but no.*

Danny took a hearty swig from a cup filled to the brim with what looked like straight brown liquor.

"All right then, Mallory. What's this about?"

"Straight up, no bullshit?" Danny nodded. "It's about you, or your family, and a friend of mine who was murdered."

"That's not what Karen told me."

"I know. I lied to her. I felt it best to first share what I have with you."

For the next several minutes Mallory laid out her story, from the friendship with Leigh to walking in on her crime scene as an investigative journalist. From the police officer's rush to judgment in declaring it a suicide to the angel of a detective, Anthony Wang, who had the foresight to preserve evidence that would have otherwise been thrown away. And finally, to the gold jigsaw puzzle, the missing piece of which had turned up in her dead best friend's belongings. "Do you know who gave Karen that artwork?"

"Maybe."

"Is that what you're doing? Why are you here in St. Louis?"

"Don't worry about what I'm doing here."

Danny's quick change in demeanor told Mallory she'd said the wrong thing. But this was no environment to be a shrinking violet.

"Fair enough," she said in a strong voice, a curt nod added to show she had balls. "What about this question. Why did somebody try to kill you?"

"I live in the hood. It's what we do."

"Seriously, Danny? You agreed to come out so we do this? Dance around dead bodies and let guilty motherfuckers go free?"

"All right, then, shorty. Stand your ground. I like that shit." For a long moment, Danny stared at her, as if he were trying to make up his mind about what to tell her, or if he should say anything at all. Mallory said nothing, not wanting to jinx the moment. At this moment, anything would be better than nothing. She was enjoying the time with this side of her family, but it wasn't exactly a vacation, after all.

Danny took another long swig of his drink, then leaned forward in a conspiratorial fashion. "I'm going to tell you a story. Because I appreciate how you're holding it down for your girl and I think you're legit. Besides, it's a damn shame what happened to her. Shit didn't have to go down like that."

Mallory swore the blood in her veins turned to ice water. She fought against shivering at the chill of impending truth.

"What happened?" she asked so quietly her lips barely moved.

"You said you were at the crime scene, right? You know

what happened. Dude crushed up a lethal amount of oxy-codone, fixed her a drink, and sent her to heaven."

"Who?" she said as Danny took another drink. "The same per-son who gave you the sculpture, and Leigh the missing piece?"

A nod, slowly.

Time stopped. The room faded away. All Mallory saw was Danny's face, and the mouth that at any moment could spew the answer to the mystery that had consumed her life.

"Christian Graham?"

"No, not Christian." Mallory's eyes bored deeply into Danny's. *Tell me!* they screamed. "His manager, the uncle, Pete."

"Pete?"

"Yep."

"But why?"

"He had one baby on the way and didn't need another."

Mallory fell silent, digested his words. *Not Christian. His uncle, Pete. Uncle Pete. UP!* Now, she got it, why the word seen several times in Leigh's appointment book often made no sense. It had been a code. Not for Christian, but for his uncle. Then finally his last sentence sank into her conscience. It was Pete's baby Leigh carried.

For a second, Mallory felt as though all breath had left her body. Her mind flashed to the picture that Sam found of Leigh, Christian and Pete. All this time she'd been focused on Christian. She never would have guessed it was the middle-aged man with the cute young wife. One sentence was all it had taken to put everything in perspective, to lay out the reason and make it crystal clear.

"You all right?"

She looked up. "No."

"I hear you. I'm sorry about your friend."

"Then why didn't you do something? Even if you didn't want to go to the police directly, you could have made an anony-mous phone call or told somebody else."

Danny said nothing. Took another drink. Mallory's eyes narrowed. "You were in on it?"

"Don't come at me all judgmental like that. He asked if I could score some pills. When I told him that I was out of the game, he offered me five stacks to get back in just one more time. I didn't know why he wanted them."

Mallory's voice dropped. It was her turn to lean in. "But you had to know that five thousand dollars was a helluva lot to pay for a handful a pills. Plus he gave you the artwork."

"I didn't know what that piece was worth until you told Karen. If I had, things might have gone differently and I wouldn't have gotten shot."

"What does that mean?"

"You're the investigative reporter. Figure it out."

"I thought you said you didn't watch the news."

"People say a lot of things. Just because we say we don't know doesn't always mean we don't know."

"You got shot because of something you did, something involving Pete. Whatever you did might not have happened had you known the value of the piece he gave you. But he paid you for the pills, right? That doesn't make sense."

"Keep on thinking about it. I'm going to go holler at my boy."

Mallory barely noticed he'd left the table. She was too wrapped up in having another puzzle to solve. By the time he returned to the table, she thought she'd done just that.

"You tried to blackmail him."

"Really?"

"Hell, yeah. You knew about Leigh. You supplied the pills. And when you heard of her death you put it together, then demanded money to keep quiet about it."

A smile spread slowly across Danny's face. "You're pretty good."

"Sometimes. But how did you know she was pregnant?"

"Butt dial."

"Shut the fuck up."

"I kid you not. A conversation that I wish I'd never heard. He invited your girl over to give her the money to have an abortion, and a little more to disappear, get the hell out of his life. I think she really loved him. She knew about the engagement, couldn't understand why he didn't choose her. They started arguing, and he let it slip that Melissa was pregnant. Your girl was upset but smooth at the same time. Asked him how she expected her to kill their child while his or her half sibling lived? Sounded like she cried a little bit and then just told him straight up it would take a mil to do what he wanted."

"Leigh demanded a million dollars?"

"Didn't stutter, either."

What Danny relayed to her sounded just like Leigh, and what she would do. Mallory knew he was telling the truth.

"That's when Pete lost it. His nephew's a baller, but he ain't rolling like that. He never would have come off of that kind of paper. Not when they already had what it took to make the problem go away.

"So after it became clear that your girl wasn't going to back down, Pete told her he'd give her what she wanted. He apologized, acted all cool, told her he would pour them both a drink so they could calm down. She told him she shouldn't drink because of the baby. He told her that one glass wouldn't hurt her."

"Then you demanded money that Leigh didn't get. And he tried to kill you, too."

Danny shrugged. "Tried and failed."

"There's always next time."

"People trying to kill me don't get a second chance."

"He's got to take you out. You can hold this story over him for the rest of his life. He knows it, and you know it. That's why you're here in St. Louis. Laying low until you come up with a plan. That's where I come in, Danny Groves. With my evidence and your story, we can put Pete away, and you can return to the city. Sell that chunk of gold and move to a new neighborhood."

"There's only one problem. I don't work with the po-po."

"I'll figure out how to jump that hurdle. For right now, just work with me."

28

It wasn't admissible as evidence, but with Danny's taped conversation, Mallory was finally ready to have a package delivered to Detective Anthony Wang, a carefully orchestrated series of events with Sam as the liaison. Two days later, she received the coded text she'd requested. Wang had the info and was proceeding toward their mutually desired goal. He'd be in touch.

With nothing to do but wait, Mallory decided to try and reclaim at least the semblance of a life. Finally out from under a constant state of paranoia, she decided to take a day trip out of the city to relax and clear her head. To be normal, a human being again. To not think about Christian or murder . . . or even Leigh. Mallory couldn't get her old one back, but she wanted a life. It was time to make a new one. Still not wanting to let down her guard in the hideout city where her father lived, she checked Google maps and some entertainment sites and decided to head west almost two hundred and fifty miles down Interstate 70 to a former jazz hotspot, Kansas City, Missouri.

Once on the highway she called Ava, who picked up after half a ring.

"Dammit, girl," she hissed in a barely audible whisper. "About time you called. I'll return it in ten. Answer." Click.

Mallory smiled and then laughed out loud. Ava could have cursed her out, and Mallory wouldn't have minded at all. She hadn't realized how much she missed her friends until just now when Ava answered. She didn't know she and Sam filled so much of her life until their absence left a great big hole in it. She popped in the CD her father had given her, his one and only album—*Top of the Hill*—the other baby birthed the same year as Mallory, 1983. The first song, a haunting melody called "Melvin's Mystique," brought a smile to her face. She turned up the volume. Seconds later the tune was interrupted by the screechy sound of her burner phone ringing through the Bluetooth.

"I'm sorry," Mallory answered.

"You should be. We've been beside ourselves wondering what's happening and if you're all right."

"What do you mean? Sam knows what's going on."

"She didn't tell me."

"I sent a text message."

"The anonymous one from an unknown number that said you're okay and would be in touch? The one that sounded like it was written by your killer? That one?"

It felt good to laugh. Mallory cracked up. "You had my number."

"Not written on my fucking forehead, you nut!" Now Ava was laughing, too. "All this worrying that you'd died, and now if you were here I'd kill you!"

"I miss you, Ava."

"I know you do. And Sam shared a little about what happened. But you know I want to hear it all."

"I'll tell you everything, but not today, okay?"

"Why not?"

"Because today I'm trying to be normal for once in my life."

"Good luck with that."

"Shut up! I'm serious. I've been consumed with this stuff every waking moment for forever, it seems, a couple weeks at least. Now that what Sam told you has happened, I feel like I can take a break. Know what I'm doing?"

"What?"

"Headed to Kansas City."

"What for?"

"Ha! Not an unreasonable reaction, given you live in NYC. Kansas City is one of the country's jazz capitols. Twelfth and Eighteenth along Vine Street was jumping back in the day."

"That's right. Your dad's a musician. How is he?"

For the next hour, Mallory and Ava talked about everything and anything light and fun. Nothing to do with murder. Later, Sam beeped in, got plugged in to the conference call, and three of them together moseyed into KC, MO.

Once into the city, Mallory bid her friends adieu and jumped straight into the tour she designed that began at Eighteenth and Vine. She toured the American Jazz Museum and the Negro Leagues Baseball Museum, the Mutual Musicians Foundation, and the Charlie Parker Memorial. After asking locals about the nearby clubs, Mallory decided to come back that night to hear live jazz. Meanwhile she ate lunch at Crown Center and then drove to and strolled through the Country Club Plaza. A couple hours of shopping and an overpriced mani-pedi made her feel like a girl again.

Later on, Mallory parked her car near the Mutual Musicians Foundation, where she looked forward to some good old jamming like her father used to do. But having been told those sessions didn't start until around midnight, she decided to get in some much-needed exercise by simply walking around. She still wore the braids, so being recognized wasn't a huge concern. Seeing there wasn't much past the attractions she'd already seen, she decided to head over to the Blue Room. The crowd was light, the band just warming up when she entered and took a place at the bar. The bartender looked more like a biker, with tattoos everywhere, a black Mohawk tinged in blue, and large gauged earlobes sporting Viking discs.

He headed over to her, wiping down the bar as he walked.

"What can I get you, pretty lady?"

"Do you have sparkling wine?"

"Yeah, it's called champagne." He smiled to reveal a row of straight, white teeth.

Mallory smiled, too. "Okay, smartass. I'll have a glass."

"Coming right up."

Mallory bobbed her head as she looked around as more people entered the club, feeling up the sparse audience. There was a mixture of cultures represented. Tables were filled with either couples or girlfriends. She found the lack of men-only tables interesting, guessed hanging out and listening to live jazz was not a male bonding experience.

The bartender returned. "Here you go, pretty lady."

"Thank you, pretty boy."

"Ha! That's a first."

"What, being called a boy?"

"Exactly." It was drawn out with sarcasm to prove to her that he was not buying whatever she sold. "You're not from around here."

"No. What gave me away?"

"That attitude. Where you from, Chicago?"

"Farther east."

"Ah. A New Yorker. I should have known. Go Navigators!"

"You're a basketball fan."

"I'm a Graham fan. Everybody's eyes are on him and the team, and the chase for history with a historic fifth win. You're not paying attention?"

"Not really. I've been on the road."

"Then you probably don't know about the lying bitch trying to pin a murder on him."

Mallory prided herself on the champagne she'd just sipped staying in her mouth.

"No, what happened?"

"Some vindictive writer wrote a piece about a woman that committed suicide, except she thought it was murder and that Christian was somehow connected to it."

"Damn, that's bold. She called him out like that?"

"Hell, no. She knew better than to use his name. He would have sued her into poverty. But another guy, probably a Navigator fan, called her out as you say. Exposed her. Can't remember her name, but she didn't write the article under it anyway. Tried to hide behind another one."

"Wow. That's crazy. Did Christian respond? Or the team? What are they doing about it?"

"They're not saying. But if I know Christian, he's gonna fry her ass."

The band started playing. Mallory turned around, not so much to listen to them but to digest what pretty boy had just said, to contemplate what would happen if she came from beneath the braids and was recognized. One thing Mallory knew for sure. She'd no longer be "pretty lady."

The band was okay, but Mallory had lost the zest for hanging out in Kansas City. Maybe another time. She turned to pay up and felt as though someone checking her out.

She pulled out her wallet, swayed to the music and casually looked around. She immediately saw a face that she thought she recognized. Mallory placed a twenty on the bar, asked the bartender a question, headed toward the bathroom and out the back door he'd told her was there. Her adventure in Kansas City entertainment had gone to hell in a handbasket. First the bartender who loved Christian Graham and wanted her head on a platter. Now seeing Christian's publicist, Zoey Girard, standing across the room.

How long had Zoey followed her? Had she seen the meetings between her and Danny? What about her father? Who knew where he lived? Mallory couldn't get to her car and Interstate 70 fast enough. Christian told her she'd entered a game with no way out, and that she'd be sorry about it. Mallory reached the interstate entry ramp and floored the gas pedal. She'd never apologize about what she believed in. And when it came to the game, she planned to win.

29

Mallory arrived back in St. Louis certain she hadn't been followed. She'd circled the hotel several times, looking and not finding any suspicious-looking vehicles before she pulled in. After pulling up Zoey's pic on the internet and remembering the woman in the club, she was no longer even sure about what she had seen. Paranoia may have painted the publicist's features on some innocent blond woman's face. An internet search seemed to further confirm this, as an article suggested Zoey was in Phoenix with Christian. Mallory crashed on the bed and went to sleep fully clothed, without any doubt on another matter. The fugitive life was not for her.

Hours later she was startled awake by a knock on the door. The fear she'd laid to rest after her time on the internet came back like a fist that punched her in the chest. She eased out of bed and tiptoed to the peephole. *What?* Covering her mouth to suppress a scream, she took a step back and then looked through it again. The person she saw was still there in real time, living color. He knocked again, this time harder.

She opened the door. "Detective Wang! What are you doing? How did you find me?"

"I could ask you the very same questions. May I come in?"

"Oh, of course." Mallory stepped back to let him enter. "I feel like I'm dreaming. Are you really here?"

"I'm really here."

"How did you find me?"

"I'm an investigator. It's what we do. Tell you what, though, took some real digging. Your people are loyal and very protective." Mallory's stare intensified. "I talked to your dad."

"And he disclosed my location?"

"Only after several phone calls and my sharing information only meant for you. Which must be pretty important, since after not being able to reach you by phone, I jumped on the first plane out this morning."

"The unknown calls last night, that was you." She told him about her near-sighting of Zoey. "I was too spooked to answer the phone and then forgot to check messages. Is this about Leigh? Are the authorities investigating her murder?"

"They've opened a case."

"Yes!" Mallory punched a fist in the air. "Come have a seat. Tell me everything."

Mallory led the detective over to a couch and sat down on the chair beside it. She leaned forward, hungry for information. She was praying this nearly two-year-long journey was nearing an end.

"What's happened?"

"Your hard work paid off. I laid out what you sent me and turned over what I'd collected the day of her death. No one could argue against the evidence. Some of the information was gained illegally and in its present state can't be used during the trial, but it points the officers in the right direction."

"These officers, who are they?"

"I know what you're thinking, and don't worry. There are officers in that precinct who for the right amount of money could shape the case for the highest bidder. This team isn't one of them. It's why I went to them and personally presented the evidence. These guys don't give a shit about Graham and his celebrity. They are bulldogs for justice who won't stop until they get an indictment."

"How long will that take?"

"Considering the judge who's hearing it? Not long. You've gathered enough information for probable cause. Someone could be charged as little as a week."

"Pete Graham, you mean." Wang nodded. "For?"

"Murder, in the first degree. Turns out there were two types of evidence on the bottle you sent to Baltimore. The DNA on the rim was verified as belonging to Christian, but his DNA was not on anything found in Leigh's apartment. Where it gets interesting is that there were two sets of fingerprints on the bottle. We don't have his prints on file but it's assumed that one set belonged to Christian. The second set lined up with the evidence I'd collected."

"Which was?"

"The two wineglasses in Leigh's apartment. After the officers left I bagged them and took them with me."

"Oh my gosh, that was genius!"

Wang nodded. "I thought so. Pete Graham's prints were on file. They're a perfect match."

Mallory fell against the chair. Could this really be happening? The moment felt surreal.

He reached out his hand. "Good work, detective."

"Thank you, boss."

"If I ever stop rolling solo and need a partner, I'll give you a call."

"I don't think so. After this murder case is over, I'm hanging up my badge."

Mallory pulled up to a BBQ joint off Martin Luther King Boulevard. She was there to grab lunch and pick up Danny.

He'd warned her the place was a hole in the wall but the ribs were the best ones she'd ever eat. About the first part, at least, he hadn't lied. Thankfully she didn't have long to ponder about how clean the kitchen was. Danny came out carrying a large grease-stained sack and two cans of cola. She unlocked the car. He hopped in, and so did a smell that immediately made her mouth water.

"If those ribs are as good as they smell, I'm already in love."

"Girl, one bite and you'll want to marry these bones."

Mallory laughed hard for the first time in ages.

"Where are we going? You're not going to be able to eat these and drive."

"Somewhere private, where we can talk."

Danny gave her a look. "I know about what. Go up to the light and make a left."

"Only just met me, yet know me so well?"

"Uh-huh."

Mallory's phone rang. Ava. She ignored it, turned off the ringer, and took the phone off the dash. She wanted to talk to her friends now but hoped to have much more to share when the meeting with Danny was over.

Ten minutes later, Mallory pulled into a memorial park. It was a wide-open space with the St. Louis Arch in the background. She was wary at first, but Danny directed her to a spot away from the more touristy area. She rolled down the windows and turned off the car. Danny handed her a paper plate bending under the weight of the food heaped on top of it. For the next several minutes the two exchanged little conversation, focused on spicy baked beans, chunky coleslaw, and meat that fell off of the bone. Danny unabashedly licked his fingers. Mallory followed suit. It was the most relaxed the two had ever been around each other. She hoped the quiet camaraderie would continue. To get a man who lived by the code of the streets to cooperate with the law, she would need it.

She reached into her purse, pulled out two twenties, and laid then on Danny's jeans-clad leg.

"What's this?"

"You pick the spot. I buy the lunch. Remember?"

"You don't have to do that. And it didn't cost forty dollars."

"It could have, and I still would have paid it. You were right. Those ribs were everything."

Danny continued to smile, but his eyes narrowed. "I'm getting the feeling this may be more than payment for ribs. This might be more like a bribe."

"*Moi?*" Mallory batted her lashes and feigned innocence. "I don't plan to bribe you. But I do have news."

"Pete Graham. I saw it. First degree murder."

"When?"

"Just now. On a TV in the rib shack. It interrupted the channel they had it on. Today's breaking news."

"Why didn't you tell me when you got in the car?"

"Wanted to see what you already knew. If that was the reason you brought me here. Obviously not, based on your reaction."

"I knew the indictment had been handed down. They've got some pretty solid evidence."

"Like what?"

"Fingerprints for one. That found Pete's on items collected at the crime scene. But it's far from an airtight case."

"What do you want me to do about it?"

"Testify. I have a confession."

"What?"

"No one else knows about it," she lied, "so don't get upset. But I had to do it."

"What the fuck are you talking about, Mallory?"

"The other night when we were talking, I taped the conversation."

"Bitch! Are you crazy?"

"Danny, calm down."

"Don't tell me to fucking calm down. What the fuck did you tape me for?"

"Habit, mostly. But also to have proof that I wasn't crazy, if only for myself. Which is all it can be, since I didn't tell you beforehand. Recordings made without the other person's knowledge are not admissible in court. There's nothing I can do with the tape, Danny. But there's a lot you can do with the information on that tape.

"Without you and the knowledge that Leigh was pregnant, and was trying to extort Pete for one million dollars, it will be hard to prove motive. The defense can claim they were dating, he ended it, and she was distraught over the breakup and his engagement. Is that really all right with you? That the man who killed one person and tried to kill you gets to live large with no repercussions while you stay in hiding and your son suffers?"

"You leave my son out of this."

"I wish I could, Danny, but he's right in the middle of it. I know about the attempted suicide." Danny's shoulders slumped. "You're not the only one who took a bullet that night. Brandon took one, too. To the heart."

Mallory poured her heart out, but she left Danny still not knowing whether or not he'd testify. It was time to make another call.

Mallory dialed Leigh's mom, Barbara and got voicemail.

"Hello, Barbara. It's Leigh's friend, Mallory. I'm sure you've heard by now that there's been an indictment in Leigh's death. I have some very important information to share with you that's also time sensitive, so if you return the call as soon as possible I'd really appreciate it."

Mallory left her number.

"I can't imagine the pain this development stirs up for your family. I'll be . . . praying for you."

Mallory hung up the phone, surprised at herself and how the message had ended. The words had seemed to come out of their own volition, seemingly appropriate given Barbara's staunch faith. Mallory had never engaged in prayer, but that's not what surprised her. It was more than the fact she'd said the words. Mallory meant them.

30

Atlanta was known for its strip clubs, and tonight following their victory against the Hawks, Christian, Pete, and a group of players were in a generous mood.

"Look at that ass!" Pete exclaimed, licking his lips as the dancer bent over and worked her muscles in a way that made her cheeks clap. He stuck a one-hundred-dollar bill in the glitter-lined crevice and slapped the rump he'd admired.

Christian was having twice the fun with a set of twin dancers. Twins were his guilty pleasure. After watching their acrobatic athleticism on the pole, he decided another, more personal show was in order. Twenty minutes later he and Pete left the club with an entourage of five exotic ladies ready to earn big dollars by dancing on poles outside the club. They reached the stretch limo Hummer with bottles of pricey bubbly and a box of condoms, figuring there was no need to wait to get the party started. They were so caught up in the moment that neither Christian nor Pete noticed the two suited men approaching them or the police cruiser discreetly parked at the end of the block.

The shorter of the two members of law enforcement stepped in front of Christian but looked to his left. "Pete Graham?"

"Yeah," Pete responded, a hard dick and liquid courage cutting his patience short. "Who the fuck are you?"

"I'm the officer who's going to tell you that you're under arrest," he calmly replied, whipping out handcuffs and placing them on Pete before anyone else could react.

"Whoa, wait a minute, guys." Christian was all smiles, his posture relaxed. The twins remained by his side, but the other girls scattered. "There's got to be a mistake somewhere. This is my manager and my uncle. Hold on, officer. You're arresting the wrong man!"

"Hey, Christian," the other officer said, stepping forward. "Good game tonight. Sorry to have to end your evening on such a bad note. But there's no mistake here. Your uncle's under arrest. He's been indicted for the murder of Leigh Jackson."

The short officer took over, all business, as he had been from the start. "You have the right to remain silent. Anything you say can and will be used against you in a court of law." He began leading Pete away. "You have a right to an attorney. If you can't afford it . . ."

"Get your hands off me! Where are you taking me?"

"Where are you taking him?" Christian repeated.

"To jail," the stern one responded. "Where he'll sit until Monday until the judge decides whether or not he'll be granted bail."

Judicially slapped sober, Christian dismissed the twins and called Nick, the name Pete called out before being placed in the cruiser. Nick called Matt Hernandez, one of the highest paid and most successful attorneys in the country. Matt pulled strings, and even though it was a weekend, Pete was out of jail and back in New York in less than twenty-four hours. In that time, a team had been gathered, and the next day, Sunday, Christian's day off, they met at his penthouse.

The group presented a somber tableau—Christian, his dad,

Corbin, Pete, Nick, Matt Hernandez, and Zoey, invited only to have the tools necessary to spin the story for the press. It was Christian's first time seeing Pete since the limousine parting. He hated to ask him in front of everyone, but he had to know.

"Did you do it, Pete? Did you kill that girl?"

Pete's head dropped. His expression remained crestfallen as he looked at Christian. "I can't even believe you'd ask me that."

"But I did. And what you just said is not an answer."

"No, Christian. My arrest is the sole result of the reporter Mallory Knight's sick imagination. She's stirred up a hornet's nest and the public's interest, and now the NYPD feel obligated to conduct a witch hunt and satisfy a mob that's out for blood. I didn't do it."

"But you dated her, though."

"Not really. She was more like a late-night hookup, how do you call it?"

"Booty call?" Zoey interjected.

"Exactly. We had sex a few times. She wanted more. I didn't. I ended it. End of story, okay?"

"Look, don't get pissed at me. You're the one who got indicted, but public opinion has us both convicted. Okay?"

Christian got up and paced. "I know you guys hate Mallory Knight, and I don't like her much either right now. But I can't understand why, out of all of the men in New York, all the athletes even, she chose me to connect to her best friend's murder and what she gave to police convincing enough for them to arrest you."

Matt held up his hands. "Guys, guys. All of those are good questions but not important. The question for the courts isn't whether or not he did it, but whether it can be proven. That's why I'm here. To disprove every piece of evidence the prosecution presents. To delay and discover and postpone this case until we drain the state's pockets and the interest dies down."

"Why go through all that if Pete's innocent?" Corbin asked. "I'd much rather have my name cleared than break the court's bank."

"To send a message," Matt responded. "Let the world know that any time you bring a Graham to court, it's going to cost you. And at the end of the day we're still going to win."

After being somewhat assured that the egregious mistake that was Pete's arrest would be successfully resolved, a very worried Corbin left to update his equally concerned wife about his brother. Pete and Matt went into another room to strategize. Nick left with instructions to find out any and everything he could on Mallory Knight and Leigh Jackson. Christian, drained and sore from last night's brutal two-point loss to the Boston Celtics, prepared to go to the training center for some much-needed therapy. He gathered his things and walked toward the elevator.

Zoey fell in step beside him. "You got a minute?"

"What does it look like?"

Zoey didn't answer, just got into the elevator, too. "I wanted to ask you something, away from the group."

"Yeah?"

"Do you believe him?"

Christian wanted to answer quickly, decisively. He wanted to feel from the pit of his gut that there was no way that his uncle could even be involved in something so nefarious, let alone commit the act himself. He wanted to, but something wouldn't let him. Something he couldn't quite put his finger on but couldn't let go.

"I want to," he finally replied, as the elevator reached the luxury living building's lobby and they stepped out into it. Christian waved at the doorman but stayed by the elevator. "What about you?"

"I want to," she parroted, looking him in the eye with an expression that said she wanted to, but didn't.

"What makes you hesitate?"

"He's not being totally honest."

The doorman took a few steps toward them. "Excuse me, sir. But should I have your car brought around, Mr. Graham?"

Christian didn't look over. "In a minute," he said. And then to Zoey: "How do you mean? He admitted to knowing her, and them having sex."

"They dated, Christian, for at least six months. He was seeing her and Melissa at the same time."

"How do you know?"

Zoey sighed, shoved her hands in her jeans pockets.

"Unh unh. Don't get quiet on me now."

"I feel badly breaking a confidence. I said that I wouldn't."

"What do you know, Zoey? Speak. Now!" It was spoken soft and low, yet with deadly force.

Zoey looked around. "Let's go into one of the meeting rooms." Christian nodded curtly and led her down a short hall.

Zoey followed him into the room and shut the door. "Okay. A few months ago, Pete went to Emma and—"

"Emma? At the center?"

Zoey nodded. "He wanted to borrow money that he said he'd pay back from the proceeds of this year's gala. A lot of money."

"What's a lot?"

"A million dollars."

"What?"

"He told Emma it was for a project happening overseas. Said that you knew about it but insisted rather forcefully that you not be bothered"—she used air quotes—"with the details. Wanted her to transfer the money into an account the foundation had never used before. She hesitated. He pressed her, seemed almost desperate to get the money right away and adamant that you not know about it. Emma was suspicious. Troubled by his actions and concerned about his demeanor. So much so that she reached out to me."

"And you went to him."

"Yep."

"And?"

"He was angry at first, threatened to get Emma fired. When I told him that wasn't going to happen, he changed his demeanor and acted as though the whole thing was no big deal. Said he'd gone to Atlantic City and gambled up a huge debt but had since paid it off. I asked him where he'd gambled, but he wouldn't tell me."

Christian's eyes narrowed. "Around what time did this happen again?"

"Beginning of the year. Just before the gala at Mandarin."

Right around the time that Danny got shot and then disappeared.

"Any of that make sense to you?"

Christian looked at his watch, answered her question with a sigh. "I gotta go."

"Yeah, me too. Pete and Matt are probably looking for me." Christian raised a brow. "Tomorrow's press conference."

"Oh. Right." He pulled her into a hug. "Thanks for pulling me out of the dark, and letting me know what happened."

"You're not angry that I didn't do it sooner?"

"You promised you wouldn't. I understand."

"Are you going to confront him?"

"I don't know, but the more I learn about that girl's murder, the more I want to know the truth."

The next morning, Christian boarded the team plane for Miami and watched the press conference on satellite TV. Pete looked impressive in a tailored navy suit, his boyish handsomeness coming through even on the serious occasion. His wife, Melissa, was by his side, having eschewed her tight miniskirt, deep-vee top, and stiletto uniform for a conservative wrap-around dress in patriotic red, white, and blue. Zoey stood next to her, the consummate professional with her black skirt, white button-down, and blond hair in a bun. But the star of the hour was clearly Matt Hernandez, charismatically handsome, poised, and commanding as he stepped up to the microphone.

"Good morning. My name is Matthew Hernandez. As all of you know I'm here on behalf of my client, Pete Graham, who has been falsely and maliciously accused of the heinous crime of murder, of which he is completely innocent. My client had a brief and casual relationship with the deceased, Ms. Leigh Jackson, but upon meeting and becoming engaged to the lovely Melissa Beckford,"—he motioned to her—"who is now his wife, he promptly ended the relationship with Ms. Jackson. She was quite distraught about the breakup and shortly thereafter was discovered unresponsive in her apartment. The police who arrived on the scene at that time noticed an open bottle of pills, later determined to be opioids, and an empty bottle of wine. It was determined that Ms. Jackson's death was due to an overdose at her own hands.

"We are extremely disappointed in Judge Oppenheimer and the prosecutor's office for cluttering an already overflowing judicial system in this state with this frivolous yet extremely serious accusation and charge. We look forward to our day in court where my client, Pete Graham, and by extension his nephew, Christian Graham, whose life is also being disrupted by these malicious charges, will be fully and totally exonerated, after which we will seek judicial retribution and punishment for those responsible for disrupting the lives of these upstanding, taxpaying citizens. Thank you very much for listening and for understanding that because this is an ongoing case there will be no questions answered at this time."

Christian finished watching and then scrolled the internet

for comments. For the most part, the press was kind, and overwhelmingly on his and his uncle's side. Meanwhile Mallory Knight was being vilified and blackballed after being fired from *New York News*. He leaned over and looked out the window, thinking it was a toss-up as to who would finally be vindicated. Her or his uncle?

31

Three weeks ago, Pamela Johnson boarded an Amtrak train on her way to St. Louis. Today, Mallory Knight returned on a late-night flight, ready to reclaim her spot in the Big Apple. She knew there might be reporters, that she might have to fight and claw past them on the way to the train. Mallory was ready, and up for the fight. After almost two years of climbing uphill someone had believed her and looked at the proof. Pete Graham had been indicted. The nation would learn the truth about how Leigh died. Mallory couldn't imagine what it may have been like for Leigh in those final moments. However it ended, nothing the media threw at Mallory could come close as a match. They had a question? She had an answer. Mallory could all but hear the *Rocky* sound track as she walked up the jetway.

I'm back, you doubting motherfuckers. Bring it on!

The return was anticlimactic. There were no cameras, microphones, or reporters. No one hid in the bushes or waited on the sidewalk in front of her Brooklyn brownstone. There were no glances of recognition or finger pointing. Mallory was relieved yet also strangely disappointed, like she had been spoiling for a fight and reached the playground only to find there was no one to punch. Later Mallory would realize she shouldn't have been worried. She hadn't seen someone watching, but someone had seen her. They'd tipped the press. By the next morning, that had all changed.

Mallory stepped out her front door dressed in a black power suit, a white button-down shirt, and pumps. She was on her way to a meeting with an attorney and a publicist, experts she'd need to handle the media attack she expected, an attack that met her at the front door.

"Mallory! Over here!"

"Mallory Knight!"

"Time for a couple of questions?"

"Ms. Knight! Any comment on Pete Graham's arrest?"

She turned on her heel and held up her hands. "I know how much you all want the story. As a fellow reporter, I truly do." This bought a few chuckles from the half dozen or so gathered around her. "I'm on my way to a meeting, after which I'll be is-suing a public statement. Until then I have no comment. Sorry, guys. Thanks."

Subway-riding Mallory instead hailed a cab and while rid-ing to Manhattan made arrangements with Ava to stay at her house until the hoopla calmed down. When she returned to Brooklyn a couple hours later, the door opened even before she could knock, with both Sam and Ava peeking their head around it.

"Hey, bitches!" They enjoyed a group hug and a few tears. When they disbanded, Mallory really looked at Sam for the first time and got a shock.

"Am I seeing what I think I'm seeing?"

"Yes," Sam said, her smile angelic as she rubbed her stom-ach. "Almost five months."

"Five! I've only been gone one, and you weren't pregnant when I left."

Ava laughed. "Not that we knew of, but the last time you saw this chick she was four months along."

"And you didn't tell anybody?"

"I didn't know," Sam replied. "No morning sickness. No sore breasts. My period's always been irregular, so that wasn't new."

"Then what was the tip-off?"

"Annual doctor visit."

"Do you know what you're having?"

"No. We want to be surprised, but we're hoping to give Joey a little sister."

"Ahh. I'll get to be an auntie once again."

For the next hour or so the friends shared girl talk, a break that Mallory relished from the murder investigation. The reprieve was over all too soon, however, as after leaving a second message Barbara returned her call.

"Sorry I didn't call earlier," Barbara said. "We were out of town at a meeting where my husband was made a bishop. It's been a rather busy time since then. But I did get your message and appreciate your prayers."

"There is still something I'd like to discuss with you, Barbara."

"What's that?"

"It's a rather delicate subject that I'd like to share in person if I could. I'm in Brooklyn right now and could come over any time. Now or whenever would be convenient for you."

"What is this about?"

"It's about Leigh and the trial coming up."

"We won't be participating in that and please, call me Mrs. Jackson."

Mallory was physically taken aback. "Excuse me?"

"Edward and I have talked about it and agreed to steer clear of that matter. Leigh is sleeping in the arms of Jehovah. Nothing that happens in the courts will change that fact."

"I must say your answer totally surprises me, Mrs. Jackson, and has caught me totally off guard. Of course, I respect whatever you and your husband decide. She was your daughter, after all. But I would still like to talk with you, even if your husband can't be there. I believe the information is important, and as a woman and her mother, something you really ought to know."

"Very well then. The bishop has a meeting tomorrow at ten. I'll be free for an hour. You can come over then."

Mallory actually made it to the block at 9:45, time enough to watch Bishop Edward back out of the driveway and head down the street. She felt a better chance of being heard without the stiff stepfather, hoped to appeal to Barbara's instincts as a mother who after learning the whole story would demand justice for her child.

Mallory drove up and parked in front of the home, went to the door and knocked softly. Barbara opened it, looking surprisingly light and happier than Mallory had ever seen her. Given her position over the phone, she shouldn't have been surprised, but Barbara's attitude, considering her daughter's suicide had been reclassified as a murder, chafed Mallory's sensibilities. She'd have to tread lightly.

"Hello, Mrs. Jackson."

"Mallory, come in."

"Thanks for agreeing to see me."

Mallory entered a room of browns and grays that looked comfortable but lacked personality.

"Have a seat, there, on the couch. Can I get you a cup of coffee?"

"That would be great, thanks."

"Cream and sugar?"

"However you're making yours is fine with me."

Barbara returned shortly and joined her on the couch. "Now, Mallory, what do you have to tell me?"

Mallory took a sip of the coffee before placing the cup on a saucer. "Mrs. Jackson, did you know that Leigh was seeing Pete Graham, the man who's been charged with her murder?"

"No, there was very little about Leigh's personal life that I knew about, which, considering that we were opposed to her lifestyle, was probably best." She looked pointedly at Mallory. "And probably best to remain that way."

"I hear you, Mrs. Jackson. I don't know much about your religion but am aware that Leigh's not being a part of it caused tension between you. What I have to share is difficult, and I'm not a mother, so I can't speak personally, but as a daughter, the news I have is something I think you ought to know."

Mallory watched Barbara physically brace herself. She straightened her back and set down the cup. "All right. What is it?"

"Leigh was pregnant, Mrs. Jackson, with Pete Graham's baby. It appears she found out just after he got engaged to another woman who he'd been seeing at the same time as your daughter. He wanted her to have an abortion, but Leigh wouldn't do it. She didn't want to kill her unborn child. We believe that's why he killed her."

"I see." Barbara was silent for a long time, then reached for her coffee and took a sip. "Would you like more coffee?"

More coffee? What? *Am I being punked?*

"Coffee? No, Mrs. Jackson, I don't want any more coffee. I'd like to know how what I just told you makes you feel. Leigh didn't commit suicide. She was murdered. And she was pregnant with your grandchild."

"What proof do you have?"

"Medical records. She was seeing an obstetrician with an office on Long Island, and was approximately eight weeks along."

Mallory watched Barbara swallow several times as if fighting back tears. She sighed deeply and looked out the window. Mallory imagined she saw nothing outside. She imagined she saw Leigh, and imagined her unborn baby. She hoped so, anyway. It would make her more receptive to what Mallory had to ask her.

"The prosecutor's office knows that the defense will deny this. Even with the medical records, they will say that the baby was by someone else, not Pete."

"Well, isn't that possible? When a person engages in that type of behavior with multiple partners, isn't it possible to not know the father of your child?"

"Mrs. Jackson, Leigh was not like that. She flirted and liked to have a good time, but when it came to love, she was very selective, and in the time that I knew her not promiscuous at all. There is a way we can be positive about the father's identity. We can have her body exhumed—"

"Absolutely not."

"It could be done very quietly, and respectfully."

"There is nothing respectful about what you're proposing. I appreciate you were friends with my daughter and respect you doing what you deem necessary regarding her death. But the bishop and I do not share your position, nor that of the courts, and we are ruled by a higher judge." She stood. "You've said what you came to say and finished your coffee. My husband will be returning soon. I wish you well."

Mallory mumbled a goodbye, too shocked to formulate a coherent sentence. She knew Barbara would be hesitant, expected to have to fight the stepfather. But that the mother of a daughter murdered for carrying someone's child would adamantly refuse to seek justice . . . Barbara might not, but Mallory would, by any means necessary.

Mallory returned to Ava's house, settled into an oversized chair and reached for her tablet. While searching the law regarding exhumations and crime, she pondered. *Since Barbara won't consider exhuming the body, can I rob a grave?*

After an hour online, Mallory felt better. She reached for her phone and called Detective Wang.

"Hello, Detective. Mallory Knight. I've got news."

"I'm fine, detective. Thanks for asking. And no, I'm not in the middle of anything. What can I do for you?"

"Sorry about that. How are you? Busy?"

He chuckled. "What's on your mind?"

"I visited Leigh's mother earlier today."

"Oh?"

"Yes. I felt she had a right to know that her daughter was pregnant when she died."

"That's unfortunate."

"Yes, it was. I told her with the hopes that the news would make her amenable to having Leigh's body exhumed so we could test the DNA of the unborn child. I couldn't believe her actions, and you won't either. After hearing that her daughter had more than likely been killed at the hands of the man who'd impregnated her, she calmly took a sip of coffee and asked if I wanted mine refreshed. Detective, you there?"

"You shouldn't have done that."

"Mentioned the exhumation? Yes, I realize that now. It would have been better to give her a couple days to digest the fact that had Leigh lived, she would have been a grand-mother."

"You shouldn't have done any of it. Gone to the house. Mentioned the baby. Anything. By doing so you may have tipped the prosecution's hand and allowed confidential infor-mation to become public."

"I didn't tell the public, detective, I told Leigh's mom. I re-vealed information obtained by putting my career and maybe even my freedom on the line. Information that the prosecution wouldn't have if not for me regarding a case that is only be-cause I forced it. And you helped," she added into the pro-longed lull.

"When I told you that I was thinking about a partner, I wasn't serious. I know Leigh was your friend. I know that you're emo-tionally and professionally invested in this case. I stand behind what I said that day in St. Louis. The investigative work you did was stellar, award-worthy. You did the right thing in turning over that evidence to licensed investigators and the NYPD. But your job is over, Mallory. In order not to jeopardize this case and allow her killer to go free, you've got to back off and let the people who need to, including me, do our jobs."

"Fair enough. I apologize for overstepping my bounds."

"Accepted."

"What are you going to do now?"

"Since you've already antagonized, excuse me, I mean spoken to the mother, and she was not receptive to having her daughter's body exhumed, I'll speak with the prosecutor's office about seeking a court order. Given that our knowledge of the pregnancy was obtained illegally, it's a touchy situation. We're going to need real finesse and a stroke of luck to proceed."

"I might have the stroke you need."

"Mallory . . ."

"I'm not going to do anything more than I've done already. I'm just saying there might be a way to have that evidence entered into the case."

"How?"

"Not sure yet. Let me think about it and get back with you."

"You back to work yet?"

"Not officially. No one will hire me. Living on my savings and 401(k) while I weigh my options and consider my next move."

"Maybe it should be to a community college and a criminal justice class."

"Thanks for the thought, but naw, teaching's not my thing."

"Teaching? Are you kidding me? You need to—"

"Reconsider? Nothing doing. Bye, Wang."

Mallory ended the call and scrolled for Danny's number. She tapped on it and connected the call. It went to voicemail.

She was not deterred. She scrolled down a little farther to Karen's number. Her thumb was hovering over the button to connect it when she changed her mind, reached for her purse and jacket, and headed out the door. There was an old saying that the way to man's heart was through his stomach. Mallory didn't cook, and a heart wasn't what she was after. She needed Danny to cooperate with prosecutors and agree to testify. Maybe the way to get that cooperation was through the mother of a son who idolized him.

32

The meeting with Karen went better than the one with Barbara. The former showing the kind of horrification at why and how Leigh had died that the latter had not possessed. Mallory had considered what Detective Wang said about the importance of protecting the prosecution's trump cards, but the rewards received from sharing the information with Karen had been well worth the risk. She was planning a trip to St. Louis so Danny could see his kids. While there she agreed to talk to him. Hopefully by next week he'd be willing to talk as well.

That out of the way, Mallory secured lodging for the rest of the month and moved out of Ava's apartment. Now tucked away in a spacious Airbnb with views of Jamaica Bay, Mallory tried to relax as she went through the personal items that had been left at her friend's house in her rush to leave town. She turned on her cell phone. After a month unused, dings and vibrations suggested at least a dozen calls. She took a deep breath and began to scroll through the missed calls. One number jumped out at her right away. A call from a couple weeks ago and then several in the past few days. The multiple calls on the screen brought out mixed emotions. One of them was anger, to the point she started not to return the call. But curiosity won out, and she decided not to put it off and wait until tomorrow. It was just after eleven a.m. She dialed the office, Charlie's direct line.

"The dead have arisen," he answered, his voice gruff and raspy.

"Yeah, you tried to kill me, but I wouldn't stay down."

"You were right, Mal. I was wrong. I'm sorry."

"No need to apologize. I was wrong, too. I went against you and ran to a rival paper. You did what you had to, what any boss would have done under the circumstances."

"You're an excellent investigator. Hell, you've got an award to prove it. Your gut instincts have rarely led you wrong. I should have listened to you."

"Yes, you should have. The good news is that somebody finally did."

"Didn't you think it was Christian, though? I was blown away that it was the uncle."

Mallory wouldn't go into details like that. Not on a phone where she might be recorded. And not with a man whom she'd tried to convince but who never believed her. "I thought a lot of things, Charlie. Some were right. Some were wrong. But for the record, I'm glad Christian's name was cleared. The golden boy is still golden, and I know you're glad about that."

"Yeah, all of New York is breathing a sigh of relief."

"You called a bunch of times. Anything besides ass kissing on the agenda?"

"There sure as hell is. I'd like to unfire you, give you back your job."

"Wow, Charlie. I don't know what to say."

"Say that you'll think about it."

"Okay. I'll think about it."

"Other than that, how are you, kid? I was highly pissed off when you went and did what you did, and with Asshole Anderson of all people, for God's sake, but I still genuinely care about you. Not only as a reporter, but as a human being. How are you holding up?"

"There've been good days and bad days, but your phone call has made this day better."

"You reached out to Rob?"

"Is that a trick question?"

"No. I can't imagine you'd let him get away with what he did."

"He will, but I'm not going to dwell on it. Unfortunately, when it comes to writing a piece in a way that avoids the possibility of lawsuits, Anderson taught me everything that I know. It'll be my word against his that what he did was deliberately malicious, or that he intended the outcome to be what it was."

"Sounds like you've already talked to a lawyer."

"Feels like I've become one."

"What about Christian? Have you talked to him?"

"I'm not discussing the Grahams, or anything related to Leigh's murder. With you, or anyone. Nothing personal, but anything related to that situation is off limits."

"Okay. Got it. Then how about them Yankees?"

"Ha! You nut." The line reminded Mallory of how much she loved Charlie, how aside from the later articles about Leigh he'd almost always championed her projects. They spent another thirty minutes talking casually about the business and other news headlines, and what shape the "Knightly News" column would take if Mallory returned.

"Honestly, Charlie, it's hard for me to think about work in that context right now. Until this conversation my professional life was in limbo, and there are other multi-layered matters crowding my brain. Can I think about it and email over a few options in a few days?"

"Sure, Mallory. Take all the time you need. But not too much."

"I appreciate the offer, Charlie. Thanks."

Mallory hung up the phone and after checking the fridge and the time decided it was time to get some fresh air. There were several eateries nearby, but after checking them out she decided to assuage her taste for a Newsroom burger. She texted her friends that she'd be there and hoped they could meet her, then jumped on the subway with visions of grilled onions, green peppers, and mushrooms dancing in her head.

Trepidations arose as she neared her favorite eatery, but Mallory ignored it and reached for the door. For all the years she'd come here, the restaurant had always been a safe haven. She prayed that today it wouldn't let her down. Inside, she was relieved to see the crowd was light, due in part to the hour, just after two. She'd missed the lunch rush and beat the happy hour crowd. Perfect. She relaxed even more as she strode to the bar and sat down.

"Hey, Mallory!"

"Hi, Joe."

"Long time no see."

"I'm sure you've read why."

"I don't believe half the crap I read. Unless it's your column."

"Good answer."

"What can I get you?"

"I've been dreaming of a Newsroom burger with sweet potato fries."

Joe, a part owner of the restaurant, smiled at her mentioning a menu staple he'd helped create. He punched her order into a computer than reached into a cooler for a chilled mug, poured a pale ale from the tap, and slid it over.

"That's the new pairing for the burger. Tell me what you think." Leaning against the bar with his massive arms folded across a chest that easily bench-pressed one-fifty, he watched and waited for her reaction.

Mallory took a sip of the light, fruity beer. "Nice."

Joe nodded. "Better than wine or vodka?"

"Works for me. And you know I'm not a beer drinker, so that's saying something."

"I'm glad you like it. It's good to see you, Mal. You okay?"

"I'm hanging in there."

"Saw that the *News* let you go. We all thought that was fucked up."

"I agree. But I kinda fucked up, too, though, so Charlie had the right."

"By giving the article to the *Reporter*?"

"Exactly that."

"But what Rob did in response to it? That was as under-handed a journalistic move as I've ever seen."

Mallory shrugged. "Made big news. I'm sure it sold a lot of papers. The end justifies the means in the cutthroat world of rags."

"If you say so."

They chatted awhile longer. The computer dinged. "That's your burger. Be right back."

Mallory enjoyed a long swig of beer as she looked around the nearly empty dining room. She wiped a frothy mustache away from her lips as a nice-looking man with windblown hair and a clean-shaven face entered the restaurant, looked around, and headed for the bar.

He sat a couple seats down from her, looked over and said hello.

"Hi."

"Not that many people here. Hope that isn't a sign that the food is lousy."

"No, the food is great."

"Ah, so you've eaten here before."

"Plenty of times."

"Cool. Recommend anything in particular?"

"The Newsroom burger. I took the subway over just to get

my fix." She looked up as Joe came out of the kitchen. "Here it is now. Take a look at that masterpiece. Want to try it?"

"Oh, no. I wouldn't want to take your food."

"There's almost a half-pound of ground round here. Joe, bring me a knife."

He did. She cut off a fourth of the burger, placed it on a napkin, and slid it to the friendly stranger. He took a bite, closed his eyes and groaned.

"You're right. That's insanely delicious."

"Can I get you one, buddy?" Joe asked.

"No, I'm waiting for someone and will just have a beer for now." He nodded at Mallory's glass. "Whatever she's having."

He finished off the slice of sandwich and reached for a napkin. "That was really kind of you to share your food." He extended his hand. "Name's Henry."

"Mallory."

"Mallory Knight?"

Mallory hesitated for the briefest of seconds. "Yes, that's me."

"Wow, that's crazy! I know who you are."

"I take it you've seen the news."

"Actually, no. I just returned from a month out of the country. But I was reading this on the way over." He reached into his jacket and pulled out a large envelope.

"What's that?"

"Take a look. I think you'll find it interesting." Mallory looked skeptical. "Okay, I admit there's parts of it that may piss you off, but overall the piece is pretty evenly balanced.

Curious, Mallory picked up the envelope and reached in to pull out the papers inside.

The man stood up. "Then again, balanced is a matter of perspective. Mallory Knight, you've been served."

"Henry" was halfway to the door before Mallory could react. He reached the door and turned around. "Thanks again for sharing your burger. It was really good."

Bites of said burger began to roil in her stomach as she looked at the document the envelope had contained. She was being sued by Christian, Pete, and one of their companies for libel, slander, and character assassination and defamation.

Just like that, her appetite was gone, replaced by a lawsuit for one hundred million dollars.

After recovering from the shock of a) being sued and b) for how much, Mallory got busy assembling a legal dream team. Two days later she stood in front of a podium in the conference room of her attorney, Valerie Kau, who had taken the case pro bono, flanked by the feminist lawyer and activist on one side and her new publicist, Micah Shore, on the other. A select group of twenty journalists had been invited to the press conference, Ava among them. Her best friend sat front and center, an anchor for Mallory, who gripped the sides of the podium and met many of the eyes trained on her steadfastly. Repositioning the prepared speech that lay before her, she took a breath, squared her shoulders, and spoke.

"Good afternoon, and thanks for coming. My name is Mallory Knight. I am an investigative journalist specializing in the unsolved murders and disappearances of women across the United States, particularly women of color, whose stories are often overlooked or ignored. Almost two years ago, I was shocked and saddened to arrive at a crime scene as I'd done dozens of times before, and recognize the woman lying on the bed before me, grotesquely displayed amid a scene set up to suggest a suicide had occurred. There was only one problem. I knew that woman, a journalist also. Beautiful, intelligent, vivacious, driven. Not only a capable journalist but my best friend. One who would not go outside without lipstick, much less take her life without clothes.

"As most of you know by now, the death was rather quickly ruled a suicide. I knew with every instinctive fiber of my being that they were wrong. That Leigh Jackson had been murdered. But at least on the surface and on the face of things, there was no proof. Now, there is.

"Because the NYPD initially ruled her death a suicide, I was limited professionally to the coverage I could give on this story. As a serious journalist, I hesitate to print conjecture. 'Just the facts, ma'am,' is often our bottom line. I was driven to keep the story going, and her memory alive in the public mind, but seeing as there was no case it was a difficult, if not impossible challenge. The *New York News*'s illustrious editor, Charlie Callahan, was brave enough to allow a couple of articles, and I thank him for that opportunity, but there was only so much I could do in that professional capacity.

"So I opened my own investigation. I followed my gut and the crumbs of evidence found along the way. I worked with a couple other people who also had doubts and followed their instincts. The path led to New York Navigator Christian Graham's uncle and manager, Pete Graham, who was indicted for her murder.

"I have not been shy in my coverage and reporting of events surrounding the death and investigation of Leigh Jackson. Much of what has printed has been my opinion. When possible, I've cited facts. Everything I've written has been within the scope of the law as it pertains to journalism and the coverage of public figures in national news. Still, earlier this week, I was served with papers naming me, Rob Anderson, and the *New York Reporter* in a lawsuit for one hundred million dollars."

Reporters had been casually writing and typing as she talked. With this news, the scribbling increased, along with the pecking on tablets and keyboards.

"Pete Graham is innocent until proven guilty, and regarding these charges, I am innocent—period. I will fight these false accusations as vigorously as I worked to uncover who killed Leigh. My sole purpose in trying to keep the story of

Leigh's death alive was to see her killer be prosecuted and imprisoned. To get justice for a woman who didn't deserve to die. Again, Pete Graham is innocent until proven guilty. But for whomever killed my friend and fellow journalist Leigh Jackson, I hope they die in prison and then rot in hell."

Attorney Valerie Kau then stepped up to the microphone, adjusted it to her height of five foot one, and then asked, "Any questions?"

There were many, most of which pertained to the case and couldn't be answered. But the next morning Mallory smiled at the front-page headline in the *New York News*—short, sweet, and true:

Knight Fights!

33

May had arrived and with it the Eastern regional finals. It hadn't been easy over the past month, but with discipline and focus honed since he was fifteen years old, Christian was able to force Pete's indictment and the media circus that followed out of his mind and focus on work. The effort paid off. The Navigators had fought their way to a place at the table, going up against the Miami Heat. The last team standing would meet up with the Western regional winners. In Christian's mind that would likely be Golden State. He didn't care who was on the other side of the tip-off when the finals began. The Navigators would beat them. That had been Christian's mind-set all year. He'd never entertained losing one time. The only picture he'd envisioned was winning it all. For Christian, losing was not an option in any area of his life.

He would have chosen otherwise, but game one wasn't happening at home. The team had traveled to Miami the night before. To make sure he was not distracted by anyone or anything, Christian had passed on staying at the designated hotel and rented a private home on the beach for him and his entourage. Besides the usual practice, physical therapy, and training, Christian's routine for the finals included meditation and yoga. By the time he got to the arena he was calm and relaxed.

When they gathered in the locker room, all the guys looking at the captain who had led them to this decisive moment, Christian spoke with the authority of a king and the certainty of a sage.

"Here we are, fellas. Heading down the last lap of our race with destiny. We already know how it's going to end. We're already holding up the trophy and feeling the confetti on our face. All we need to do is stay focused, remember what we've practiced, and have each other's back for forty-eight seconds.

"We're in Miami, but tonight, this arena's our house. The court's the same size. The net's the same distance from the floor. And we're the same badass muthafuckas who've won this bitch eight times. Let's go out there and do it again!"

The speech worked. The men went out determined to set the tone for what they hoped would be a conference sweep in just five games.

That's not what happened.

The Navigators lost, and badly.

Afterward, Christian didn't want to talk with anyone. He wanted to be alone to figure out what the fuck had happened from them being up by five at the end of the first half to him fouling out and them losing by fourteen points less than an hour ago. He wanted to punch walls, and maybe a few people. But he didn't do any of that. He had a responsibility. So he followed his coach into a packed room for the mandatory press conference to a barrage of camera flashes and questions that started almost before he sat down.

"Christian, what happened?"

"What do you mean, what happened? We lost, that's what happened. Did you not see the game? Or the score?"

"Sorry for being so general, Christian. You guys came out firing on all cylinders in the first half but struggled overwhelmingly in the second. What factors led to the two halves being so different?"

Christian took a sip of water and leaned into the microphone on the table. "We lost our focus. Became impatient. Got into foul trouble. Got off our game and started playing theirs."

"Speaking of foul trouble, Christian, you've only fouled out of a game twice this whole year. It was clear that Navigator fans felt you were being singled out by the officials. Do you agree with them?"

"I'm not going to sit here and blame our loss on anyone outside of our locker room. No matter what anyone else does, at the end of the day I am the master of my fate. If we'd won, I wouldn't be blaming the officials for that. So win, lose, or draw, I am always going to accept responsibility for what happened."

There were a few other questions about Christian's performance and that of his teammates. When the organizer signaled there was just time for two more questions, Christian chose a reporter with whom he wasn't familiar, a pretty young woman with an engaging smile.

"Hello, Christian. Tough loss tonight. Many would say that considering everything happening in your life outside of the arena, it's impressive that the Navigators are here at all. What impact has your uncle's indictment had on your ability to keep your head in the game?"

Christian fell back against the chair. "Next question."

"That's a fair one," another reporter said. "Along with the foul trouble there were several shots that while impossible for most have up until this point been makeable for you. It's a fair assumption that your uncle being accused of murder would have an impact."

"Doesn't seem like I need to answer the question, then. You already have it all figured out." Christian stood up and walked out. When his coach walked into the locker room a few minutes later, he had only one thing to say before he went back to the house.

"That's my last press conference until the championship, the one that we win."

Video from the press conference went viral. The young reporter, who happened to be an intern for ESPN, was dismissed by the network and vilified by the public. Christian thought it a fair outcome. He felt that she'd asked the question to stand out, make a name for herself. She'd done that.

Christian used the anger at losing game one in the conference to raise his game to another level. Changes were also made when it came to outsiders and access. A wall of protection was built around him. From that interview until game seven of the NBA Finals, he didn't go anywhere alone. On the rare moments he'd gone out publicly, his entourage protected him as fiercely as his bodyguards, two of whom were also with him at all times. There was slight concern that some misguided fan might try and hurt New York's savior. But the bigger reason for the stalwart efforts to provide him sanctuary was basketball. The love of the game.

Game seven happened at home, in New York, in the Navigators' arena that Christian had built. Tickets were advertised online and sold for six figures. Every A-list celebrity was in the house. All eyes were on Christian.

He didn't disappoint. The Navigators won. After that, everything changed. Christian Graham was god again. Leigh's murder? Pete's indictment? Forgotten.

34

After the press conference with her celebrated activist attorney and powerhouse publicist, Mallory had felt hopeful, even fairly confident that the defamation lawsuit would be dropped within months and that Pete's trial would begin shortly thereafter. There were newspaper articles and requests for radio and television interviews, one from a well-known national talk show host. There seemed to be renewed interest in not only how Leigh died but who was she before that. The woman. The journalist. Mallory felt she was finally getting the type of treatment that should have happened all along, that the lie of Leigh being a woman distraught enough to commit suicide was being replaced by the truth of her strength.

Mallory even became something of a media darling. Women and men alike admired her loyalty to friendship. Women sympathized with what Mallory felt was a misrepresentation of her character with the defamation lawsuit. She went back to work, and instead of a singular focus on serious topics with "Knightly News," she and Charlie decided to expand her platform with a segment called "Mallory Matters." There was a meeting with a cable network where discussions were held about a combination news and lifestyle show with the same name. She moved back into her brownstone and became a regular again at Newsroom. Two months of happiness.

Then the Navigators won the championship. Made history. And everything changed.

Overnight, interview requests dried up. The cable TV company changed their mind. She remained at *New York News*. Charlie remained her advocate. But where "Mallory Matters" had started with promise, tons of emails, responses, interest, once June arrived and the Navigators won the championship, it seemed that all of New York and the world came under a spell and Christian Graham was the magician. Mallory wasn't totally immune to the magic. She woke up one morning and a year had passed. The defamation lawsuit was dormant but still on the table. But Pete's trial had been granted its third delay, and Mallory had a feeling that when it came to this tactic, the defense team was just getting started. Life hadn't proceeded according to her plan, and she wasn't happy about it.

That's what Mallory found herself telling her mother during a late-night call on yet another Saturday night when she had nobody. And yes, she'd just gotten paid.

"It's just not fair, Mom. It's been a year since the indictment was handed down. Over two years since Leigh was murdered. But the Navigators won the championship, and it's like the entire judicial system got amnesia. Nobody remembers. Nobody cares. I can't take it!"

"Mallory, hon. I'm worried about you."

"Don't be. I'm a big girl. I'll get through it. It may take therapy and prescription drugs, but I will be sure to keep it together until the trial at the very least."

"And then?"

"What do you mean?"

"I don't want to upset you further than it sounds like you might be already. But have you given all of the possible outcomes due consideration? Like the trial taking five, ten years to happen? Of Pete not being convicted? What will you do if that happens? What will your life be like if you do all this work, make all of these strides, win all of these victories, and the outcome remains unchanged?

"Mallory, you are an incredible young woman. Over the past year I feel I've gotten to know you in a way that I didn't and, quite frankly, it's a shame. But your tenacity, your perseverance, the way you champion a cause, is admirable. The one big concern that I have, however, is that this situation has consumed so much of your life, and when it's over the void will seem as wide as the Grand Canyon, one that may seem impossible to fill. And then what?"

"I don't know, Mom. I've tried to block out the possibility of him not being convicted."

"But it is a possibility. One that you need to reconcile your feelings with so that if it indeed happens, you will be okay."

"Okay? How do you propose I do that?"

"By knowing that no matter what happens, you've done everything in your power to get justice for Leigh. To honor her by embracing the life she was robbed of. By living your every moment, every second of your life. Fully. Completely. With no regrets. By finding a way to be happy. I don't know much about your friend, Leigh Jackson. But from what you've told me and what I've read it's what she would do, and what she would want for you."

Mallory thought long and hard about what Jan said. In doing so she realized that for the past year that was the lesson life had been trying to teach her. Her friends, too. Not verbally, but by their actions. After years of complaining that there were no good men, Ava was almost six months into a relationship with a guy from Chicago that she met online. Their main communication had gone from in person to by text and email as she commuted back and forth between New York and the Windy City where he owned a hair products company and a string of successful barbershops.

Sam's daughter, Jasmine, was almost walking, her family of four now taking up much of her time. Mallory visited her every now and then, but more and more they had less and less in common. What she realized, after hours of deep, authentic contemplation, was that Jan was right. Life was passing by, with or without her. Whether convicted or acquitted, Pete's life would go on. In that moment, Mallory decided that hers would, too. Help in jumpstarting that life would come from the unlikeliest of persons.

Mallory went online and after searching a variety of options decided to get into something she hadn't enjoyed since college. Two weeks after the conversation with Jan, she walked into a cycling class. Five minutes later the instructor arrived.

It was Zoey Girard.

To leave in that moment would have been too conspicuous, but seconds after the final song ended, Mallory slid off the bike, grabbed her things, and made a beeline for the exit.

She got about halfway down the hallway before her name was called out.

"Mallory, wait." She didn't. Zoey hurried to catch up with her. "Mallory!"

"Look, I had no idea that was your class. Don't worry. I won't be back." She started walking again.

Zoey placed a hand on her arm. "I'm glad you didn't leave."

"Why?"

"I don't consider you the enemy. Yes, I'm Christian's publicist and as such his protector, too. I admit to warning him about you, and blocking your attempts to contact him. Knowing that you were an investigative journalist, I always felt there was an ulterior motive. And there was."

"That's not quite true."

"How do you dare stand here and say that?"

"Because interviewing Christian was not my idea and when it happened, I wasn't sure who killed Leigh. But she was a huge Navigator fan and I knew she'd met Christian. And even though she denied it, I thought they'd dated. So when the opportunity presented itself to get more information, I did. My best friend had been murdered. And nobody gave a damn. Each time another tidbit got dropped, I followed the trail."

"I can't say that I agree with your methods, but I don't blame you for defending your friend."

Mallory didn't know what to say. So she said nothing, just turned and started walking toward the door.

"I'm here every Saturday," Zoey called out after her. "And most Tuesdays and Wednesdays, too. Come back and in no time, I'll have you in shape."

Mallory didn't respond. She didn't go back. A week later Zoey called her.

"Look, Zoey. I appreciate what you said the other day. I don't hate you, either. But considering the circumstances and the plethora of cycling classes, I think my attending another one is best."

"Okay. I hope you change your mind, but I get your point. But the class isn't the only reason I called you. Have you ever been to Kansas City?"

Mallory was immediately defensive, believing she was finally going to learn the reason behind Zoey's perceived kindness.

"Why, have you?"

"Hundreds of times. Used to spend summers there as a kid, all the way until high school."

"Hmm."

"Anyway, I was there a while back at this club with my cousin. I saw this woman about your height and complexion. She had a little different style, though. A little funkier. Wore these long braids. But I swear she could have been your twin."

"My relatives live in Omaha," was Mallory's noncommittal answer.

"Well, look at that," Zoey said. "Something in common."

She hung up, no goodbye, in the brusque, businesslike way with which Mallory was familiar. The following Tuesday Mallory went back to Zoey's cycling class. Six months later, Zoey had kept her word. Mallory was in the best shape of her life.

Little by little, Mallory's life changed. It became more balanced. She kept in touch with Sam and Ava but made new friends. Several months after that, while Mallory was busy minding her business, something else happened. The judge came down on Pete Graham's defense team, called them out on their tactics and set a date. Almost three years after Leigh Jackson was murdered, her case was going to trial.

35

Some had advised her against attending, felt her presence would detract from the justice she sought. But when the trial for the case of the *State of New York vs. Peter Franklin Graham* got underway, Mallory was an invested spectator in a jam-packed Manhattan courtroom.

The first two weeks were brutal. The prosecution presented evidence. The expert defense team dismantled it with the precision of a Swiss army knife. Expert witnesses battled against each other. And the worst news? Prosecutors had failed to submit evidence creating probable cause for the court to grant an order demanding the exhumation of Leigh's remains, which made the fact she'd been pregnant when she died and that Pete was believed to have been the father inadmissible evidence. Mallory had reached out to Leigh's parents. So far, they had not attended the trial.

By week three the defense filed a motion to dismiss. The judge denied it but admonished the prosecution that if no witnesses were brought to add to what had already been presented, they needed to rest their case. That Thursday, for the first time since the trial began, Mallory didn't walk into the courtroom alone. A newly engaged Ava, back for a visit after having relocated to Chicago, sat beside her.

"Look at his smug ass," Ava whispered, shooting daggers that should have pierced the back of Pete's neck and those of his defense team. "Sitting there as though he's in a business meeting instead of on trial."

"It is business," Mallory responded. "And he's got good reason to be confident. I hate to say it, Ava, but the prosecution is no match for that guy's dream team. I know they're lying. They know they're lying. But in our court system it's not what you know. It's what you can prove."

"All rise."

The buzz of conversation dwindled as the judge entered and the bailiff announced that court was once again in session. The prosecution was asked to call their first witness of the day to the stand.

Alex Weiner, the astute, well-educated prosecutor who with any other defense team might have already won the case, stood.

"Your honor, the prosecution calls Charles Callahan to the stand."

Mallory's jaw dropped. She'd begged the attorneys to let her testify, to at the very least be a character witness for her friend. But they'd declined her offer, believing that putting her on the stand and opening her up to the defense's cross-examination was too much of a risk. That would have opened up the door for the defamation suit to be mentioned, which would have weakened Mallory's credibility and by extension the prosecution's case. But Charles could tell the jury what she'd told him!

Ava leaned over. "Did you know?" she whispered. Mallory shook her head. "Brilliant."

Charles was sworn in and took the stand. Mallory had a feeling he knew exactly where she sat, but he looked straight ahead, determined yet slightly vulnerable. It struck Mallory that this was the first time she'd seen Charlie in a subordinate position. For the second time in her life, she said a prayer.

The questions began.

"Mr. Callahan, what is your position?"

"I'm the senior editor for the *New York News*."

"Did you know the victim, Leigh Jackson?"

"No, I did not."

"Did you know of her?"

"Yes."

"Prior to the media attention surrounding this trial, what did you know about her?"

"Objection, your honor. Irrelevant."

"Overruled."

"Go ahead, Mr. Callahan."

"I knew she was a journalist who was found dead in her apartment, at the time deemed the apparent victim of suicide."

"How did you obtain this information?"

"It was reported on in our paper by one of our investigative journalists, Mallory Knight."

"How long have you known Ms. Knight?"

"I've known her work for about seven years, and her personally for five."

"In the time that you've known her, would you describe her to be a capable journalist?"

"Much more than capable. She's an award-winning investigator. One of the best in her field."

"Objection, your honor," the defense groaned as if becoming ill with the line of questioning.

"Overruled," the judge said. But then to the prosecutor, "Get to the point with this witness."

Weiner nodded. "Did there become a time when your opinion changed as to how you believe the victim, Leigh Jackson, died?"

"Yes."

"When was that, and why?"

"It was several months following her death. My employee, Mallory Knight, was writing a series on unsolved murders and questionable deaths. She came to me with what she believed were inconsistencies in Jackson's official cause of death from what she'd seen."

"What she'd seen?"

Charlie nodded.

"Verbalize your answer," the judge said.

"Yes. Because of the series Mallory was often alerted when a murder was suspected. She was called the morning of Ms. Jackson's death and went to the scene."

The defense attorney stood. "Your honor, may we approach the bench?"

They did. Mallory couldn't hear what was said, but from the look on the prosecutor's face whatever it was wasn't good. He conferred with his partners before addressing the court. "I have no further questions."

Matt Hernandez stood and slowly approached Charlie, his very countenance that of supreme confidence and legal expertise of the highest order.

"Did you join your employee, Mallory Knight, at the home of the deceased, Ms. Jackson?"

"Excuse me?"

"Were you there, Mr. Callahan, in the home of the deceased Ms. Jackson, at the time the death was investigated?"

"No."

"How were you able to corroborate your employee's account of what happened, what she told you she saw that convinced her that the police officers and detectives trained and licensed in such capacities were wrong in their assessment and she was right?"

"It wasn't a matter of—"

"I'm not asking for what wasn't. I'm asking for what was. What was the method you used to corroborate your employee's story at the time her piece on Ms. Jackson was printed?"

"It wasn't fact-checked, if that's what you're asking."

Matt turned toward the jury. "It wasn't fact-checked. A major, legitimate newspaper in one of America's largest cities allowed their employee to run an article as one would run their mouths without knowing what they were talking about, and appear on the printed page as fact when, in fact, it was not fact-checked. This witness is done."

"Objection," the prosecution said, after shooting up from the chair. "That was a leading comment designed to—"

"Sit down, attorney Weiner. Objection overruled."

The morning continued with the ducks lining up in the defense's favor, no more so than when Christian entered the courtroom and a recess had to be called to reestablish order. By the end of the morning Ava began preparing Mallory for the very real likelihood that Pete would be acquitted. Remembering her mother's words, Mallory considered the possibility. The mere thought made her heart hurt.

"Your honor, the prosecution would like to call a surprise witness."

"Your honor," Matt began, smiling condescendingly at Weiner, "with the time we've had to prepare this trial, there should be no surprise witnesses."

"He's feared for his life, your honor, and has only recently agreed to be a witness for the prosecution."

"That doesn't matter, judge. The defense must be given advance notice."

"You're being given notice now!"

The courtroom buzzed with spectator comments. The judge hit his gavel. "Attorneys, approach the bench."

After a couple moments of heated whispered exchanges, the judge announced that he would allow the witness.

"The prosecution calls Daniel Groves to the stand."

Mallory's head jerked up. *No, it couldn't be.*

From the moment Danny started talking, Matt's cockiness began to drain away. Danny testified that Leigh had asked Pete for a million dollars to keep their affair a secret from his new wife. When the prosecutor suggested the testimony could be corroborated by an employee at Christian's Kid Foundation, the defense called for a recess. When they returned it was with a plea deal for murder in the second degree.

Just like that, it was over. Peter Graham pleaded guilty to second-degree murder and received a twenty-year prison sentence with the stipulation that at least ten years had to be served before he was eligible for parole.

Pandemonium broke out in the courtroom. The judge repeatedly struck his gavel, to no avail. To Mallory it sounded like the beat for a one-word rap. Guilty. Guilty. Guilty.

36

Christian had always done everything possible to not wind up in prison. Yet here he was, preparing to walk into the Eastern Correctional Institute to visit the uncle who'd been more like a brother for Christian's whole life. An uncle in prison for taking a life. The whole situation felt unreal. Usually visitors met inmates in a communal visiting room. Because of Christian's high profile, however, and a few hundred types of green encouragement, the warden made an exception and allowed Christian and Peter to visit in a private room with a guard present. Just being behind the fence made Christian uncomfortable, yet he maintained a casual conversation with the remaining guard while another brought his uncle from the cellblock.

A few minutes later the door opened, and a handcuffed Peter walked through with the guard just behind him. Christian worked hard to mask his surprise. He'd only been behind bars a couple months, but his uncle had aged ten years. No words were exchanged as the guard removed the handcuffs and Peter walked to where Christian now stood by the chair.

"One brief hug," the guard who'd waited with Christian informed them.

"I'll be just outside this door," the other warned, as if

Christian were going to play Superman and try to bust his uncle out of a maximum-security facility.

The two men shared a strong embrace. Both sets of eyes were damp as they sat at the round table across from where the guard stood, giving them a modicum of privacy.

"How are you, man?" Christian finally said.

"What can I say? This isn't the Four Seasons."

"No."

"It's a shithole, Christian. I need to get transferred out of here. They're all a bunch of animals. Trying to extort me, I'm in fear of my life."

"Maybe you should have thought about that before."

"Before what? You don't believe what happened in that crooked courtroom? I pled guilty because the lawyers forced me to, not because I am."

"Save it, Pete."

"I'm not lying. Ask Matt. Somebody got to Danny and paid him off to lie on the stand. I was looking at a very real chance of life without parole."

"Danny lied, huh? What about that tape? Were you lying on that? Were you lying when you told that girl you'd come up with the five million she was asking for?"

"Her plan had been to blackmail me all along. I think it had been Danny's idea, and the two of them were in on it together."

"Oh, really."

"Damn right. I know you have a soft spot for that criminal because of his son, but believe me when I tell you, he's bad news."

Christian's eyes were sad as he looked at his uncle. "I admired you, man. Looked up to you my whole life. Dad always had doubts about you working with me, but I defended you at every turn. Who better to work for you than family, someone who's known you from the time you were born."

"I'm still that man."

"You're the man in here that you were on the outside. Not the one I imagined, but the one who showed up when I wasn't around. The one who felt the heat when Danny wanted to sell you that tape and tried to borrow money from the organization."

"What? I—"

"The one who made the payment with a gold sculpture instead, only Danny didn't believe the value you told him. Surprised I know about that, huh? They didn't even get to present that evidence in court. Or the missing piece you gave Leigh, worth almost forty thousand. Even though she was a woman you barely knew."

Pete jumped to his feet. "I don't know who you've been listening to, but I won't sit here and listen to those lies come out of your mouth. Guard, I'm ready to go back to my cell."

Pete walked over to where the guard was. When the door was open for him to be led back to his cell, Pete did not look back.

Christian watched him, as a single tear ran down his cheek. For the uncle he loved and the murderer he knew, it would be the only one he shed.

The week after Pete's plea deal, Mallory entered the cycling class unsure of what to expect. If Zoey was upset about what had happened, it didn't show. She acknowledged Mallory when she entered the room and conducted the class with the same mixture of cheerleader and drill sergeant that she had all the others. Her actions didn't change until the end of the class, when she walked over and asked, "Can I buy you a drink?"

Zoey didn't drink alcohol, so Mallory joined her at the publicist's favorite juice bar and at her suggestion ordered a mean green drink that Zoey swore would add years to Mallory's life. They settled into a table by the window and for the first few moments watched the pedestrians hurrying to the rest of their lives.

"I assume there's a reason you wanted to buy me a drink," Mallory said at last.

"To offer my congrats."

Mallory paused, looked up. "You're congratulating me for helping to put away your client's manager and uncle?"

"You didn't put away anyone. Pete did himself in when he decided to play God and become the dispenser of life and death. You did what needed to be done, what I wanted to see happen."

Zoey had Mallory's full attention. "Wait, you knew Leigh? You knew Pete killed her?"

Zoey shook her head. "I didn't know her, but I knew they dated. Saw them in a rather compromising position one night and asked him about it. He denied it, then downplayed it. Always bothered me that he'd make such a big deal. When she died, it bothered me even more. And then when the indictment was handed down and he lied to Christian, I knew there was more to the story. I also knew that if anyone could get to the bottom of the sordid mess and uncover the truth, it was you. The Prober's Pen winner: Mallory Knight."

"You knew about me before the media blowup?"

"I'd read your series, 'Why They Disappear, Why They Die.' That's why when you first contacted me about interviewing Christian, I was suspicious and leery of your motives. I thought you suspected him of having something to do with Leigh's death, and I didn't believe that wasn't true. I was ready to do whatever I had to do to protect him. At the same time, I wanted your help in finding out what was going on with Pete, who I never trusted because he was jealous of Christian. That's why . . ."

Zoey paused, looked at Mallory and then looked away.

"That's why what?"

"That's why I accused you of drinking the Kool-Aid and becoming another worshipper at Christian's throne."

"The anonymous emails. It was you."

"The way fans worship Christian is almost the way he viewed his uncle. There was no way I would have been able to convince him that Pete was capable of anything close to what actually happened. But I knew that you could. I also thought that you and I were a lot alike and that if I goaded you in just the right way, you'd be like a dog with a bone and not stop until you knew the truth. I was right."

"I spent months trying to figure out who was behind those anonymous emails. They were different than the other mail I received. But after Rob exposed me and in turn exposed Christian, you sent a congrats. Why, since you knew he was innocent?"

"Because I knew if they shined the spotlight on Christian, they'd see the blood on Pete's hands."

"You may not drink alcohol but after everything you told me just now, I need a shot."

The two walked a few blocks to a small, neighborhood bar. They talked for hours, almost closed down the place, finding out that they were more alike than different, and understanding that, while it had appeared otherwise for almost three years, all along the two had been on the same team.

37

Mallory rushed around her apartment, performing last-minute straightening in an already immaculate living room. She stopped short of chiding herself for being nervous. It wasn't every day her dad came for a visit. In fact, it had never happened before. Not when she lived in Omaha with her mom, stepfather, and half sister. Not even when she chose the University of Missouri at Columbia to get her journalism degree, a choice she now admitted was made in part due to its proximity to the Gateway City and her father just one hundred and twenty-five miles away. The hidden blessing found in her St. Louis hideout just months before was the time it allowed her to spend with a man she hardly knew and bond with the half brother she'd seen only a handful of times. It was going to be hard leaving New York and her beloved Brooklyn brownstone, harder still to leave the paper where she'd made a name for herself in less than ten years. But for every door she was closing, she believed another one would open. Doors to her future and to her past. Doors to the family that, in recent years, she'd all but ignored. Family that she now knew meant much more than she'd ever realized, or admitted. Family that she wanted to know again, to love again, and to feel their love.

Mallory had spent half of her life in denial during the contentious relationship that began when Jan divorced her father. The threat of an opportunity for restoration had thawed the icy relationship shared with her mother. Hopefully this visit and her relocation back to the Midwest would be the foundation for a meaningful relationship with her dad.

The phone face lit up on a nearby table. Melvin was in a taxi and on his way. The airport was at least a thirty-minute ride this time of day. Mallory walked to the fridge to see what kinds of drinks there were to offer. Milk. Flat soda. Old wine. *Lovely.* She reached for the wine and soda bottles, poured them into the sink. Time for a trip to the corner grocer. Tonight's plans were dinner and a Broadway show, but it would be good to have something to snack on in case Melvin was famished. She pulled out her debit card, slipped it into her back pocket, and reached for her sunglasses and house keys. Just as she neared the foyer, the doorbell rang.

Dad? Maybe so. Mallory had assumed he'd texted from the airport, but they could have been in transit. A mixture of excitement and anxiety played ping-pong in her stomach as she reached the door. She put her hand on the knob and out of habit took a quick peek through the side pane before she opened the door.

She snatched her hand from the knob as though it were on fire. *Christian.*

The doorbell rang again.

She set her jaw, squared her shoulders, and opened it. "What are you doing here?"

"I tried to call. Left a couple messages."

"How'd you know where I lived?"

"Couple phone calls. Wasn't hard."

"What do you want?"

"To talk about what happened."

"I don't think you and I have anything to talk about.

Besides, I was just headed out." She stepped outside and turned to lock the door.

"I think he did it."

Her hand paused with the key in the lock. Her shoulders slumped, but she didn't turn around.

"I think my uncle aided in your friend's death. Or caused it." Mallory looked back and saw the sincerity in Christian's eyes. "I'm sorry it happened and was hoping to talk with you to try and better understand what happened, why it happened, anything at all."

"I'm expecting company."

"I understand."

"But I've got a couple minutes." She opened the door and held it so that Christian could come inside. He followed her into the living room. She sat down and motioned for him to have a seat, too. She thought about offering him a drink, then remembered she had nothing. Probably best. This wasn't a social call.

"What made you finally believe it?"

"Pete."

"He admitted it?"

"More like the guilt was in what he wouldn't say." Christian told her about his recent prison visit and the coded conversation he and his uncle had shared. "I still don't understand why."

"She was pregnant."

Christian visibly started. "What?"

Mallory remained calm. "I believe the baby was his."

"Are you sure?"

She nodded. "You can ask Danny. He heard it all. Those pricey lawyers you paid for successfully fought to keep out the evidence. They were further aided by Leigh's parents' unwillingness to disturb her 'sleep' "—Mallory used air quotes—"by having her body exhumed. Had we done that, I believe the evidence would have been allowed and would have provided conclusive proof that Leigh was pregnant with your uncle's child at the same time his new wife was also preparing to have a baby."

Christian sat forward, put his head in his hands. "This situation is beyond fucked up."

"Tell me about it."

"You don't understand." Christian's jaw was set, the words spoken as though it hurt to do so. "Melissa slept her way through half the NBA before snagging Pete and turning him out. Word on the street was she never stopped screwing around. My family doubts the baby is his, but Pete is too in love to have the boy tested."

"Then you can't be sure the baby isn't his."

"No, but I do recognize that the older he gets, the more he looks like a dude that plays for the Hawks."

"Good Lord. In some ways, I guess this is as hard on you as it is on me."

"I can't even tell you what acknowledging the truth has done. When I was growing up, Pete was everything to me, at times even more than my dad. He was the brother I never had, an alibi when I needed one, and my first best friend. It's killing me to know that he's where he belongs and that there is nothing I can do."

Christian placed his head in his hands once again. Mallory watched him take a couple deep breaths before his shoulders began shaking. Instinctively she walked over to him, placed a hand on one of the shaking shoulders. Christian's arm snaked around her waist and brought her down to his knees. She didn't resist, but sat on his legs and wrapped her arms around the broadest shoulders she'd ever felt. She squeezed and whispered, "I'm sorry."

Two words that broke a dam. Christian bowed his head. Silent tears plopped on her exposed arm. She held him tighter, blinked back her own tears. His arms held her tighter, then slid to her shoulders. He lifted his head. She looked down. Sensuality seeped into the sadness. He lifted his head. She lowered hers.

Ding-dong.

The bell snapped Mallory out of a Christian-induced fog. An urgent whisper. "My dad." She slid off his lap, straightened her clothes, and wiped her eyes. Christian stood, too, suddenly embarrassed.

"Sorry about that. Emotions got away from me."

"No need to apo—"

"Where's your bathroom?"

It was as though Mallory could literally see a door close. The vulnerable, feeling basketball star had been pushed back into the closet, replaced by a man fully in control.

"Down the hall to your right."

The doorbell rang again. "Coming!"

She rushed to the door and opened it. "Hi, Dad."

"Hello there."

She pulled him into an embrace. Harder than she'd intended, longer than she'd planned.

He stepped back. "You okay?"

"Fine. Excited!" She forced a big smile on her face and looked at the carry-on bag he held by the handle. "That all you brought?"

"That and my horn." He stepped back and retrieved the case leaning against the building, then passed by her and entered the home, looking around the whole time and talking nonstop.

"New York! Whew wee! It's been a minute since I've been here and, man, how it's changed. Brooklyn looks nothing like it did in the eighties. Came close to asking the taxi driver to head straight to Harlem but then I said, naw. Came here for my baby girl. Gotta make that my first stop. Harlem will be my second, though. This is nice, Mallory Anne."

His enthusiasm was contagious, her smile genuine as she answered. "Thanks, Dad."

"You own this or just renting?"

"Renting."

"I bet this place would cost a million dollars."

"Two, actually."

He whistled. "Got damn!"

He paused at the window, looked outside, and then again around the room. "This sure is nice, baby girl. You must be doing a grand up here. I know none of it is because of me, but . . . I'm proud of you."

The comment brought about an unexpected emotion that Mallory quickly dismissed as the remnants of what had happened just before Melvin arrived.

"You came to see me just in time."

"What do you mean?"

"I'm moving. I'm leaving New York."

"What?" A single question asked by two voices. Mallory turned to see Christian fully emerge from the hallway as her father turned as well.

"Christian Graham? The Don't-Give-a-Damn telegram?" He closed the distance between them in three long strides. His hand was outstretched, his smile wide. "Got damn! I feel like I've died and gone to heaven. Man, I watch you every time you play!"

"Christian, my dad, Melvin. He obviously already knows who you are."

"You'd have to be dead not to know him. This man is the best thing that happened to basketball since Jordan and Johnson ruled back in the day."

The accolades further secured Christian's armor. "It's a pleasure to meet you, sir."

"The pleasure's all mine. Hey, can I get a picture. Whew wee! The boys back home aren't going to believe this!"

Melvin whipped out his phone and snapped off a few selfies. "Come on over here, baby girl. I want people to know this ain't no Photoshop right here!"

"They'll know, Dad."

"Come on," Christian said. "You should be in the shot."

After taking a few more pictures, Mallory tried to regain control. "All right, guys, enough with the photo op. Christian, I'm sure you have somewhere you need to be while Dad and I have a date with Broadway."

"Broadway?" her dad said, with a scowl.

"What are you going to see?" Christian asked.

"*After Midnight.*"

"Ah, that's a good one, Melvin. Great music. You'll enjoy it."

"I know you play ball, man. But what do you know about music?"

A slow smile spread across Christian's face, much like when he'd pulled a player out of the zone to lay up an easy two. "Kansas City, 1983. 'Melvin's Mystique.' I know about that."

"Whew wee! Boy, whatchu talkin' 'bout!" Melvin walked over and slapped Christian on the back. The two men traded handshakes and fist bumps, bonding on sight. Mallory wasn't quite sure how she felt about the spectacle unfolding before her. In five minutes Christian seemed closer to her dad than she had her whole life. Even so, she refrained from pouting, stomping her feet, and reeling off every song on the one and only solo album her dad had ever recorded. Though her true feelings had remained hidden until Christian looked at her face, then turned to her dad.

"Look, I need to run." He pulled a card out of his wallet. "But here's the name of a private club I hang out at sometimes when I want to nourish my inner musician. Doesn't heat up until midnight but then jams all night. Will you still be here on Friday?"

"Damn straight!"

"Drop my name at the door. Maybe we'll play a tune or two together."

"I'd love that, man. Would love it!"

It turned out to be one of the best days of her life. Her dad, already on a high from being in the city that never slept, went to a whole other level after meeting Christian. He loved the city, the food, the play. Loved Harlem and the private club where he indeed jammed with Christian—saxophone and guitar. They even talked about doing a recording together. Melvin invited Christian to St. Louis. Christian promised tickets to her dad when the Navs played the Bulls. The two men made plans as if they'd be in each other's lives for the long haul. Mallory definitely planned to build on the new relationship begun with her father. When it came to Christian and her future, however, she wasn't so sure.

38

The city was different and the setting was new. But for Mallory, Sam, and Ava it felt like old times.

The three were in the backyard of Sam and Fritz's newly purchased home in Montclair, New Jersey, drinking spiked tea while sunbathing and catching up on each other's lives. Ava rolled off a lounge chair and walked over to a table with a healthy lunch spread.

"Anyone else want a sandwich?"

"I'm good," Mallory said, placing a toe in the backyard pool to test the water.

"You going in?" Sam asked her.

Mallory shook her flat-ironed locks. "I've got a hot date tonight. Don't want to mess up my hair."

"I knew it!" Ava said. "Any time we see you with straight hair there's an event happening.

Sam sat up. "Okay, spill the secret. Are you and Christian dating or what?"

"We're friends," Mallory said, her tone noncommittal.

"With benefits?" Ava suggestively munched on a pickle. "Has he visited the basement? Is he cleaning out dust?"

Mallory ignored her. "Sam, where are the kids? I have a gift for Jasmine."

"With their dad and his parents. They purchased a cabin. He went there to fish. It'll be my first time not having my kids for forty-eight hours."

"Think you'll survive?' Mallory asked.

"Maybe not. But don't change the subject. We want to know who you're banging."

"Nobody. But I am open to the possibility of maybe starting a relationship if the right person came along."

Ava rolled her eyes. "Who can be more right than someone like Christian?"

"Someone like Eddie."

Sam laughed. "Careful, Ava. Mallory might go after your man."

"I'll be damned. No way I'd leave New York to live in Chicago. Ava has nothing to worry about."

"I sure don't. You can deny all you want to, but I know things are heating up with you and Christian. I saw the picture in the society page with you all cozy with his family. Who was it, Sam? The mom and that publicist we all know Christian's fucking."

Mallory laughed. "Contrary to popular opinion, Christian doesn't fuck every woman he meets."

"Maybe not, but he's fucking her. What's her name?"

"Zoey."

"Have you ever seen her at one of his press conferences? Hardly ever calls on a woman reporter. If they're pretty, she can forget it. Girlfriend is guarding that dick."

"Like you're guarding Eddie?"

"I'm not worried about my man. I gave it to him good before I left. Once this morning and twice last night. That's like a marathon for a man over forty. After the workout I gave it, he'd have to use a pump to make his dick hard again."

Everyone laughed, Mallory the loudest.

Sam walked over and sat beside her, threw an arm around her shoulder. "It's good to see you happy, Mallory. It's been so long I'd almost forgotten this carefree woman I met all those years ago."

"She's back," Ava said. "Her hard work paid off, Leigh can rest in peace, and Mallory can go on with her life knowing that she was victorious. You know what? We never formally acknowledged your victory. Everybody grab a drink. Let's give a toast to our girl for being the baddest investigative journalist after me."

"Ha! Shut up." Mallory gave Ava a shove.

"You guys drink the bubbly, I'll stick to sparkling juice."

Ava and Mallory looked at Sam and then at each other.

"Not again," Ava deadpanned.

Mallory's eyes dropped to Sam's cloth-covered stomach. "So that's why you're wearing the one-piece. Mr. Baby Maker has struck again."

"Yes, and this time I want him or her to have a playmate from one of you. Preferably you, Mallory, with Christian, so Fritz and I can finally get season tickets."

"You'd better say Mallory. Because the only playmate you're getting from me is a dog." Ava poured Mallory a glass of sparkling wine. Sam held up her juice.

"Mallory, I'm quick to bullshit with you, but right now I'm totally serious. You are the best friend a woman could have. You had Leigh's back from the beginning, and no matter the consequence or the cost, you never stopped trying to get justice. You epitomize true friendship. You are a ride-or-die chick for real. So first,"—Ava poured a little of her drink on the patio—"to Leigh Jackson. May you truly rest in paradise, sister."

Sam and Mallory followed suit in the ritual libation.

"To Leigh, and to Mallory." Ava raised her glass.

Sam repeated it.

"We did it, Leigh," Mallory said as they toasted.

The friends hugged as the sun broke from behind a cloud and enveloped them in a warm, sunshine hug.

A new day had dawned. Hear, hear.

39

On Saturday before the Fourth of July, Mallory finished dressing and stared in the mirror with a critical eye. The twenty pounds lost with regular cycling were evident in the flat stomach and toned body beneath the tan halter dress that gently hugged her body as it flowed from her neck to the floor. The gentle dip in the bodice showed off a tear-shaped tiger eye, a congratulatory present from Jan that Mallory received in the mail just that day. It seemed to glow against her sun-kissed skin, the color enhanced by her afternoon by Sam's pool. It hadn't happened in a long time but tonight Mallory felt sexy, daring, a fact made even more evident by the grouping of colorful bangles on her arm, the ones from Leigh's duffel bag that Mallory never thought she'd wear. Her hair was combed away from her face, except for flat-ironing, a gentle curl on the end the only styling. The doorbell rang. She pushed her pedicured feet into a pair of beaded flats, grabbed her purse and opened the door.

"Hey, Christian."

"Hey, beautiful."

She smiled. "Thanks."

He opened her car door. "Ready for our date?"

Mallory gave him a look but before she could say anything he closed the door and bounded over to his side of the car.

"This is not a date," she finally answered.

He smirked, while oozing confidence and charm. "Yes, it is."

For today's trip, Christian had left his sporty Porsche Panamera parked and drove the late-model white SUV he'd recently purchased. While barely taking his foot off the gas, he exited the I-495 freeway toward Uniondale, Long Island. Less than ten minutes later it parked in front of a newly renovated, two-story home with an ample manicured lawn and a two-car garage with a basketball hoop secured above the doors. Three young boys riding ten-speed bikes raced toward the driver's side door as it opened.

"Christian!"

"Ah, man. It really is him!"

The third kid just stared.

"What's up, Eric?" He held out his fist.

An eleven-year-old kid with a forest of twists atop an otherwise shaved head smirked as he tapped the fist of his idol and side-eyed his friends. "Told y'all I knew him."

"Eric goes to my center," Christian explained. "All of you are welcome to come, too. There is an application process to be admitted full-time, but weekends are open to everyone." He introduced himself to the other boys as Mallory exited the car and joined him. "Where's Brandon?"

"With his dad." One of the other kids had retrieved a basketball and tossed it to Eric, who now bounced it continuously. Christian looked at Eric, raised a brow. "Am I the only one you see?"

Eric's grin was impish as he bowed his head. "Um, no. Hi."

"Hello. Eric, right?"

Eric nodded, surprised "You remember me?"

"Sure. You're Justin Bailey's friend."

"Wow, you've got a good memory."

"Only for important people," Mallory said with a wink.

"Is that your girl?" the more boisterous of Eric's friends asked.

"That ain't no girl. That's a woman," the other chided.

"Mallory is a good friend," Christian offered. He looked up and waved at Karen, who'd come out of the house and stood on the porch.

"Come on in here, y'all. Those kids will keep you out there all day."

Eric fell into step beside Christian. "Will you play ball with us later?"

Christian rubbed a hand across Eric's close-cropped curls. "You been practicing your layups?" Eric nodded. "What about your free throws?" No response. "Uh-huh. What'd I tell you? Fifty free throws every day. All right?"

"I'll do fifty," Eric's friend offered.

"Let's do them right now." The boy's faces lit up as Christian reached for the ball. They raced toward the hoop. Mallory continued up the drive to the front door, where Karen waited.

"It's good to see you again," Mallory said while accepting Karen's embrace.

"You, too. Come on in."

Mallory followed Karen down a short foyer that led to a large, airy living room. She could see a kitchen beyond it and to the left a dining room with seating for six.

"Karen, your place is beautiful."

"Thank you. I was scared at first. Didn't know what I'd do with all this room. But a friend of mine helped me choose the colors and then a few more helped me pick out the furniture and before I knew it"—she shrugged and looked around—"the place felt like home."

"You did an awesome job."

"Come on. Let me show you around."

"I'd love that. But first, this is for you." She held up a large, brightly colored gift bag.

"What's this?"

"Nothing too fancy. Just a house-warming gift I thought you'd like."

Karen walked over to an oversized recliner and set down the bag. She pulled out a tissue-wrapped package and glanced at Mallory before peeling it back to reveal the picture. Her gasp and the tears that sprang to her eyes were proof that the gift choice was a good one.

"My kids look so beautiful! I've never had anything like this."

"I asked Harmony if there was a picture of the three of you that I could borrow. I passed the one she gave me on to an artist friend of mine. Told him about Brandon's love for basketball, Harmony's gardens, and your love for the children. He took it from there."

"I know just where to hang it." Karen pointed to a space to the right of the fireplace. "Right on that wall."

Karen proudly led Mallory through the four-bedroom, three-bath home with a full basement and large backyard. Once back in the living room, she pulled out her cell phone.

"Are y'all in a hurry? Harmony is down the street. She'll be so sorry she missed you."

Mallory looked at her watch. "I don't know about Christian, but I've got time."

"I'll tell her to hurry." Karen used a stiff forefinger to tap out a text. "Meanwhile you two can enjoy a slice of pie I made just for y'all. Well, actually a woman named Marie made it, but I heated it up in my brand-new oven."

Mallory laughed. "Works for me."

"Let me get Christian. Those boys will have him out there all day."

"I'll get him."

Mallory walked to the door and was surprised to see about twenty to thirty people crowded around Christian, who conducted an impromptu basketball clinic. Again she was struck with his easy camaraderie and relaxed posture as he entertained the crowd.

"Christian! Karen has something for you."

He tossed the ball to Eric as others came toward him with pieces of paper and cameras for a selfie. Still more people approached from down the street.

"That's it for now, guys."

He jogged up the steps.

"That's quite a crowd you drummed up in ten minutes."

"Comes with the territory of being a star," he said with a shrug that suggested no bragging, just fact. He walked into the kitchen. "What are you cooking?"

"Nothing. Just heating up some pie."

"Eric said Brandon and Danny went out of town."

Karen nodded. "Uh-huh. Driving their granny to Vegas."

"Danny's mom?" Mallory asked.

"His grandmother. Brandon's great-grand. With the money Danny gave her she could finally realize her dream to retire out west in her favorite city. Found a senior community out there near Danny's sister, a nice little one-bedroom apartment that she said was perfect. Big enough for her and someone to visit, yet too small for anyone to stay any length of time."

"It's nice that Danny took the time to drive her out there," Mallory offered. "And took Brandon with him."

"That was my suggestion after finding out his plans. Figured it would be some good father-son bonding time. Brandon had never been out of New York, and Danny never went farther than DC. So it's an adventure for both of them."

"So Brandon . . . he's doing all right?"

"Much better, Christian, with his daddy on the mend."

"But still in therapy."

"Yep. Him and Harmony, too."

At that moment, the front door opened. An exuberant Harmony ran into the kitchen and over to Mallory, who enveloped her in a big hug.

"Wow! Suburban living obviously agrees with you! I don't think I've ever seen you so excited."

"I love it out here," Harmony said, giving Christian a hearty hug, too. "I've got a garden, Mallory. A real one! Come on, let me show you."

It was almost an hour later when Mallory and Christian returned to his SUV and headed to Brooklyn.

"It's a great thing you did for them," Mallory said.

"Considering the pain my uncle caused them, I felt it was the least I could do."

"Yeah, but you didn't have to. And you did. Which shows that underneath all that blubbery arrogance is a good heart."

"I've been trying to tell you that." He glanced over. "No response?"

"Nope." She said it with a smile, though.

"The game is over. Your team won. We don't have to act like opponents anymore. You agree?"

"I agree with that."

"Good. Then you'll have no problem hanging with me tonight."

"I didn't say all that."

"Do you have plans?"

"Depends."

"Don't matter to me. I can always find somebody else for this ticket to the jazz festival."

"You're not serious."

"Dead serious."

"That concert's been sold out for months."

"Mr. Arrogant over here has connections. Wanna go?"

"Heck, yeah!"

* * *

A little past one in the morning, after hanging backstage with musicians she'd admired from afar for years, Christian and Mallory returned to the white stretch limo waiting in the parking lot for VIPs. The evening had been more perfect than either could have planned.

Mallory fell back against the cushioned back seat. "I could die right now a happy woman. I've been to heaven and back."

"That was pretty dope," Christian said, more subdued as he sent out pics on his cell phone.

"The whole night was amazing." Mallory sat up and impulsively kissed Christian's cheek.

"What was that for?"

"Everything. Especially tonight. Thank you."

Christian's hazel-tinged eyes turned dark brown as his smoldering look swept the length of Mallory's body. He thought she'd dressed appropriately weirdly in cutoff blue jeans, a torn tee, and high-tops, her hair swooped into one big afro puff. Now, as she sat up with chest heaving, eyes at half mast, and lips a kissable shade of pink, the spontaneously casual look took on a quality of sexy unlike that manufactured by the women he'd dated. As the limo inched forward and eased out of the crowded parking lot, he shifted his body, aligned his shoulder with hers. He laid his head on her shoulder.

"You're beautiful, you know that?"

"You make me want to believe," she whispered.

He lifted his head. "I think you really mean that."

"I do."

Christian lifted his finger and ran it along Mallory's jaw. He turned her head toward his, slid his hand to the back of her neck, and urged her forward. The kiss was soft, tentative, but Christian wanted more. He shifted his body again, prepared to take everything—the kiss, the night, the relationship—to another level. Mallory resisted, and then gave in. She opened her mouth and enjoyed the kiss. The first one. But when he contin-ued and his hand slipped from behind her neck to her shoul-der and on to her breast, she broke it off.

"Stop, Christian." She scooted over to put distance be-tween them. "It's not you. It's me. I'm not ready for that yet."

"You're not a virgin, are you?" The question was asked lightly, but the mood remained bleak.

"My opinion has changed about you. When this whole thing started, you were a bit of a jerk. But I get it now. You're a good guy. Once you decide to settle down, I think you'll make some lucky woman very happy."

"Who says I'm not ready to settle down now?"

"Oh, I don't know. Probably a half dozen women or so."

Christian smiled at her honesty. "Yeah, you're probably right."

Conversation eased into safer territory after that. The con-cert. The foundation. The "Knightly News."

"I downloaded your column's app," Christian said, almost proudly.

"You did?"

"Indeed. I like it. Makes me think in ways I haven't before."

"Yeah, well, that app is going to be pretty useless for the next eight weeks. I shouldn't say that. There will be a column. I just won't be writing it."

"How can there be a 'Knightly News' with no Knight?"

"Easy. By dropping the 'K.'"

"You quit your job?"

"Taking a leave of absence. I've eaten, slept, and lived jour-nalism for over fifteen years, since my junior year in college. Researching my friend's death again reminded me how short life is, and how precious the time. I want to take a break, step back, and access how mine's going, and if the direction it's headed is still the right one."

They reached her brownstone.

Christian nodded toward her walk-up. "Will you still be here?"

"Not for a while."

"Will you be back?"

"We'll see."

"Will you keep in touch?"

"Absolutely."

The hug was filled with unasked questions and unmasked desires. Mallory allowed a brief kiss on the lips as they parted, then tapped the window as a signal for Treetop Thomas to open the door.

"Thanks for tonight, Christian. I'll never forget it."

"You won't have to. It won't be the last one."

She waved and walked away. Christian watched her joke with Treetop as she climbed the steps to her door. She entered her home without looking back, and soon the limo cruised through the streets toward Midtown Manhattan. But Christian's thoughts and heart stayed back in Brooklyn, on a girl with curly hair, a loyal heart, and a sharp tongue. He'd answered honestly when he said he wasn't ready to settle down. But when he did, he could imagine it being with someone who'd push him to be a better man. Someone like Mallory Knight.

40

Mallory's steps were steady and sure as she walked through freshly cut grass, clutching her purse tightly against her as she navigated the plaques and tombstones that marked the final resting place of a family's beloved. Her steps slowed as Leigh's stone came into view. The granite seemed to gleam beneath the rays of a bright sun, setting her apart in death as much as her beauty and vivacious personality had in life. The hand of grief clutched Mallory's heart. Neither time nor a guilty verdict had yet healed the scar of her loss, but she hoped the news she came to share would at last allow Leigh to truly rest in peace. She stared at the writing on the stone for a moment, then sat down and rested her back against the cool slab.

"You probably know already, but . . ." Mallory faltered as an unexpected lump arose in her throat and tears threatened before she finished with an anguished whisper. "We did it! We got that motherfucker, Leigh. Against all the money and high-powered attorneys and courtroom bullshit, Pete Graham was convicted and will be in prison for the next twenty-five years. I'll be at every parole hearing to make sure of that. And as much as I hated the assignment of solving your murder, it was some of our best work. Yep, you and me, Leigh. I never could have done it without you."

Tears fell. Mallory let them.

"He deserved the death penalty, but your parents' refusal to get involved and the state prosecutor's weak performance was no match for Graham's top-tier team. But Christian believes the truth, Leigh. That surprised me. I'd been dodging his calls because I thought he'd try and make a case for his uncle. Convince me that he was innocent somehow, or excuse what happened. But he didn't. He was shocked, hurt, and after learning that you were pregnant, very angry. Your number one New York Navigator is on your side, Leigh. Now he's cheering for you, and admits that his uncle is exactly where he should be. The irony isn't lost on me, nor are the reasons you adored him. I get why you were such a fan, and makes me wonder why he wasn't the one you dated. I now believe it when you say that you didn't. Christian remembered you from the picture, but swears you and him never went out. It's weird because I can see you with Christian, but his uncle? The reason may have been the child you died with inside your womb—Pete's child. A baby coming would definitely alter whatever choices you'd made till that point. I wonder how that happened, you and Pete, and how you felt when a baby forced you to make a choice. Did you love him, Leigh? So many questions that still linger around this. So many answers we'll never know.

"We do know the role that Danny played, Brandon's father. I guess you know, too. Christian is helping out his family, too. It was wrong what he did, supplying the pills Pete used to spike your drink. But in my heart of hearts I don't believe that he's a bad person, and not even sure he knew how Pete would use the pills. He's like so many guys up against life with limited choices, kids to feed and bills to pay. But at the time you were . . . that everything happened . . . he'd actually gotten out of that life. He'd stopped dealing drugs and was working at an automotive shop. Pete offered him five thousand dollars for a couple of pills. He'd sold many more for much less."

Mallory looked up as a funeral processional passed by, the

hearse shiny and black beneath a cloudless blue sky. Several black town cars followed, regular cars, too, their headlights beaming the message that another soul had earned their angel wings. Her eyes traveled the length of the line and continued to a grove of trees with her car parked just beyond them. A car that held her future, and reminded her it was time to say goodbye to her past.

"So . . . I guess that since you may have already known all that I just shared, you probably also know about my new friendship." Mallory heard Leigh's voice in her head and laughed out loud. "Not friends with benefits, silly, we are strictly platonic, I swear! You always pushed me to get back in the dating game, to be open to love. So it feels nice and totally appropriate that you played a large part in bringing us together. But before getting into anything serious, I need to spend time hanging out with me, getting back in touch with who I am and what really matters. Getting out of the city, the rat race, the media madness, will help me do that. It's also time I bridge the gap that's existed between me and my mom, my whole family really. I love New York. My heart will always beat to its rhythm, but for the first time since I stepped off the train at Penn Station after college, I can imagine myself living somewhere else. I'm going to take the break and then . . . we'll see. I need time to just breathe. Now that I feel you're truly resting, I can relax, too."

Mallory stood and placed her hand on the tombstone, surprised at its coolness despite the late June heat. When she'd left the house, it had been early and cool but now, nearing noon, the sun had risen high in the sky and positioned itself directly above her head.

"I guess I'd better be going. My flight leaves in a couple hours and a part of you is coming with me." Mallory held out the arm where a single silver bangle caught the light of the sun. "I wear at least one of them every day. No, I am not a bangle girl. Yes, you should feel special. And while I'll never come to this city without thinking of you, this will be my last visit here. I finally agree with Sam. I don't need to come here to talk with you. You're in every ray of sunshine on my skin. In every gentle breeze. Your voice will always be in my head, giving me advice and helping me navigate the twists and turns of life. I love you always, Leigh, my best friend. Please continue being my angel for the rest of my life."

Mallory reached inside of the bag she'd clutched during much of the visit. She pulled out the garden spade purchased while planting herbs with Harmony on her brownstone's windowsill and laid it on the tombstone. Then she pulled out a handkerchief, unfolding it to reveal the shiny gold item inside. The puzzle piece. She picked up the spade and knelt down one final time to dig a small hole on the right side of the stone. Once it was deep enough that she felt the piece wouldn't be disturbed, she removed it from the colorful cloth. For a long moment, she held it in her hand, turned it over and ran her fingers across its smooth, cool surface, much as she had after finding it in the clutch. Finally, she placed it to her lips, set it in the six-inch-deep hole, and covered up the treasure.

"Thanks for giving me a clue, girl. Literally and figuratively. I give it back to you now, as a constant reminder of the puzzle you helped solve. The biggest one of all, and in the end, the only one that mattered. I have other items to remember you by, and memories that can never be taken away.

"I love you, Leigh." Mallory wiped away a tear and touched the tombstone one last time. "Goodbye for now."

Mallory walked swiftly across the grassy lawn without looking back. She wiped away the last remnant of tears, straightened her shoulders, and whipped her head about, causing her bouncy curls to dance as if shaking off the visit and the last of her sadness. Sunshades back in place, she emerged from the grove of trees between her and the car with a smile on her face.

She walked over to the passenger side, opened the door and got in. For several seconds, silence ensued.

A hand slowly slid over and gripped hers. She gripped back.

"You okay?"

Mallory nodded, offered a sigh. "It's hard, but I will be. Thanks for convincing me to come and say goodbye. I didn't think I needed to, but I'm glad I did."

"Do you mind if I go up and have a word with her? I didn't want to infringe on your time alone, but would love to tell her I'm sorry and to . . . you know . . . to rest in peace."

Mallory looked at Christian, felt his sincerity and saw the regret in his eyes. A sudden lump in her throat prevented her from speaking. She nodded, wiping tears as she watched him retrace the steps she'd just taken, and stand solemnly for several minutes before returning to the car. He got in. They hugged. No words were spoken. None were needed.

Christian started the car and eased out onto an empty side street leading out of the cemetery. A few lights and turns later, he eased on to the highway toward JFK. Christian scrolled through his MP3 music list and clicked on a song. Mallory recognized the tune immediately, Tivon Pennicott's "It's About Time," the song that was playing when he'd picked her up at the Philadelphia airport. He winked at her, obviously grooving as he tapped out the funky jazz beat on the Porsche's steering wheel. Mallory smiled, bobbed her head, and couldn't help but imagine that Leigh smiled, too. Her BFF had often called Christian a triple threat—smart, successful, gorgeous.

You might be right, Mallory thought to herself as she stole another glance. *You just might be right.*

Don't Miss

Stiletto Justice
Available wherever books are sold

*Camryn King's sizzling debut novel delivers an intriguing tale
of three resourceful women with a ruthless senator in their
sights—and even more explosive ways to take him down . . .*

A successful businesswoman who used to play by the rules.
A cautious single mother who never took chances. A gorgeous
rebel out of money and almost out of time. Each loves a man
unjustly sentenced to long prison terms by former prosecutor
Hammond Grey. They've tried every legal remedy to get justice—only to see Hammond climb ever higher up the political
ladder and secure himself behind power and privilege. So
when Kim, Jayda, and Harley meet in a support group, they've
got no options left. It's time for them to launch Plan B. And
they won't stop at infiltrating Hammond's elite world and uncovering mass corruption. Exploiting his deepest weakness is
the ultimate delicious payback—and the kind of justice they'll
gamble everything to get . . .

Enjoy the following excerpt from *Stiletto Justice* . . .

PROLOGUE

"Is he dead?"

"I don't know, but seeing that lying trap of a mouth shut is a nice change of pace."

Kim Logan, Harley Buchanan, and Jayda Sanchez peered down at the lifeless body of the United States senator from Kansas, Hammond Grey.

"I agree he looks better silent," Kim mused, while mentally willing his chest to move. "But I don't think prison garb will improve my appearance."

"Move, guys." Jayda, who'd hung in the background, pushed Harley aside to get closer. She stuck a finger under his nose. "He's alive, but I don't know how long he'll be unconscious. Whatever we're going to do needs to happen fast."

"Fine with me." Harley stripped off her jacket and unzipped her jeans. "The sooner we get this done, the sooner we can get the hell out of here."

"I'm with you," Kim replied. Her hands shook as she unsnapped the black leather jacket borrowed from her husband and removed her phone from its inside pocket. "Jayda, start taking his clothes off."

"Why me?" Jayda whispered. "I don't want to touch him."

"That's why you're wearing gloves," Harley hissed back. "Look, if I can bare my ass for the world to see, the least you can do is pull his pants down. Where's that wig?"

Kim showed more sympathy as she pointed toward the bag holding a brunette-colored hair transformer. "Jayda, I understand completely. I don't even want to look at his penis, let alone capture it on video."

Harley had stripped down to her undies. She stood impatiently, hand on hip. "I tell you what I'm not going to do. I'm not going to get buck-ass naked for you two to punk out. It's why we all took a shot of Jack!"

"I'm too nervous to feel it," Jayda said as she wrung her hands. "I probably should have added Jim and Bud."

"Hold this." Kim handed Jayda the phone and walked over to the bed. After the slightest of pauses, she reached for the belt and undid it. Next, she unbuttoned and unzipped the dress slacks. "Jayda, raise him up a little so I can pull these down."

Harley walked over to where Kim stood next to the bed. "Don't take them all the way off. He looks like the type who'd screw without bothering to get totally undressed."

Kim pulled the pants down to Hammond's knees. The room went silent. The women stared. Kim looked at Harley. Harley looked at Jayda. The three looked at each other.

"Am I seeing what I think I'm seeing?" Jayda asked.

Harley rubbed the chill from her arms. "We're all seeing it."

"*Star Wars*? Really, Hammond?" Kim quickly snapped a couple pics, then gently lowered the colorful boxers and murmured, "Looks like his political viewpoint isn't the only thing conservative."

She snapped a few more. Harley donned the wig, looked in the mirror, and snickered. "Guys, how do I look?"

"Don't," Kim began, covering her mouth. "Don't start to laugh . . ." The low rumble of muted guffaws replaced speech.

The liquor finally kicked in.

"Come on, guys!" Jayda harshly whispered, though her eyes gleamed. "We've got to hurry."

"You look fine, Harley. As gorgeous a brunette as you are a blonde."

Harley removed her thong and climbed on the bed. "Remember . . ."

"I won't get your face, Harley. What the wig doesn't cover, I'll clip out or blur. You won't be recognizable in any way."

"And you're sure this super glue will work, and hide my fingerprints?"

Jayda nodded. "That's what it said on the internet."

"I'm nervous." Harley straddled the unconscious body and placed fisted hands on each side.

"Wait!" Kim stilled Harley with a hand to the shoulder. "Don't let your mouth actually touch his. We don't want to leave a speck of DNA. I'll angle the shot so that it looks like you're kissing."

"What about . . . that." Jayda pointed toward the flaccid member.

"Oh, yeah. I forgot. Look inside that bag." Harley tilted her head in that direction. "With the condom on, it looks like the real thing."

Jayda retrieved a condom-clad cucumber and marched back to the bed as though it were a baton. "He won't like that we've filmed him, but he'll hopefully appreciate that we replaced his Vienna sausage with a jumbo hot link."

The women got down to business—Jayda directing, Harley performing, Kim videotaping. Each job was executed quickly, efficiently, just as they'd planned.

Finally, after double-checking to make sure her work had been captured, Kim shut off the camera. "Okay, guys, I think we've got enough."

Harley moved toward the edge of the bed. "Pictures and video?"

"Yep. Want to see it?"

"No," she replied, scrambling into her jeans. "I want to get the hell out of here."

"That makes two of us," Jayda said, walking toward the coat she'd tossed on a chair.

"Three of us." Kim took another look at the footage. "Wait, guys. I have an idea. Jayda, quick, come here."

"What?"

"No time to explain. Trust me on this . . . please?"

Five minutes later they were ready to go. "What should we do about him?" Jayda asked, waving a hand at his state of undress.

"Nothing," Kim replied. She returned the phone to its hiding place in her pocket. "Let him figure out what may or may not have happened."

They'd been careful, but taking no chances, they wiped down every available surface with cleaning wipes, which they then placed back in the bag that once again held the condom-clad cucumber. Harley almost had a heart attack when she glimpsed the wineglass that if forgotten and left behind would have been a forensic team's dream. After rinsing away prime evidence, she pressed Grey's fingers around the bowl, refilled it with a splash of wine, and placed it back on the nightstand. After a last look around to make sure that nothing was left that could be traced back to them, the women crept out of the bedroom and down the stairs. Harley turned off the outside light and unbolted the side door.

Kim turned to her. "You sure you don't want to come with us?"

Harley shook her head. "I have to leave the way I came. Don't worry. The car service is on the way. See you at the hotel."

After peeking out to make sure the coast was clear, Jayda

and Kim tiptoed out the back door as quietly and inconspicuously as they'd arrived. A short time later Harley left, too.

Once down the block, around the corner, and into the rental car, Jayda and Kim finally exhaled. The next day, as the women left the nation's capital, hope began to bloom like cherry blossoms in spring. Until now their calls for help and cries for justice had been drowned out or ignored. Maybe the package specially delivered to his office next week would finally get the senator's attention, and get him to do the right thing.